SHADOWBLACK

THE SPELLSLINGER SERIES

SPELLSLINGER
SHADOWBLACK

Look out for

CHARMCASTER

Coming in May 2018

SHADOWBLACK
SEBASTIEN DE CASTELL

HOT
KEY
BOOKS

First published in Great Britain in 2017 by
HOT KEY BOOKS
80–81 Wimpole St, London W1G 9RE
www.hotkeybooks.com

A CIP catalogue record for this book is available from the British Library.

HARDBACK ISBN: 978-1-4714-0667-6
TRADE PAPERBACK ISBN: 978-1-4714-0613-3
also available as an ebook

1

Typeset by Palimpsest Book Production Ltd, Falkirk, Stirlingshire

Printed and bound by Clays Ltd, St Ives Plc

Hot Key Books is an imprint of Bonnier Zaffre Ltd,
a Bonnier Publishing company
www.bonnierpublishing.com

To Doctor Sukanya Leecharoen of the Royal Angkor International Hospital in Cambodia, whose wit and kindness turned what began as an agonizing affliction into a strangely entertaining experience.

WAY of WATER

The way of the Argosi is the way of water.

Water never seeks to block another's path, nor does it permit impediments to its own. It moves freely, slipping past those who would capture it, taking nothing that belongs to others. To forget this is to stray from the path, for despite the rumours one sometimes hears, an Argosi never, ever steals.

1

The Charm

'This *isn't* stealing,' I insisted, a little loudly considering the only person who could hear me was a two-foot-tall squirrel cat who was, at that moment, busily picking the combination lock that stood between us and the contents of the pawnshop's glass display case.

Reichis, one furry ear up close to the lock as his dextrous paws worked the three small rotating brass discs, chittered angrily in reply. 'Would you mind? This isn't as easy as it looks.' His tubby little hindquarters shivered in annoyance.

If you've never seen a squirrel cat before, picture a mean-faced cat with a big bushy tail and thin furry flaps of skin between his front and back legs that let him glide through the air in a fashion that somehow looks both ridiculous and terrifying. Oh, and give him the personality of a thief, a blackmailer and, if you believe Reichis's stories, a murderer on more than one occasion.

'Almost done,' he insisted.

He'd been saying that for the past hour.

Thin lines of light were beginning to slip through the gaps between the wooden slats in the pawnshop's front window and beneath the bottom edge of the door. Soon people would be coming down the main street, opening their shops or standing outside the saloon for that all-important first drink of the morning. They do that sort of thing here in the border-lands: work themselves into a drunken stupor before they've even had breakfast. It's just one of the reasons why people here tend towards violence as the solution to any and all disputes. It's also why my nerves were fraying. 'We could have just broken the glass and left him some extra money to cover the damage,' I said.

'*Break* the glass?' Reichis growled to convey what he thought of that idea. 'Amateur.' He turned his attention back to the lock. 'Easy . . . easy . . .'

A click, and then a second later Reichis proudly held up the elaborate brass lock in his paws. 'See?' he demanded. '*That's* how you pull off a proper burglary!'

'It's *not* a burglary,' I said, for what must have been the twelfth time since we'd snuck into the pawnshop that night. 'We *paid* him for the charm, remember? He's the one who ripped *us* off.'

Reichis snorted dismissively. 'And what did you do about it, Kellen? Just stood there like a halfwit while he pocketed our hard-earned coin. That's what!'

To the best of my knowledge, Reichis had never actually *earned* a coin in his life. 'Shoulda ripped his throat out with your teeth like I told you,' he continued.

The solution to most thorny dilemmas – to squirrel cats anyway – is to walk up to the source of the problem and bite it very hard on the neck, preferably coming away with as much of its bleeding flesh as possible.

I let him have the last word and reached past him to pull open the glass doors and retrieve the small silver bell attached

6

to a thin metal disc. Glyphs etched along its edge shimmered in the half-light: a quieting charm. An *actual* Jan'Tep quieting charm. With this I could cast spells without leaving the echo that allowed bounty hunters to track us. For the first time since we'd fled the Jan'Tep territories, I felt as if I could almost – *almost* – breathe easy again.

'Hey, Kellen?' Reichis asked, hopping up on the counter to peer at the silver disc I held in my hand. 'Those markings on the charm – those are magic, right?'

'Kind of. More like a way to bind a spell onto the charm.' I turned to look at him. 'Since when are you interested in magic?'

He held up the combination lock. 'Since this thing started glowing.'

A set of three elaborately drawn glyphs shimmered bright red along the cylindrical brass chamber. The next thing I knew, the door was bursting open and sunlight filling the pawnshop as a silhouetted figure charged inside and tackled me to the floor, putting an abrupt end to a heist that, in retrospect, could have done with more planning.

Four months in the borderlands had brought me to one irrefutable conclusion: I made a terrible outlaw. I couldn't hunt worth a damn, got lost just about everywhere I went, and it seemed like every person I met found some perfectly sensible reason to try to rob me or kill me.

Sometimes both.

2

The Way of Fists

Getting punched in the face hurts a lot more than you might expect.

When somebody's knuckles connect with your jaw, it feels like four tiny battering rams are trying to cave in your mouth. Your own teeth turn traitor, biting down on your tongue and flooding the back of your throat with the coppery taste of blood. Oh, and that crack you hear? It sounds a lot like what you've always imagined bone breaking would sound like, which must be why your head is already spinning a quarter-turn clockwise, trying to keep up with your chin before it leaves the scene of the crime.

The worst part? Once your legs recover their balance and your eyes flicker open, you remember that the devastating opponent beating you senseless is a skinny freckle-faced kid who can't be more than thirteen years old.

'Shouldn'a stolen my charm,' Freckles said.

He shuffled forward, causing me to lurch back instinctively, my body having apparently decided it preferred the embarrassment of collapsing in on itself over the risk of getting hit again. Laughter erupted all around us as the crowd of townsfolk who'd come out of their shops and saloons to witness the fight began placing wagers on the outcome.

No one was betting on me; my people might be the best mages on the continent, but it turns out we're rubbish in a fist fight.

'I paid you for that charm,' I insisted. 'Besides, I put it back in the case! You've got no cause to –'

Freckles jerked a thumb up to where Reichis was perched on the swinging sign outside the pawnshop, happily inspecting the silver bell on the charm. Every time Freckles hit me, Reichis rang the bell. This is the sort of thing squirrel cats find hilarious. 'You think I spent all night picking that lock just so you could give the charm back?'

'You're a damned thief,' I told the squirrel cat.

Freckles's face went an even brighter shade of red; he must've thought I was talking to him. I keep forgetting that other people don't hear what Reichis says – it all just sounds like a bunch of grunts and growls to them.

Freckles gave a yell and barrelled into me. The next thing I knew, I was on the ground with the wind knocked out of me and my opponent pinning me down.

'Best get on your feet, kid,' Ferius Parfax suggested in that frontier drawl of hers. She was leaning against the post where we'd tethered our horses, black hat dipped low over her forehead as though she were taking a nap. 'Can't dodge when you're flat on your back.'

'You could help, you know,' I said. Well, that's what I *would* have said if I could've got any air into my lungs.

Ferius was my mentor in the ways of the Argosi – the mysterious, fast-talking card players who went about the world

9

doing . . . well, nobody had yet told me exactly what it was they did. But Ferius was *supposed* to be helping me learn how to survive as an outlaw and stay clear of the bounty mages who were hunting me. She did this mostly by dispensing such brilliant axioms as, 'Can't dodge when you're flat on your back.' That one annoyed me almost as much as her calling me 'kid' all the time.

'Told you to forget about the charm, kid,' she said.

I might have heeded her warning if she hadn't then started up on some Argosi nonsense about 'the way of water' that irritated me so much I'd ended up taking advice from a squirrel cat whose solution to everything – when it didn't involve ripping someone's throat out with your teeth – was thievery. So really it was both of their faults that I'd ended up on the ground with Freckles on top of me doing his best to knock me senseless.

One thing I've learned about non-magical fighting is that you need to protect your face, which I was trying to do. Unfortunately my opponent just kept swatting my hands away and then proceeded to punch me again. *Ancestors, how does this kid hit so hard?*

Freckles shifted his hips, shimmying forward as he grabbed my wrist and wrapped one of his hands around my index finger. 'Everyone knows the price for thievin',' he said as he slowly bent it back.

Panic overtook me even before the pain. Every Jan'Tep spell requires forming precise somatic shapes with your hands. You can't do that with broken fingers.

I bucked my hips as hard as I could and desperation gave me just enough strength to throw Freckles over the top of me, sending him face first into the dirt. I quickly flipped myself over and got to my feet. Freckles was already waiting for me. 'Gonna bleed you,' he said.

Gonna bleed you. Three words that perfectly summed up the hot, arid hellhole they call the Seven Sands: a patchwork desert that wasn't much more than an endless dusty quilt stained with backwoods little towns filled with people who were rough, mean and gave up any pretence at being civilised at the drop of a hat. Not that most of them could afford a hat.

Freckles, evidently concerned that I hadn't heard him the first time, declared even louder, 'Gonna bleed you real good.'

My hands dropped to my sides – a reflex developed from a life spent learning magic rather than getting into physical altercations: you can't cast a spell if your hands are balled up into fists like a barbarian's. I relaxed my fingers, letting them reach into the powder pouches attached to the sides of my belt. Just a pinch was all I needed: a dash of red, a smidgen of black. Toss them in the air, form the somatic shapes with my hands, utter the one-word incantation, and Freckles would get a taste of what he'd been dishing out to me up till now.

Most Jan'Tep mages have bigger and better spells than I do, but I make up for my lack of ability with fast hands. I'm what my people derisively call a spellslinger – a mage who combines whatever paltry magic he can muster with every trick he can learn to stay alive. In my case that means a bit of breath magic mixed with a touch of exploding powders. Individually they don't amount to much, but put them together with perfect timing and you can create a blast that'll tear through an oak door like it was wet paper. So yeah, Freckles was about to get the surprise of his life.

'No magic, kid. Remember?' Ferius said.

Oh. Right.

The reason I'd wanted that quieting charm in the first place was that every time I cast a spell, it sent out a sort of mystical echo that let hextrackers – mages who specialise in hunting down other mages – follow our trail. Since avoiding them was kind of my life's ambition at this point, Ferius had insisted I stop relying on magic to get myself out of trouble. Problem was, Freckles was coming at me again, fist cocked and ready to send me to my ancestors.

'You win,' I said, putting up my hands and backing away. 'I'll give you back the charm and you can keep the money.' Possibly not my proudest moment.

'Gonna take the charm, gonna take the money,' Freckles said. Then he gestured to where Reichis was perched on the sign. 'Gonna skin that animal of yours too. Make a hat out of his fur or maybe just light him on fire and watch him run till he can't run no more.'

Those words sent a cold, hard knot twisting in my stomach. Not long ago I'd witnessed a mage using ember magic to set fire to Reichis's tribe. That image was still burned into me, and so was the look of glee on the killer's face. It was a lot like the one Freckles wore right now.

Ferius says fear and anger are two sides of the same coin. Freckles had just flipped mine.

A stabbing pain started to build in my left eye, like a head-ache, only a lot worse. I tried blinking it away, but the ache kept getting stronger. The morning sun faded, but the shadows remained, grew, became bloated as the world darkened all around me, the way it does when dreams drift into nightmares. Only I was fully awake.

'Get a hold of yourself, kid,' Ferius warned. She'd seen this happen to me before, but her warning came too late, because now her voice sounded as if it were coming from far away, like she was just a memory of someone I once knew.

Freckles's laugh, on the other hand, kept getting louder and louder in my ears. His smile got bigger and bigger, contorting his appearance. When I get like this, all I can see are the ugly parts of people. The mean parts. It was as if I were watching Freckles turn into the worst version of himself he could ever become: the one who liked to hurt things, the one who would giggle as he set fire to Reichis.

The rage inside me got so bad I stopped feeling the pain in my eye and didn't even notice that I'd dug my hands back into the pouches at my sides until I saw the particles of red and black powder floating in the air in front of me. Just before they collided, my hands formed the spell's somatic shape: bottom two fingers pressed into the palm in the sign of restraint; fore and middle fingers pointed straight out, the sign of flight; and thumb pointing to the heavens, the sign of, 'Ancestors, please don't let me blow my hands off.'

'Carath,' I said, my lips perfectly enunciating each syllable. A fiery bolt of rage and fury shot out – not enough to kill, but more than enough to hurt. The red and black flames entwined in the air like two angry snakes and flew right past Freckle's shoulder, scorching the outer wall of the pawnshop. It would have been an impressive display of power if that had been my target. Turns out that getting hit in the head is really, really bad for your aim.

The pain in my eye disappeared all at once, and the dark visions assailing me faded, leaving behind the plain, dusty street and the dismayed faces of the onlookers. The attacks come and go quickly like that, leaving me shaken and stumbling – not exactly the best condition to be defending yourself.

13

Whatever shock and outrage Freckles had felt, he quickly set it aside. Before I could get my arms up to protect my face, he delivered a sharp right hook just above my left cheek. His fist came away with a trace of blood on it. His look of smug self-satisfaction turned to confusion when he noticed smudges of pale beige *mesdet* paste on his knuckles. He glanced back at me, and I guess that's when he saw the black markings encircling my left eye like twisting vines made from pure darkness.

'Shadowblack,' he whispered.

The word spread through the crowd like fire on dry leaves.

'The demon plague!' one of the onlookers declared.

Most of them drew back in horror, but Freckles was evidently made of sterner stuff. He didn't even sound scared when he said, 'Figures a thief would be devil-cursed.'

If they'd given me a chance to explain, I could have told them that the shadowblack wasn't actually a plague or even a curse, but more of a mystical disease that afflicted a small number of my people and wasn't, to the best of my knowledge, contagious. I would've left out the parts where it gradually drives you insane with maddening visions until your magic becomes a danger to everyone around you and that any Jan'Tep mage who crossed my path was duty-bound to kill me.

None of that mattered though, because by then Freckles had grabbed me by the throat with both hands. I yanked at his wrists, desperate to break free, but his grip was too strong. My throat spasmed, fighting for breath. The world started to shrink around me. It occurred to me then that there's probably an ingenious way to get out of a chokehold.

I should really learn it sometime.

14

3

The Red Price

I couldn't have blacked out for more than a second, because just before my head hit the ground, my eyes opened and I saw Freckles flying backwards away from me. At first I thought maybe I'd somehow triggered a new and highly useful spell, but then I saw Ferius gripping the collar of Freckles's shirt and realised that all that had happened was that she'd hauled him off me.

Too bad. I could've really used more magic.

I coughed up dust, and the next thing I knew, my opponent was flat on his back a few yards away and Ferius was standing between me and some big, broad-shouldered thug, who was probably a close relation of Freckles's because he shared both his skin condition and his attitude.

'Best you move away, woman,' he said, peering down at her through squinty little eyes. 'A devil owns that boy's soul and I'm gonna send him to the Dark Place.'

The Dark Place. The borderlands are full of sophisticated spiritual expressions like that.

'Now, friend,' Ferius said, 'let's not get all excited over a plain old birthmark.' She lent her next words the perfect mix of scolding and amusement. 'Imagine all you enlightened and educated folks fallin' for that old superstition.'

Calling these people 'enlightened and educated' was highly optimistic, but a few of them liked the sound of it. A woman in the crowd took a small step forward and peered down at me. 'If it's just a birthmark, why does he hide it?'

Ferius walked over to me and reached down to rub some of the paste away, revealing more of the twisting circular markings. 'Cos it's unsightly, that's why. Boy's sensitive about his looks!' She started laughing uproariously.

The crowd found her light-hearted mirth infectious. I don't know how she does it, but Ferius always knows just what to say to sway people to her point of view.

Well, most people, anyway.

Squinty jabbed a finger in my direction. 'I say he's got the demon plague, and even if he don't, that stuck-up little Jan'Tep tried to steal from my kin. Now he's gotta pay the red price.'

In the Seven Sands, 'the red price' means roughly the same thing as 'gonna bleed you'.

'Seems to me Kellen already paid plenty for that trinket,' Ferius said, nodding up to where Reichis was still perched on top of the shop sign, delightedly examining his silver bell. 'Then your boy went and asked for more.'

'Don't matter. A thief is a thief, and the red price says he's gotta lose his fingers.'

Ferius offered him one of her easy smiles. 'Good sense says to leave things be. Right now what everyone's going to remember is that your boy fought off a fella twice his size. That's a good story. A proper one to tell your friends when you're tossin' back a drink at the saloon.'

Squinty grinned back at her. 'It's gonna be an even better story when I show them your boy's finger bones.'

A sour taste rose up in my mouth. I'd been terrified at the

16

prospect of Freckles breaking my fingers; having them cut off would mean I'd never cast a spell again for the rest of my life.

Ferius lowered her voice so that only the big man and I could hear her words. 'Don't think it'll be nearly as impressive a tale when your friends point out that after you tried to take an innocent boy's fingers, you got your ass kicked by a woman barely bigger than your left arm, do you?'

For a moment there, it looked like Squinty was giving her words careful consideration, but then he rolled up his sleeves before squeezing his big, meaty hands into fists, making the knuckles crack. 'No quarter just because you're a lady.'

'Oh, I'm no lady, so don't you worry about that.' Ferius removed her black frontiersman hat and set it on the ground, sending a tumble of red curls down to her shoulders. 'You want to dance with me, friend? Tell you what –' she tapped a gloved finger on her jaw – 'you give me your best shot, right here. Then, if you're still not satisfied that things are settled, well, I'll take my turn and we'll see where that leads us.'

The crowd started whispering excitedly, and more coins changed hands, but they weren't betting over *whether* Ferius would win or lose, just on how quickly and how badly.

In the short time I'd known her, I'd never seen Ferius Parfax back down from anyone or anything. Maybe that had something to do with her being an Argosi, but I tended to think it was just that she was crazy. Problem was, so was this guy, and he looked as if he could tear her head off.

I rolled onto my side and got my hands under me, preparing to get back on my feet.

Ferius gave a subtle twitch of her fingers, signalling me not

17

to interfere. 'Whenever you're ready,' she told Squinty. Her right foot was behind her as she leaned forward, giving the big man a clear shot at her jaw.

He glanced back as though he were going to share a joke with his friends, then suddenly came round with a punch that could've knocked down an eight-foot tamarisk tree.

All along I'd just assumed that Ferius was going to dodge or duck or otherwise avoid the blow, that maybe she'd planned to come up underneath it and deliver a swift kick to Squinty's groin or a jab to his throat, but he was too fast. She took that punch square on the jaw, her head spinning to the right, shoulders and the rest of her body following along until she was turned right around and facing me.

She just stood there, looking lost, as if she'd been knocked unconscious but her body hadn't figured it out yet. I dug my hands into the pouches at my sides. If Squinty tried to hit her again, I was going to blast him into oblivion and deal with the consequences later. I doubted he'd need to though, because I'd never seen anybody get hit as hard as Ferius had just been hit.

All of a sudden the corner of her mouth rose up and she winked at me.

Before I could even breathe a sigh of relief, Ferius Parfax turned back to the man who'd struck her and said, casual as can be, 'Let's call that a practice round. You want to go one more time before it's my turn?'

Squinty looked as if he'd just swallowed his own tongue. 'How . . . ? How did you . . . ?'

Ferius reached down and picked up her hat. 'Now, I appreciate you goin' so gentle on me. Maybe since you're feeling generous, you could just let us be on our way now?'

An uneasy stillness fell over the street. The crowd watched and waited for someone to make a move. A few more bets changed hands, and more than one onlooker loosened a knife from its sheath. Squinty had friends ready to take his side. Too bad we didn't have anybody on ours. All the while the big man just kept looking at Ferius, and she at him. Reichis chittered down from his perch, 'Why do they keep staring at each other like that? Are they going to mate now?'

The last thing you want to do in a situation like this is giggle like an idiot, but that's just what I did. Everyone glared at me, all except for the two combatants. I couldn't see what was in Ferius's eyes, but whatever it was made Squinty reconsider his position on the subject of the red price. 'Reckon you've learned your lesson,' he mumbled. 'Give back the charm and you can go on your way.'

'Deal,' Ferius said. She walked over and untethered our mounts. 'Kellen, kindly tell the squirrel cat to get down here and return the man's little trinket.' She turned and led the horses along the street towards the edge of town.

I was still trying to make sense of what had just happened when Reichis leaped off the sign, spread his paws wide and let the thin furred membranes between his front and back limbs catch the breeze. The crowd broke out in gasps and worried whispers, a few of them holding their hands up in front of their chests, fingers intertwined in the shape of tiny houses. Must have been some kind of folk sign against evil. People get superstitious around Reichis sometimes.

The squirrel cat glided smoothly to the ground, the gracefulness of his landing diminished by the angry glare he gave me as his dextrous paws went about unclasping the silver charm from the little bell. 'If you'd just ripped that kid's throat out like I told you, we'd be eating his eyeballs right now.' He tossed the charm on the ground behind him and then tinkled the bell at me. 'I'm keeping this.'

He took off after Ferius, leaving me sitting in the dirt and dust, surrounded by a crowd of people who were no doubt wondering if it might not still be worth trying to cut off my fingers.

'Best you not come round here again, Shadowblack,' someone said.

A few others grumbled their agreement.

I nodded and slowly pushed myself up to my feet.

Sixteen years old and already I had a price on my head in half the places I'd ever been. No money, no skills, and without that charm I'd be announcing my location to every mage in the borderlands any time I cast the one spell I was any good at.

Oh, and my travelling companions were an Argosi gambler who never gave me a straight answer and a homicidal squirrel cat whose favourite food was human eyeballs.

Welcome to the life of an outlaw spellslinger.

4

The Art of Winning a Fight

We spent the rest of that day riding along an ancient cobbled road that cut a winding path as it climbed through the desert hills, a stiff wind sending the sand on either side drifting ahead of us like waves across an endless ocean.

Ferius says the Seven Sands got their name from the way the mineral content gives the soil in each region its own colour. When we'd first left my home in the Jan'Tep territories four months ago, the sand had been mostly yellow-gold from the mix of iron and quartz. Further north the olivine-rich particles had reflected a bright emerald green, but now we were moving east where rich deposits of lazurite turned the sand a deep blue. I might have found the landscape pretty if people here would just stop trying to kill me.

Having lost the charm, the money and most of my dignity, I was starting to have serious doubts about my future as an outlaw. 'I'm going to die out here, you know.' The words had sounded more dramatic in my head, but with my bruised jaw and swollen tongue, all that came out was, 'Argh . . . yeaow . . . ugh.'

Ferius seemed to get the general idea. 'The borderlands are the safest place we could be right now, kid, what with you having the shadowblack and all; fewer mages than in the Jan'Tep arcanocracy, less assassins than in the Daroman empire, and don't even get me started on the Berabesq viziers. Those fellas would set you on fire soon as look at you.'

'Whereas these barbarians just want to cut off my fingers.'

I rubbed at my cheek again, wishing I was back in my clan city among the Jan'Tep. My mother could've taken away the bruising and pain with healing balms. Instead I was stuck out here in the borderlands, where what passed for modern medicine was a rusty bone saw and an admonition to toughen up and take the pain.

Of course, if I *were* back home, my younger sister Shalla would have mocked me for getting hurt in the first place. I could just see her, arms crossed, looking up at me with one eyebrow raised disapprovingly. 'A Jan'Tep mage of the House of Ke does *not* go around being terrified by frontier hicks and pathetic hextrackers, Kellen.'

I missed Shalla. Even though we fought about, well, everything, she was family. Sometimes I even missed my mother and father too, despite what despite the way they'd counter-banded me and taken away my magic when they'd discovered I had the shadowblack. Most of all, though, I missed Nephenia. I missed her dark hair and shy smile, the way every time I was sure I had her figured out, she'd prove me wrong. We'd only kissed the one time, but I swear that even under the bruises on my face I could still feel the soft, tentative brush of her lips on mine.

Ancestors, but I *really* wanted to go home.

Of course, there were more people who wanted me dead there than in the entire population of the borderlands. How was I supposed to defend myself from war mages and hextrackers when I couldn't even hold my own against a skinny thirteen-year-old kid?

Reichis gave a loud snort from atop my shoulder. Despite being slightly too tall and heavy to make it comfortable for either of us, he'd taken to perching there sometimes. It wasn't from any sense of affection for me; the little runt just likes being high up. 'Should've followed my advice,' he said, slurring his words. He sometimes gets into the flask of liquor that Ferius keeps in her saddlebag.

I worked my mouth open and closed a few times until I could speak properly, if painfully. 'Remind me again?'

Reichis made a 'huff' sound in my ear. It's his version of a sigh. 'First, clamp your teeth around the other guy's neck.' He opened his mouth wide to reveal his fangs and jutted out his jaw. 'Then shake until his throat comes apart. Simple.'

'Right. I'll try to remember that for next time.'

It doesn't do to get into an argument about fighting with the squirrel cat. Any time I did he just bit me and said, 'See? See? *Now* who's the dumb animal?'

'Or you can rip his eyeballs out,' he added. 'That also works.'

'Got it.'

'Ears are good too. You wouldn't think so, but tearing the ears off a guy really puts a hurt on him.'

Ferius chuckled. 'Is the little bugger going on about eyeballs again?'

She doesn't share whatever bond with Reichis it is that lets my mind translate his chitters and growls and farts into words, but evidently she's been around enough squirrel cats to know that they all think they're the apex predators of the animal world. 'He's onto ears now,' I said.

Ferius shook her head, curly red hair following along for

23

the ride. 'It's always something with his kind. Eyes, ears, tongues. You'd think they'd find something new once in a while.'

'Hey, shtick with what works, I always shey.'

I turned my head to look at Reichis. 'Are you drunk? You sound weird.'

Ferius chuckled. 'He ain't drunk, kid.'

'Then what . . . ?' The hint of a self-satisfied smirk had begun to light up the squirrel cat's fuzzy face. 'What did you do, Reichis?'

He didn't reply at first, so I kept my eyes locked onto him. Staring contests make him uncomfortable. After a few seconds he opened his mouth wide and lifted up his tongue to reveal the three coins hidden there.

'You rotten . . . You snuck back in? While I was getting my ass handed to me, you went back inside that shop and stole a *second* time?'

Reichis hopped off my shoulder and onto the front of the saddle, reaching into his mouth with a paw and taking out the coins. 'Hey, those townies stole from *us*, remember?' he mumbled. '*Someone* needed to retrieve our hard-earned money.' He proceeded to stuff the coins into a small black bag hidden under the horn of the saddle. He'd asked me to buy him the bag so he'd have somewhere to keep his private treasures and had made it clear what would happen to stray fingers that found their way inside it. So much for 'our' hard-earned money.

We rode on a ways until the sun was getting low on the horizon before Ferius asked, 'You ready to talk about what happened back in town, kid?'

'You mean when I nearly got choked to death?'

'I mean when you almost took that boy's head off with that spell of yours.'

For someone who was supposed to be teaching me how to stay alive, Ferius spent a lot more time worrying about other people. 'It wasn't enough powder to kill him,' I insisted. 'Just enough to . . .'

'Just what? Set him on fire? Scar him for life?'

'It was the shadowblack,' I tried to explain. 'Sometimes it—'

'The shadowblack shows you an ugly world, Kellen,' she said, cutting me off. 'It don't give you an excuse to be just as ugly. That ain't the Argosi way.'

The Argosi way. Whatever that means.

I started to turn away, but she reached out a hand and took hold of my chin, holding it steady even as we rode. 'Those markings of yours grow just a touch each time you use magic, you know that, right?'

'It's just your imagination,' I said, shaking her off. 'Besides, how else am I supposed to defend myself if you won't teach me any of your Argosi combat techniques?'

'I keep telling you, kid, there *ain't* no such thing.' She reached into her black leather waistcoat to pull out one of her long, thin smoking reeds. 'Wrastlin' ain't the Argosi way either.'

Wrastlin' is what Ferius calls it any time I get into trouble. 'I *saw* you beat that guy back there, remember? He was huge!'

'He was a big one all right,' she conceded. 'But I didn't fight him. I just danced with him a little.'

'That punch would have taken a normal person's head right off. Your jaw must be made of iron!'

She smiled as if I'd said something funny, then lit her reed with a match retrieved from the cuff of her linen shirt. After a long, slow drag, she let out a thick puff of smoke that enveloped us in blue-white fog. 'Kid, my jaw ain't any tougher than yours or anyone else's. Think back to what you *really* saw, not what you expected to see.'

I have a good visual memory – it comes with a lifetime of training in how to perfectly envision spells before casting them. When I thought back to the fight, I saw Ferius, leaning forward, presenting her jaw to her opponent, her right foot behind her. Squinty's fist came at her, all the strength of his hips and shoulders channelled into that punch. Then . . . There was something odd about my recollection of that moment. Events had taken place too fast to really see, but thinking on it, I could swear that by the time the blow landed, Ferius had not only turned all the way around, but her body was leaning back. Which meant that the instant the man's fist had connected with her face, Ferius had spun, following the line of his punch perfectly to dissipate the force. 'You tricked him,' I said suddenly. 'It *looked* like he hit you, but the blow barely landed at all, did it?'

Ferius reached up a hand to rub at her jaw. 'It landed well enough. Any less and he'd have figured out that I dodged most of it.'

'But to move that fast, that's . . .'

'Dancin',' she said.

When you study magic, above all else you learn precision. Spellcasting is an exact science. Every syllable, every somatic shape you make with your fingers and the image you hold in your mind, has to be impeccable. But nothing I'd learned could compare to how skilled Ferius would have to be to pull that manoeuvre off. 'The timing had to be flawless,' I said, my voice barely above a whisper.

'Timing's part of dancing,' she said, as if that explained everything.

I still couldn't wrap my head around it. 'You'd have to know exactly where he was going to land the punch. Only how could you, unless . . . ?' Then it came to me: she'd tapped a finger right at a spot on her jaw, and leaned forward so it was the only good target. Still, everything – the movement, the angles – had to be perfect. 'That punch could have broken your neck.'

'Maybe.'

I felt my cheeks flush from a sudden wave of shame. 'You risked your own life to save me. Again.'

Ferius adjusted her hat and pushed loose curls up underneath. 'Well now, that makes me sound proper noble, don't it?' Before I could reply she nudged her horse into a trot and mine followed along. 'Come on,' she said. 'Let's put some more distance between us and that town so I don't end up havin' to be noble twice in one day.'

5

Fireside Tales

That night we made camp the way we usually do: Ferius sent me off to find firewood, while she set up her collection of traps around our campsite. She never let me see them, which annoyed me no end. For his part, Reichis went hunting, and brought back the slightly mangled remains of a rabbit to add to our dinner. His fur had taken on a greenish-brown colour, his stripes now looking like the thin angular lines of sage brush.

Squirrel cats can change the colours of their coats to match their surroundings, making them particularly skilled hunters. Reichis's favourite tactic is to hide behind whatever greenery is available, and by the time a rabbit or other small animal gets close enough to see that he isn't just some slightly tubby shrub, it's too late.

Rabbit isn't a common food among my people, but I found I liked it well enough. Mind you, nothing will put you off the taste of an animal faster than hearing Reichis kill it. The problem isn't so much the ferocity with which he tears into them, but the fact that he keeps talking to his prey even after it's dead.

'That's right, you dumb rodent. Who killed you? *I* killed you.' Reichis was standing over the animal's carcass, its blood still dripping from his face. 'When you get to the afterlife, be sure to tell your stupid rabbit god that I ripped out your throat and now I'm feeling a craving for divine bunny flesh.'

He waxes poetic sometimes. Mostly on the subject of violence.

An hour later, after the meal was cooked and we were halfway through eating it, Reichis kept on extolling his great victory, describing every detail at length, making the story grander with each repetition.

'Did you see the teeth on that rabbit?' he asked us. 'Huge. Lion's teeth, that's what this one had. I'm not sure it even *was* a rabbit. Must have been some kind of hybrid half-rabbit, half-bear.'

At times like these, it's best to just stay quiet, eat your food and let Reichis talk himself out. It helps to think of him not as a two foot-tall squirrel cat but more of an eight-foot pissed-off lion.

Sometimes I don't mind listening to him brag though; there's not much to do at night in the open countryside once the horses are settled and the fire is going strong. Most of my evenings were spent staring at the flames, trying not to shake as my mind turned over one near-disaster or another. I used to shake a lot more, but I guess lately I'd gotten used to being scared all the time.

Ferius would sit cross-legged on one side of the fire, strumming the little guitar she carried with her as she told us stories – she has hundreds of them. I'm pretty sure most of them are made up, especially the daring, improbable adventures she claims to have had with remarkable people in exotic locales I'd never heard of. Given that I'd learned plenty of geography in school, I was fairly sure she was making up her settings too.

29

Reichis is highly competitive by nature, so likes to try to one-up her with his own stories. These come in two varieties: impossibly large animals he's killed, and incredible treasures he's stolen. There isn't much evidence for either, but he nonetheless makes me translate his tales of squirrel-cat valour for Ferius in painstaking detail, always demanding that I emphasise, 'And this next part, which is all true by the way . . .' Ferius does an excellent job of pretending to believe him. After a couple of nasty bites on my forearm, I learned to pretend too.

That night Reichis had just launched into a particularly gruesome account of his slaying – and devouring – a creature that I was fairly certain had actually just been a big mouse, when Ferius uncharacteristically cut him off and set her guitar back in its cloth bag. 'I think we're done with stories tonight.'

'Really?' Reichis asked. 'How about the tale of the Argosi who got her face bitten off for interrupting?'

She ignored his chittering and got up, walked over to her saddlebags and reached inside. When she pulled her hand back out, she was holding a deck of cards I recognised: steel, thin and razor sharp. In her hands, those cards were as deadly a weapon as any I'd ever seen. She cut the deck and handed me half of them.

'Are we going to practise card throwing now?' I asked. She'd taught me the basics on the first night we'd met, and I'd developed a pretty fair hand for it.

'In a manner of speaking.' She gazed out onto the long road that wound down the slope back towards the town. 'No more talking now, okay, Kellen?'

'What's –'

She shook her head, signalling me to keep quiet. Something

was up. I closed my eyes, trying to hear whatever it was Ferius had heard. The wilderness always seems quiet, but if you listen close enough it's full of noises: animals shuffling about in the hills, insects chirping, wind rustling the leaves and the sand. It took me a while before I made out the sound of a horse's hoofs underneath it all. One rider, I guessed, though I wasn't particularly good at judging this sort of thing. I caught Ferius's gaze, wondering why she was so concerned. Even if one of the townspeople had decided to try to attack us, I doubted we had much to fear.

I heard a growling noise and looked down to see Reichis next to me, his fur now black and rising in hackles, sniffing at the air. 'Crap,' he said.

I kept my voice below a whisper as I asked, 'What is it?'

'The air stinks of magic,' he replied. 'Jan'Tep magic.'

I had to stop myself from gripping the cards too tightly and slicing open my palms on the sharp edges. There was only one reason why one of my people would be out here in the borderlands alone in the middle of the night: a hextracker had found me.

6

Silk and Iron

The man who'd come to kill me rode a pale horse and smiled as if we were old friends, though I was certain I'd never seen him before. He was tall, and his immaculately styled blond hair draped down over broad shoulders covered by a long red cloak that defied all the dirt and dust of the road. He was ridiculously handsome.

That probably shouldn't have bothered me so much. You would think that impending death would lessen a person's vanity, but truth be told, if I had to die, I'd rather be killed by an ugly person.

The mage dismounted smoothly, as though he'd spent a life in the saddle, which was odd because my people aren't usually very good riders. When his feet hit the ground, they made no sound at all. 'The ancestors must be smiling on me,' he said. 'The trail had gone cold on my original quarry and I feared I'd travelled all this way for nothing. Now who should drop in my lap but Kellen, son of the House of Ke.'

'He makes a good entrance,' Reichis said, clambering up to sit on my shoulder. 'You should learn to make an entrance like that.'

'I'll get right on it.' My stomach clenched uncomfortably, not just out of fear from what was about to happen but because it was my fault. The hextracker hadn't even been looking for me until I'd stupidly used my magic trying to fight off a scrawny thirteen-year-old in a street brawl. If I'd listened to Ferius, the mage never would have known we were here. Instead I'd brought him right to us.

'Reckon you've got the wrong kid,' Ferius said, offering the bounty hunter an easy smile, relaxing her stance as if this was all a misunderstanding. 'My nephew here is called Mutt and he's no more Jan'Tep than I am.'

Reichis gave a quiet chortle in my ear. 'Mutt. Heh.'

The mage stopped about fifty feet away from us, still too far for me to use my powder magic on him but close enough that he could cast any number of unpleasant spells on me. 'A misunderstanding, you say? How odd.' He bent over to pick up a handful of sand from the ground and whispered a few syllables before tossing it in the air. Instead of falling back down, the tiny particles drifted there, suspended, and began to rearrange themselves until they formed a floating likeness of my face. Two sigils appeared beneath the image, written in the elaborate court script of my people. The first one meant 'shadowblack', the second, 'death'.

I'd never seen a spell warrant before, though every Jan'Tep initiate is taught to recognise them: transient curses that, once cast, could be reinvoked by any sufficiently trained mage to identify the fugitive they were pursuing. It's not an easy spell, and to work this far from my city it would have to have been cast by one of my clan's lords magi. Apparently my people hated me even more than I thought.

'You should be flattered by the bounty on your head,' the

mage said. 'It's almost three times what I would have got for apprehending my original prey.'

'Well now, if you ask me,' Ferius began, letting the deadly sharp steel cards in her hand shift and turn around her fingers with practised ease, 'that fancy sand picture don't look a thing like old Mutt here. Best you look elsewhere for your bounty so we don't come to any further misunderstandings.'

The flicker of a smile drifted over the mage's face as he let the sand fall back to the ground. I shouldn't have been able to see him so clearly in the darkness, but the magic swirling around the tattooed bands on his forearms cast six colours of light on his features.

'Hey, Kellen?' Reichis asked.

'Yeah?'

'The last guy who tried to kill us – how many bands had he sparked?'

'Three,' I replied. Every Jan'Tep initiate is banded using special metallic inks that connect them to the primal forces of the different forms of magic: iron, ember, breath, blood, sand and silk. Most mages will spark two or three of their bands, using those to choose the particular paths they study. Iron and ember might lead to a life as a war mage, for example, whereas iron and silk were the perfect combination for a chaincaster. I couldn't tell what sort of mage this man had become, because all six of his bands were sparking with ghostly light.

'So . . . six is worse, right?' Reichis asked.

'Yeah.' Six bands meant we were screwed.

I glanced over at Ferius, hoping to discern her plan. Ferius always has a plan. Right now she was just staring at our enemy, waiting for him to make his move.

'You set traps around your campsite,' the mage said, beginning a slow, circuitous path towards us, his steps utterly silent, casually evading snares and sharpened spikes that I couldn't spot even now.

'Now what would give you that idea?' Ferius asked.

The mage tapped a finger to his temple. 'Silk magic. I've been scrying you for hours, waiting for your thoughts to turn to your preparations.' His eyes narrowed as he stared at her. 'It's quite remarkable, really, the way you manage to keep yourself from thinking about your tricks and traps. Makes it almost impossible to perceive your plans. You have an incredibly disciplined mind.'

'Nah,' she said. 'I'm just forgetful is all. Clumsy too.' She sent one of her steel cards whisking through the air, flying fast as any throwing knife right for the mage's neck. Just before it reached its target, the card fell harmlessly to the ground.

'Impressive,' he said, his hands still at his sides.

This made no sense. Shield spells require specific somatic shapes; you can't just wish one into existence. How had he done it?

'Hey, wake up,' Reichis said, his front claws digging into my shoulder. 'Time to blast this guy.'

Despite my creeping doubts, I slid my half-deck of steel cards into my pocket, then dug my hands into the pouches attached to my belt and sent pinches of red and black powder into the air as my fingers formed the somatic shapes. '*Carath*,' I said, invoking the spell.

Fire from the blast tore through the darkness, a roar erupting from it that echoed through the open countryside even as the flames faded to nothingness inches away from their target.

It wasn't possible. There's only one way to maintain a shield

35

without the somatic forms: stand inside a circle of spelled copper sigil wire. Problem was, the mage was walking towards us.

'Something's not right with this guy,' Reichis growled.

'Any idea what it might be?' Sometimes Reichis can perceive things I can't.

'Yeah. He's way too good-looking for a human.'

Okay, maybe a squirrel cat's insights aren't always that useful.

The mage watched us, clearly amused. 'So it's true? The nekhek speaks to you in the way his kind did with the Mahdek centuries ago? What does the little fellow say, I wonder?'

I considered my response carefully. Ferius says that when faced with certain death it's important to project confidence. 'He says you smell bad and wants to know if you've been eating rotten meat.'

The mage shook his head, looking rather disappointed in me. Evidently he didn't appreciate my sense of humour, because the next thing I knew I was doubled over in pain. My internal organs were being crushed.

Several observations came to me at once. The first was that I should really be running away right now. Of course that wasn't possible, because running isn't something you can do when your stomach, kidneys, heart and liver feel like they're being squeezed for juice. The second observation was that I should stop listening to Ferius when she talks about acting confidently. Third was really a question: how could this guy keep casting spells without having to make the somatic forms or say the words?

Reichis growled and leaped off my shoulder to race across the sand. When he was within leaping distance of the mage he sprang off his hind legs, only to fall back to the ground as if he'd slammed into a wall. The mage nodded – not even gestured, mind you, just nodded – and Reichis went flying through the air, landing on his side just a few feet away from me. I tried to reach out to him, but the pain was such that I couldn't so much as move my arm.

Ferius began creeping slowly towards the mage, stalking him as though he were a skittish animal. 'Best you stop tormenting the boy. I'd hate to have to muss that pretty hair of yours.'

The mage laughed at the empty threat, but nonetheless the pain in my guts suddenly disappeared. 'You amuse me, woman, and frankly I've no interest in making an enemy of the Argosi. Your kind are fond of bartering, are they not?'

'I've been known to make a trade now and then.'

'Then allow me to offer you the bargain of your life: walk away from this place. In exchange I will put the boy to sleep before committing his soul to the depths to which he is destined.' He looked over at Reichis. 'The nekhek must be destroyed as well. After that, this unpleasant business will be done.'

Ferius took another step towards the mage. 'Afraid I can't accept your generous offer, friend.'

He looked at her quizzically. 'The child is Jan'Tep. He's nothing to you, and yet you'd throw your own life away in a hopeless bid to protect him?'

'Nah, the kid's annoying,' she replied, 'but the squirrel cat's starting to grow on me.' I barely saw her hand move and all of a sudden half a dozen steel cards were tearing through the air towards the mage. Even before they'd bounced off his shield, she'd already leaped after them, diving into a shoulder roll and coming up behind him. Her hand came up and I could see the rest of the cards fanned out like the edge of an axe. She swept them in a horizontal arc that should have sliced right through the flesh on the backs of his legs, only . . . nothing happened.

'Are you quite done?' he asked.

'Told you there was something unnatural about this guy,' Reichis said, back on his feet now, front paws clawing at the dirt as he prepared to attack a second time. 'Nobody's that good-looking.'

'Really not helping,' I said. Our attacker's looks weren't the problem; it was his . . . *Wait a second* . . . Here he was, standing in the middle of nowhere with all the dirt and dust of the borderlands swirling around him, and yet his clothes were as clean as if he'd just emerged from his private sanctum. That wasn't the only weird thing either: the glow of his tattooed bands was way too bright even for a lord magus, never mind a bounty hunter who spent his life trudging through the borderlands looking for Jan'Tep fugitives. And then there was his boots, which made no sound when he walked. So of course this guy didn't need somatic gestures or invocations to cast spells. He wasn't really here.

'He's using illusions against us,' I shouted. 'He's in our heads.'

'Actually, it's more that you are all inside mine,' the mage said. 'A rather clever contrivance, if I do say so—'

'Oh, shut up,' Ferius said, picking up the rest of the steel cards she'd tossed at him and running back towards me. She closed her eyes and spread part of her deck in each hand to form a pair of razor-sharp fans. They moved in a graceful, sinuous pattern like stalks of grass dancing in the breeze.

'What are you doing?' I asked, my own fingers in my pouches, ready to fire off another spell but having no idea where to aim.

'He's playing us,' Ferius said, still keeping up the swift movements with her hands. 'You don't waste all that time with illusions just to show how clever you are: he didn't come here alone.'

Two of them. I swore silently to myself. That was why this man wasn't attacking us directly. He wasn't some impossibly powerful lord magus who'd sparked all six of his bands – he was just using silk magic to mess with our heads while his partner got in close enough to strike.

Ferius stayed in constant motion, the sharp steel cards moving in unpredictable patterns, making it hard for anyone to strike at her directly. *Except if the other guy is a war mage. Then he'll just be getting into position to fire off a spell.*

'Spread out,' Ferius said. 'Don't let him take more than one of us out with a single spell.'

Reichis growled at the apparition before us. 'I can smell them both now. One is nearby, but the other one must be half a mile away.'

A sudden stab of pain in my stomach confirmed that our other opponent – the one the silk mage was making invisible to our eyes – was using simple iron magic. *Which means he's probably only sparked one band.* That would be good news if I could actually see him. A scream tore itself from my lips.

'Kid, duck!' Ferius said.

It was easy enough to comply since I was already doubling over in agony. One of her cards flew past my head and a second later I heard a grunt from somewhere behind me. The pain in my guts faded away again.

'Stay down, Kellen,' Ferius said, sending several more of her cards flying through the air. None of them found their target. Iron magic is good for both attack *and* defence, and the heart shield is one of the few invocations that can be cast in combination with a second spell.

'Argosi bitch,' a voice called out. I looked around and saw nothing.

Ferius groaned and suddenly dropped to her knees, a tight grimace on her lips. She tried to throw another card but couldn't; her muscles were spasming from the agony the iron mage was inflicting on her.

'You should have taken our deal,' the silk mage said, the apparition he'd created for himself fading now that the pretence was no longer needed. 'I really would have let you live, Argosi.'

Ferius writhed on the ground, her features twisted in anguish, so unlike the cocky, swaggering woman who'd moments before launched herself into danger to protect me. 'Stop it!' I screamed into the darkness. 'I accept your deal. *I'm* the one in the warrant, not the Argosi or the squirrel cat!'

The laughter that rang in my ears came from nowhere and everywhere at once. 'I think not, Kellen of the House of Ke. It's obvious now that she's the one who's been keeping you alive all these months, and that is a sin against our laws and our people. But don't worry, we'll get to you shortly.'

Reichis was racing around in frustration. 'I can't find him,' he growled. 'Gods-damned Jan'Tep magic!'

'Kid . . .' Ferius wheezed, 'stop talking and listen.'

'I'm listening. What do you want me to—'

'No.' She gasped for breath. 'Not to me, stupid. Listen to *him*.'

All of a sudden I understood what she meant and why, even as the iron mage was slowly crushing her insides, Ferius was forcing herself not to scream. She was giving me the chance to find our adversary. 'Reichis, don't move,' I said. I closed my eyes and focused my attention on the sounds around me the way I'd seen Ferius do. The iron mage might be invisible, but he still had to breathe. I just had to listen for him.

I let the desert noises wash over me. Buzzing insects. Burrowing animals. My own heartbeat. The breeze. *No . . . not the breeze.* With nothing more than a guess at his location, I pulled powder from both pouches, a lot this time.

There's a second variation of my spell that I'd once used to break through a Jan'Tep shield. The red powder in my left pouch still carried some of Reichis's mother's blood mixed in it. '*Carath Chitra,*' I said, and sent the spell screaming into the air before me.

The fiery blast broke through my enemy's shield the way Reichis tears through rabbit flesh, but my guess at the iron mage's position had been off by nearly a foot. His shield fell, but the man himself was unaffected. Before I could try again, he set his gut sword spell on me and the next instant I was in too much pain to recast. I turned my head and saw Ferius lying unconscious on the ground. The iron mage could focus all his attention on me now.

Five seconds, I thought. If I'd just been five seconds faster, if my spell was just a fraction stronger, if I were just a bit cleverer, my enemy would have been defeated. But I was too slow, too weak and, above all else, too dumb. Now Ferius and Reichis were going to die because of me.

'It's over,' the silk mage said in my mind. 'You've had a

good run, Kellen, but no one escapes Jan'Tep justice for long. When you reach the grey passage, beg our ancestors for mercy that they don't send your soul to the hell it so richly –'

His words disappeared, cut off somehow. My guts were still being twisted in knots, but my mind began to clear and the landscape all around me became sharper, the colours less muddled. I still couldn't see the silk mage, but about twenty feet to my right stood a stoop-backed man in a long grey travelling coat, his right hand out in front of him holding the somatic shape for the gut sword. Whatever had caused his partner's spell to fade hadn't affected the iron mage. 'Reichis . . .' I moaned, struggling to stay on my feet.

'He's mine!' the squirrel cat growled, racing across the dirt. At the last instant he leaped, the strength of his powerful back legs launching him over eight feet into the air. He spread his limbs wide and the thin fur-covered flaps between them billowed out, catching the breeze for just an instant before he descended onto the iron mage. If you've never had a squirrel cat fly at your face, the effect is more than a little disconcerting. The mage kept his shield up, but his focus on the gut sword spell wavered.

I took in a quick, desperate breath, my hands grabbing more powder from the pouches at my belt even as my mind reached for the calm and clarity I would need for the spell. 'Reichis, get away now.'

The squirrel cat raced away into the darkness. 'Light him up, Kellen!'

The mage turned his attention back to me, but before he could summon up his gut sword again, I had tossed the powders into the air, formed the somatic shapes with my hands and invoked the spell one last time. 'Carath Chitra,' I said.

42

The twin fires, black and red, ripped at the mage's shield a second time, tearing it apart to get to him. The flames broke through, surrounding him, biting at him until he screamed in agony. The spell didn't last long, but neither did the mage. What little had remained of his shield spell had been enough to keep him alive, but I could see the burns on him as he fell unconscious to the ground.

The sound of my lungs huffing and puffing for air as if I'd been running for miles filled my ears even as tracks of sweat began to drip down my forehead. I forced myself to breathe more slowly, willing my legs to shake off their paralysis so that I could go to make sure Ferius was still alive.

Reichis ambled over to me, his fur a dirty mess of reds and blacks like the colours of my spell. 'Nice shot, for once.'

'Thanks. For once.'

'Only we have a problem.'

'Just one?'

'Yeah.' He gestured with a paw towards the robed man I'd just taken out. 'If that's the guy who was casting the attack spells, where's the one who was messing with our heads?'

Oh. Right.

7

The Traveller

The two of us stood there in the darkness, waiting for whatever calamity would head our way. 'Maybe the other guy just had a heart attack,' Reichis suggested.

'Could be.'

I rubbed my fingertips together, trying to work away the numbness caused by using my one spell too many times in a row. If I cast it again now I'd just end up blowing my own hands off. Reichis glanced back at the iron mage lying unconscious on the ground behind us. 'That guy looks pretty old, Kellen. What if the other guy was old too? Magic's got to be hard on the body, right? Maybe he just keeled over and died.'

'Anything's possible.' A few yards away, the dying embers of our campfire cast just enough light where Ferius lay for me to see that she was still breathing. Maybe she was okay. Maybe she was going to stand up any second now, dust herself off and say something that sounded clever but made no sense. 'We have to get lucky some day, right?'

Reichis sniffed the air and then pulled at my trouser leg. 'Kellen?'

'Yeah?'

'It's not today.'

The sounds of footsteps drifted towards us from down the road. 'How many?' I asked, keeping my voice low, still frantically rubbing my fingertips together.

'Three. One male and two females.' He sniffed again. 'The male is old. One of the females is fully grown and the other is a pup like you.'

'I'm sixteen. I'm not a "pup".'

'I call it like I smell it.'

Three figures appeared at the edge of the road, barely more than silhouettes in the dim light shed by the half-moon above. I blinked several times until I could make out a few details. The first was a woman, tall, dressed in loose-fitting white and brown linen tied in place with straps of leather, most of her face covered by the same linen fabric as her garments. She carried a skinny man in a filthy white coat over her shoulders like a sack of wheat. A donkey trudged reluctantly after her, ridden by a girl in the sort of trousers and riding jacket common to the borderlands. A single strip of pale cloth was tied around her head, covering her eyes.

'You think she's a prisoner?' Reichis asked. He has a thing about captivity.

I didn't reply, figuring we'd likely find out the answer soon enough. 'Not another step,' I called out. 'Not if you want to live to see the sunrise. I've already set one of my enemies on fire tonight and I'm happy to do it again if you come any closer.'

It had sounded like a perfectly serviceable threat to me, but the woman approaching us showed no sign of being intimidated. 'That would be exceedingly unwise.'

'Yeah? Why's that?' I asked, doing my best to appear faintly amused.

'Look down at your hands.'

I did, and saw how badly they were shaking. The problem with nearly dying is that, once you *haven't* died, you start trembling uncontrollably. It's hard to get your body to stop after that.

'Well, I ain't shaking,' Reichis growled, hackles up, stalking towards her.

'Kindly ask the animal not to attack until I've rid myself of this rather unpleasant-smelling burden.' The masked woman came to within a few feet of me and deposited the man she'd been carrying on the ground.

With the silk spells gone, I saw the mage for what he really was: a frail old man with flat, homely features and wrinkled skin that had seen too much sun. Keeping one eye on the new arrivals, I reached down and lifted the sleeves of his coat one at a time. His bony forearms revealed that he'd only ever sparked the silk band and no others. The same was likely true for his partner, who'd been using iron magic against us. These two would have been a running joke among our people; they might even have been outcasts like me, hoping to buy their way back into their clans with the bounty for hunting down a shadowblack.

The woman gazed down at the unconscious man between us. 'Such fragile things we are, stripped of our illusions.' Her expression – what little I could see of it beneath the fabric covering her face – was neither derisive nor sympathetic, merely curious. 'How odd that a mage should go to the trouble of making himself appear youthful and handsome in our minds. Do you suppose that if he'd spent less attention on his appearance he might have noticed me coming up behind him?'

46

Not a question I needed to be concerned with right now, given that my fingers were numb, my hands were shaking and Ferius was still unconscious. What I really needed to know was whether this woman was a danger to us. People rarely answer the question 'Are you here to kill me?' honestly, so instead of asking it I called out to the blindfolded girl on the donkey. 'Are you being held captive?'

'She is in my care,' the woman said.

'I'd rather hear that from her.'

The girl on the donkey held up her hands to show they weren't bound and said, 'Who lets their prisoner ride while they walk, idiot?' Her accent carried only a faint trace of the drawl I'd come to associate with borderlands folk, and her diction was more precise – a bit like the Daroman envoys I'd seen pass through my homeland. If I had to guess, I'd say this girl was close to my age, wealthy and probably well educated. 'Is he staring at me?' she asked the woman.

'He appears to be.'

'Tell him to stop. It's impolite.' She dismounted and fumbled for something attached to the saddle. Once she'd got it loose, I could see it was a thin stick of wood around three feet in length. She held it out in front of her, swinging it back and forth a couple of inches off the ground.

That explained the cloth covering her eyes. 'You're blind,' I said.

'No, you're blind. I just can't see.' She turned to the woman. 'What does he look like? He sounds stupid.'

'Forgive my charge; we have been travelling many days now. These have been trying times for the child and she—'

'Seneira,' the girl said. 'Not "my charge", not "the child". *Seneira*.' She strode forward only to have her right foot slip

47

on a flat stone in the sand. Fearing she was about to fall, I instinctively reached out to steady her. Unfortunately for both of us, at that precise moment she shifted her weight to catch her balance. Our foreheads collided with a painful thud, and worse – much, *much* worse – it's entirely possible that my lips brushed against hers in the process.

'Did he just try to kiss me?' she demanded loudly, her head turning left and right as she held the stick out in front of her like a sword.

I backed away quickly. 'I didn't! I would never . . . I mean, you're blind! I wouldn't want to . . .'

'Wouldn't want to what?' she asked, her voice suddenly cold as the night air. 'Wouldn't want to kiss a *blind* girl?'

Ancestors, please just send another bounty hunter to kill me now. I swear I won't even try to fight back this time.

'If you could see the boy,' the woman in the linen garb said, 'you would realise that he is confused, injured and frightened after fighting the iron mage.'

'I'm not frightened,' I said, but no one was paying attention to me.

'Well, maybe he should keep his hands – and his *lips* – to himself.'

The woman sighed. 'Child, you know perfectly well he was only trying to keep you from falling flat on your face. His obviously poor reflexes and clumsiness are cause for pity, not an excuse for you to torment him.'

'Thanks for sticking up for me,' I said.

She ignored my sarcasm and looked past me at Reichis. 'Is the animal unwell? He seems to be . . .'

'He's fine,' I said. 'That's just what it sounds like when he giggles.'

The girl, Seneira, seemed to come to a decision as to my culpability in our unfortunate encounter. 'Fine,' she said at last, letting the point of her stick drop and extending a hand towards me. 'Let's start over. I'm Seneira.'

I took her hand and shook it for the shortest possible time I could. 'Kellen.'

'Nice to meet you.' She turned to her guide. 'See? That's how people greet each other – normal people, anyway. They have names like "Seneira" or "Kellen" or . . .'

'Reichis,' the squirrel cat chittered. Now that he was done laughing at me, he sauntered over to give each of them a sniff followed by a brief growl. 'I don't like them.'

'You don't like anyone,' I muttered.

'What was that?' Seneira asked. 'I heard something growl.'

'That was Reichis,' I said. 'He's my . . .' I hesitated. I hate sounding half-witted in front of strangers.

'Say it,' the squirrel cat snarled. 'Say it, unless you figure you can cast spells with only nine fingers.'

'Fine. Reichis is my business partner.'

Seneira turned her head this way and that. 'Business partner? I didn't hear any other people. Who's there?'

'He refers to the animal,' the woman explained. 'A squirrel cat.'

The blind girl stood there for a while. 'Perfect,' she said, then promptly sat down in the dirt. 'I'm just going to sit here until the world starts making sense, if that's all right.'

'You might be waiting a long time,' I said.

Despite the linen covering most of the woman's face, I had the distinct sense that she was smiling when she said, 'At last, words of wisdom. Seven drops of water in an otherwise dry desert.'

Seneira rested her head in her hands. 'Will you *please* stop talking like that?'

I felt a touch of sympathy for her. Ferius had used lines like that on me enough times to . . . 'Wait a second . . . Who are you?' I asked the woman.

'A traveller with no end to my journey. A guide without destination but never lost. A follower who follows none but the road in front of her. I am the Path of Thorns and Roses.'

I had no idea what any of that meant, but the fact that her reply made no sense told me who she was, or rather, *what* she was. 'You're an Argosi.'

Without bothering to indicate whether or not I was right, she walked over to Ferius and knelt down to examine her. 'Ah, sister. Why must you always be such a terrible disappointment to us all?'

8

The Path of Thorns and Roses

'Build up the fire,' the Argosi woman commanded. Very gently, she lifted Ferius in her arms and carried her over to the campfire. 'We must keep her warm tonight.'

'Is she going to be all right?' For some reason it had never sunk in for me that Ferius Parfax could really be hurt. She was too quick, too smart, too obstinate to let anyone kill her. Seeing the concern in the eyes of the other Argosi suddenly made me aware that even Ferius could die.

'The iron mage's spell broke three of her ribs. There is some internal bleeding, though I cannot yet determine how severe. Should her internal organs be damaged . . . No, let us make no maps of lands yet unseen. If she recovers consciousness by morning, there will be reason for hope. Now, the fire?'

I ran over and put the rest of the wood onto the glowing embers, then laid a few bits of tinder on top. When it didn't light right away, I peppered it with a bit of the black powder, then sprinkled some of the red on top, causing it to ignite. Within seconds the flames began to rise.

'Good,' the woman said, setting Ferius down next to the campfire. 'Now, if you could do me one further service?'

'What?' I asked.

She gestured over my shoulder. 'Kindly ask your . . . business partner to stop whatever strange ritual it is that he's performing upon my prisoner?'

I turned to see Reichis sitting on top of the silk mage's chest, one paw reaching out to push up the old man's eyelid, the other curving to scoop out his eyeball. 'Come on . . . come on . . .'

'Reichis, stop that!'

The squirrel cat turned and gave me a warning growl. 'Are you kidding me? These Jan'Tep skinbags nearly killed us all. No way am I waiting for them to wake up so they can try again. Also, I'm hungry.'

'What does he say?' the Argosi asked.

'He's . . . reminding me that two mages, unconscious or not, will soon become a serious problem.'

'The animal has a point.' She sighed and rose to her feet. 'Keep watch over the Path of . . . forgive me. She is Ferius to you, is she not?'

'Who is she to you?'

'I know her as the Path of the Wild Daisy.'

'Stupid name,' Reichis grumbled, still eyeing the silk mage.

The Argosi walked over to the squirrel cat, then got down on her knees and propped herself up on her elbows until her head was at the same height as his. 'Leave the men to me, warrior of the treetops. I will do what must be done.'

Reichis snarled and thrust his muzzle forward before sniffing at her again. I'm not sure what he was looking for, but the little monster is a sucker for compliments. 'Warrior of the treetops. I like that.' He hopped off the silk mage's chest and headed into the darkness. 'I'm going to go murder a rabbit or two,' he informed me. 'It's what we treetop warriors do.'

After he was gone, the Argosi reached into the folds of her garments. I figured she was going to pull a knife and almost considered objecting. Ferius did whatever she had to in a fight, but I'd never seen her kill someone who couldn't fight back. Then again, I wasn't entirely sure I agreed with that position. *Ancestors, now the squirrel cat's got me acting bloodthirsty.*

It turned out that the Argosi woman wasn't drawing a knife, but a tight bundle wrapped in cloth. She unwound the fabric to reveal a small mortar and pestle along with several jars. Two of these she opened, and began mixing some of the contents together.

'What are you doing?' I asked.

'The iron mage's burns aren't fatal, but they will be if I leave them untended.'

'Wait . . . *that's* your plan? You're going to treat the wounds of the men who tried to kill us?'

'I find it's rarely productive to negotiate with a corpse.'

'Negotiate? Are you serious? These men are hextrackers. Bounty hunters. Jan'Tep mages who only get paid if they bring back a body. Now you want to heal their wounds and try to talk them out of it?'

The Argosi's eyes narrowed even as she continued preparing her mixture. 'You travel with my sister and yet she has not taught you the Way of Water? It is not our custom to end the journey of another without first offering them a different path.'

I tried and failed to come up with an appropriate response to this lunacy and eventually gave up, instead keeping watch on Ferius and making sure my fingers stayed warm and my hands limber for when I'd inevitably need them. Seneira, swinging her stick a little wildly in front of her, came and joined me by the fire. 'So, I guess your life is about to become as stupid as mine.'

'Good evening,' the Argosi said to the two men as their eyes blinked open. She spoke in the casual tones you might use upon encountering fellow travellers on an empty road, rather than when facing mortal enemies who'd tried to kill you only hours before.

After she'd worked on their wounds, the woman who called herself the Path of Thorns and Roses had sat the two men up, back to back, resting against each other. I'd assumed she was going to tie them up that way, and had been about to point out that unless she was carrying spelled copper or silver wire with her, there were still a number of spells they could use against us. But she *didn't* bind them. Instead she withdrew a tiny jar barely bigger than her thumb from inside the folds of her garments and popped the cork from the top. 'You and Seneira kindly wait over there,' she said, nodding to a spot several yards away from the fire that was shrouded in darkness.

'Why?' I asked.

'These men have reason to kill you, do they not? Let us not add to the temptation.'

Once Seneira and I had done as instructed, the Argosi tapped a pinch of white powder from the jar onto her fingertip and then gently placed a few grains beneath each man's nose before replacing the cork and sitting back to watch. A few seconds later, both men had coughed into wakefulness.

The silk mage's first act was to bring his hand up, fingers forming a somatic shape I didn't recognise but which I doubted would be good for any of us. I started reaching for

54

my powders but the Argosi shot me a warning glance. Since there was no way she could see me where I stood in the darkness, she must have anticipated my reaction. 'You are in no danger,' she said.

The silk mage smiled, making the wrinkled skin of his face twist along the lines of his mouth. 'You are.'

The Argosi nodded. 'Always. It is a dangerous world we live in.'

'Perhaps, but considerably less dangerous for mages of our power than for wandering philosophers who meddle in the affairs of others.'

Had I been part of the conversation, I might have been tempted to point out that neither of these men had sparked more than a single band, which made them just about the least powerful kind of mage my people produce. Next to me, of course.

The Argosi made no such comment. Instead her expression was thoughtful, as though she were giving careful consideration to the silk mage's words. 'I believe you are right. The world is more dangerous for wandering philosophers, as you say.'

The iron mage, a man with thin red hair, perhaps ten years younger than his comrade, gave a hoarse laugh. 'See how quickly the famed Argosi back down? The woman wishes to bargain for her own life.'

She shook her head. 'Forgive me, but you are incorrect. I wish to negotiate for *your* life.'

The silk mage's fingers began to twitch. 'You would threaten a Jan'Tep mage? Lie upon your belly, woman, and kiss my feet before I draw you inside a spell that will tear your mind apart. Your soul will be shredded into a thousand pieces as your empty spirit watches, helpless and screaming until the heart within your chest sheds its last wasted beat.'

Not bad, I thought. My people aren't big on poetry but we appreciate a well-composed death threat. The Argosi, however, returned a soft, almost musical laugh. 'I do not think you want me in your head, master mage. I'm told I have an unpleasant disposition.'

The look in the man's eyes told me she'd gone too far. Before I could do anything to help, the silk mage locked his gaze on her. With the whisper of a single word the air between them began to shimmer. He was pulling her into a silk spell – not an especially powerful one, if I understood it correctly, but one that would soon destroy her mind regardless. I was just about to ignore the Argosi's demand that I do nothing when the silk mage shouted into the night sky. 'Stop! Let me go!' The air between them became still as the spell broke. His breathing was shallow as he slowly recovered his composure. 'How is this possible?' he asked.

The Argosi shrugged apologetically. 'We are travellers. It is in our nature to accept each journey for what it is, without fear, without judgement.'

The man glanced over at the fire and Ferius's unconscious form. 'But she . . .'

'You took my sister unawares. I do not suggest you attempt it once she wakens.' The Argosi leaned forward and whispered conspiratorially, 'Many find her disposition even more dis-agreeable than my own.' She reached out a finger and tapped the mage's forehead. 'Fill your mind with brighter thoughts, master mage. It is unwise to carry so much ugliness inside you.'

The iron mage growled at his comrade, 'Stop letting her

distract you with her words. Cast another spell and destroy her!'

The silk mage shook his head slowly, his eyes never leaving hers. 'I will not touch her thoughts a second time.'

'Fine, then I'll deal with her.'

The iron mage raised his right hand, forming the sign of the gut sword he'd used to attack us before. The Argosi held up a finger. 'That too would be unwise.'

The mage ignored her, stabbing his fingers out in a thrusting motion as he spoke the incantation for an iron spell we call the blood hammer. At first nothing happened, but then he doubled over and vomited onto the ground. 'What have you done to me?' he groaned.

The Argosi spread her hands wide, revealing empty palms. 'Nothing, master mage, save to apply a healing salve to your burns. Alas, the mixture requires powdered nightbloom leaves to speed recovery and numb the pain.'

'Weakweed?' the iron mage shouted. 'You poisoned my magic!'

'Hardly. I assure you the dosage was carefully considered. Within two or three days you'll be able to work your Jan'Tep spells once again. As your physician, however, I'd advise against it. Give yourself time to heal, and in that healing, perhaps a chance to find new insight.'

The silk mage, seemingly having recovered now, asked, 'And what insight do you suppose that would be, Argosi?'

'Only this: that there are things in this world more dangerous than spells, master mages.' She held each man's gaze in turn. Even from where I sat, a dozen yards away in the darkness, I found her calm terrifying. Finally she said, 'I am one of those things.'

57

For a long time no one spoke. The Argosi seemed to be waiting for something, some hidden acknowledgement in the two men's eyes that I couldn't see. She must have found it, however, because when she sat back, she said, 'Good. Now, shall we begin those negotiations?'

9

The Two Decks

I didn't think it was possible to feel bored so soon after having nearly died, but the Argosi proved me wrong. I'd assumed her version of 'negotiations' would amount to a few carefully worded threats. It turned out to be a verbal contract that must have been almost as long as the final peace treaty that ended the last war between the Daroman empire and the Jan'Tep arcanocracy. By the time the two mages had started making their way back down the road, I was fairly sure they'd forgotten why they'd come here in the first place.

My own legs and back were stiff from sitting silently next to Seneira for the past two hours. She'd dozed off a couple of times, leaning her head against my shoulder. It felt odd to be so close to someone about whom I knew nothing – especially someone who seemed quite convinced I was the local village idiot. For her part, she seemed to have decided that life was already as unpleasant as it could get and she might as well sleep through as much of it as she could.

'What'd I miss?' Reichis asked, dropping a partially eaten rabbit carcass on the ground next to where Seneira and I sat.

'Oh spirits of earth and air, what is that smell?' she asked, pushing herself up and swinging her stick in wild arcs as she stumbled away, swearing about idiot farmhands and their stupid talking animals. I didn't bother mentioning that I'd never been to a farm in my life.

Reichis was profoundly offended by her outrage. He picked the rabbit back up in his mouth and muttered, 'None for her, I guess.'

'Will you people keep it down?' came a weary, croaking voice from near the campfire. 'Can't a body die in peace?'

I jumped to my feet and ran to Ferius. Her face was pale and her hair lank, but when her eyes found me she gave me a little smirk that loosened the clamps around my chest and let me breathe easier for the first time since the fight. 'Hey, kid,' she said, reaching up a hand to put it against my cheek. Her eyes narrowed as she listened to the incessant stream of Seneira's swearing. 'Your little friend's got quite the vocabulary.'

'Her name's Seneira,' I replied. 'She doesn't think much of me.'

'Well, you take some getting used to.' Ferius passed a hand over her ribs, her fingers stopping at the bandages wrapped around her torso. 'Did you take up medicine ways while I was napping?'

'Hello, sister,' the other Argosi said, coming to stand next to me. She reached behind her neck and unfastened the clasp holding the wide strip of cloth that hid the lower half of her face. I guess I'd assumed she must have some kind of disfig-urement, but underneath the covering she looked perfectly ordinary to me. Her skin was darker than Ferius's, more Berabesq than Daroman, but she could just as easily have been Jan'Tep or one of the borderland folk. Centuries of migrations across the seas had led to a mix of cultures on this continent, bonded more by purpose than by racial origin.

'Kid?' Ferius asked.

'Yeah?'

'During the fight, did I get hit on the head real hard?'

'Not that I saw.'

She sighed. 'That's what I figured. Hey, Rosie.'

I turned to the other Argosi. 'Rosie? That's your name?'

The woman looked pained. And annoyed. 'The Path of the Wild Daisy is one that too often takes solace in simple amusements.'

'Got that right,' Ferius said. She reached out a hand to me. 'Help me up, kid. No sense putting this off.'

Something about her expression made me wary. 'Putting what off?' I asked.

She struggled just to sit up, wincing from the pain. 'Gotta kick Rosie's ass.'

'Wait – what? You can't be serious. She helped save us! Besides, you have three broken ribs. You nearly died!'

'Yeah, well, life is short. Gotta get to the important things while you still can.'

I glanced over to where Seneira was running a brush across the donkey's coat. *Maybe she can tell me what the hell's going on.*

The other Argosi seemed neither concerned nor amused. 'I'm afraid we'll have to put off our – what is that word you find so entertaining? "Wrastlin'"?' She knelt down and reached into the folds of her garments once again, this time pulling out a deck of cards. 'I have news.'

Ferius pursed her lips, staring at the cards, then reached into her black leather waistcoat and pulled out her own deck. This one I recognised as her true deck – each suit a representation of a people and its ways, the 'concordances' as she called them. The deck held other cards too, special cards that Ferius said were unique to each Argosi; the so-called 'discordances' that depicted people or events that could change the course of history. 'Let's get to it then,' Ferius said. 'But next time you and me are goin' round and round, Rosie.'

The other woman sat opposite her and began laying cards from her deck face down between them. Ferius did the same.

'What are you doing?' I asked. 'A minute ago you were ready to fight and now you're—'

Ferius looked up at me. 'What does it look like we're doing, kid? We're playing cards.'

The first time I'd met Ferius she'd taught me dozens of card games. I had a good memory for this sort of thing, and I was pretty sure I remembered them all. Whatever game she played with Rosie was something I'd never seen before. It seemed to consist of picking up seven of your opponent's cards at random, examining them and laying them out in a pattern. The other player would then do likewise. The process would repeat itself with new cards and, once they ran out, they would reshuffle the decks, never seeming to arrive at an end point.

Seneira sat next to me. 'Don't suppose *your* Argosi ever told you why they use the cards instead of talking to each other like normal people?' she asked.

'I think . . . I think there's more in the images on the cards than we might recognise,' I said, my eyes still glued to the strange game playing out before me. 'And the patterns they use when they're arranging the cards . . . maybe they can convey things that can't be spoken with words.'

Seneira groaned. 'Now you sound like one of them. I was really hoping there would be someone sensible I could talk to.'

62

'She can talk to me,' Reichis chittered, sauntering over to sit next to us. 'I'm the most sensible one here.'

'Reichis says you can—'

'Please don't tell me when your squirrel cat speaks to you,' Seneira said.

'Um, okay. Why not?'

'Because I'm pretty sure squirrel cats don't actually talk and I was hoping to pretend you weren't crazy for a little while longer.'

Reichis snorted. 'She has a point, Kellen. I always thought you were a bit—'

'Shut up, Reichis.'

The bizarre card game went on for another hour or so. Periodically Ferius would break the silence with some offhand comment like, 'Well, well, who knew the Gitabrian merchants' guild would ever sort that mess out,' or, 'Figured some Daroman general would get to that old fool eventually.'

The other Argosi – I was still having trouble picturing her as a 'Rosie' – seemed to prefer silence, so much so that after Ferius had spoken aloud for the ninth or tenth time she asked, 'Does it serve some purpose to go on prattling like this?'

'Serves me just fine. You feelin' a touch antsy? You could always get on that donkey of yours and ride into town to find us some liquor.'

'Liquor. Smoking reeds. This silly borderland slang you put on. You lose your way, sister.'

Ferius set her hand of cards down on her lap. 'A body don't get lost unless it gets too fixed on one destination, *sister.*'

The other woman gave a soft snort that managed to convey an ocean's worth of derision as she nodded towards me. 'Is this how you teach him the Argosi tenets? By turning them into country sayings and amusing anecdotes?'

'You think if I say them fancier it'll make some kind of difference?'

'From what I've seen of your student, I doubt it will make any difference at all. He used magic when he shouldn't have, drawing the Jan'Tep mages right to this area and risking my charge's life in the process. Then he panicked in the fight, and all of you would have died had I not been there to save you. Were he to live a hundred years I doubt you'd make an Argosi out of him.'

Reichis pawed at my leg. 'Hey, Kellen, I think that Argosi bitch just insulted you.'

'Yeah,' I whispered back. 'I don't think she likes me much.'

'She likes you just fine,' Ferius said. I always forget how good her hearing is. 'Rosie's just trying to distract me so I won't figure out that she's been holding back a card this whole time.'

A hint of a smile crept over the other Argosi's features. 'And you seem to think you can goad me into ignoring the fact that you're obviously holding back one of your own.'

'What, this old thing?' Ferius flicked her wrist and a card appeared between her thumb and forefinger. 'Must've fallen into my sleeve when I was shufflin' the deck.'

She handed the card to the other woman, who examined it for a long time before turning it over and dropping it to the ground. It was one of Ferius's discordance cards – the one she'd painted to look like me, the one with the word 'Spellslinger' written at the bottom. 'You've given it the right image, but the wrong name. That's the difference between you and me, sister. You follow the path of sentiment rather than enlightenment.'

'Yeah? Why don't you enlighten me then?'

The other Argosi held a card in the palm of her hand. She flipped her hand over once . . . twice . . . on the third time the card was face down. Even I could see from the back that it wasn't the same card that had been there a second ago. 'This is the sign we must follow now.'

Ferius started to reach for it, but then pulled her hand back. 'The difference between you and me, sister, is that I've never needed to pretend to see the wind in order to know which way it's blowin'.' She called over to Seneira. 'Hey, little miss. How about you come on over here for a proper introduction?'

Seneira complied, standing up and swinging her stick in wide arcs as she slowly approached them. I followed along, nervous that exhaustion and the uneven ground might lead to a fall – though absolutely determined not to repeat my previous disastrous attempt at chivalry. Ferius watched me with a raised eyebrow and asked, 'You really buying the whole blind thing, kid? Thought you were sharper than that.'

'What? You mean she's—'

'Blind people get real good at making their way through the world – they don't stumble around the way she does. They find themselves a proper cane, not some broken stick they picked up off the ground.' To the Argosi she said, 'You told a falsehood a minute ago, sister. It wasn't Kellen who drew the bounty hunters here; it was the girl they wanted. You brought this trouble to us.'

Seneira stopped a few feet away. 'I'm sorry,' she said. 'I didn't mean for anyone else to get hurt because of me.' Tears began to appear at the bottom edge of the cloth covering her eyes, sliding down her cheeks.

'Ain't nobody's fault exactly,' Ferius said, slapping a hand against the bandages covering her ribs. 'I don't reckon you asked for this trouble any more than Kellen did.' She nodded to Seneira. 'You can go ahead and take that silly blindfold off now, girl.'

'Wait . . . What's going on here?' I asked.

Ferius reached over, plucked the card from the other Argosi's hand and sent it spinning high up into the air at the same time as Seneira untied the knot holding the cloth around her head. Just as the blindfold came loose, the card landed at my feet, face up. It depicted a girl with black marks twisting around her right eye. When I looked up, I found myself staring into Seneira's green eyes and found those same markings.

'Told you I wasn't blind,' she said, letting the strip of cloth fall to the ground. 'I just couldn't see.'

I reached down to pick up the card, the discordance that the Argosi woman had painted because she believed it signified a force that could change the course of history. I saw now the word she'd written at the bottom of the card.

'Shadowblack'.

WAY of WIND

The way of the Argosi is the way of wind.

There are many winds that travel across the land: winds of change, winds of sorrow, winds of joy, winds of war. To know the truth of the world, an Argosi must listen to these winds, awaken to their touch upon the skin and follow every discordance, for any one of them could grow into a hurricane that could change the course of history. It is for this reason that the arrival of an Argosi is sometimes seen as . . . troubling.

10

Diplomacy

'Tell me again why you've got us escorting Seneira all the way back to Teleidos?' I asked, pulling on the reins in an effort to nudge my horse back on the path. He had a bad habit of drifting off the road for no particular reason – a character trait he shared with Ferius. 'And don't start up with that nonsense about "following the wind" again. That's *not* an answer.'

Ferius angled her frontier hat forward to keep the sun out of her eyes. 'Sure it is, kid. It's just not the one you're looking for.' She shot me a warning look. 'So how about you take my advice and leave it alone?'

I glanced back to where Rosie and Seneira rode a little ways behind us, just out of earshot. 'But she's not even Jan'Tep. How could she have the shadowblack?'

'First of all, kid, quit talking as if you Jan'Tep were a race. You're just a bunch of magically inclined folk who came to this continent searching for the kind of power that had faded from your own lands.' She reached out a finger and flicked my cheek. 'Different skin colours, different faces, eyes, noses . . . you're like a big bowl of beggar's stew.'

That got my back up. 'That "beggar's stew" you're talking

about happens to produce the finest mages on the continent, who just happen to live in the most beautiful cities in the world.'

Ferius snorted. 'That sure would impress me if your people had actually *built* those cities.'

She had a point. Why was I sticking up for the Jan'Tep? My ancestors had started a war with the Mahdek, massacred their people and stolen their cities, all so they could take control of the oases that gave us our magic. There probably weren't a hundred full-blooded Mahdek left in the world.

Ferius was one of them.

'Sorry,' I said.

'Sorry for what?'

I whispered, 'Because *you're* Mahdek.'

'I'm *Argosi*, kid. Mahdek blood is something I was born with. The path of the wild daisy is what I *chose*.'

Reichis, lying on his back between the front of the saddle and the horse's neck, staring up at the cloudless sky wistfully, decided to chime in. 'Squirrel-cat blood is what *I* was born with,' he said. 'And the path of the wild squirrel cat is what *I* choose. Why overcomplicate things?'

When I translated for Ferius, she chuckled. 'Well, well, squirrel-cat philosophy, right there in a nutshell.' She tipped her hat to him. Reichis loved that and mimed the gesture back at her.

I felt oddly left out. In some ways Ferius and Reichis had more in common with each other than either did with me: they'd both chosen a path for themselves. They were . . . *something*. Me? I'd made a grand total of *one* important decision in my life: to walk away from my people, and I was starting to think that that had been a mistake. Outlaws are nobodies, with no families, no friends and no real purpose. Calling yourself one is just a faster way of describing all the things you *don't* have.

'You all right, kid?' Ferius asked.

'Just great.' I tried to shake off my morose thoughts and turn my attention back to the question that Ferius had – yet again – managed to dodge. 'Regardless of whether or not the Jan'Tep are a race, the shadowblack only manifests among mages. Seneira swears she isn't one, so either she's lying or—'

'Leave it alone, kid.'

'No!' I realised I'd shouted and glanced back to see if Rosie and Seneira had noticed. Fortunately they both seemed pretty intent on ignoring me. 'I'm the one with a price on my head, not you. Seneira's got bounty hunters after her and they won't hesitate to kill me too, so I at least deserve to know why you've got us riding into even more danger than usual.'

'Fine. You remember back in that town when those folks saw the shadowblack around your eye and they all reckoned you had some sort of "demon plague"?'

'Yeah, but that's just superstitious nonsense. There's no such thing as a—'

Ferius gave me a sharp look. 'Is that so? You really figure four months outside your own lands is enough to make you an expert on what can and what can't become an epidemic?'

There was a tension in her face, and in the tone of her voice, that was at odds with her usual glib demeanour. A thought occurred to me that made my guts go cold. 'You've seen a mage plague before, haven't you?'

She wouldn't meet my eye, but stared straight ahead at the road in front of us. 'Yeah, kid. I've seen a plague. Can't say for certain whether it spread through magic or infection or something else, but people had a name for it: the Red Scream. And it was just as bad as it sounds. Until it got dealt with.'

'Dealt with how?'

Ferius glanced back at Rosie, and the two of them shared a look that didn't seem friendly at all. 'Ask me some other time, kid.'

I might have pressed her on the subject, but at that precise moment my eyes landed on Seneira for just a second. Apparently it was a second too long. 'Are you staring *again*?' She glowered.

Usually it takes people at least a full day to decide they dislike me, but Seneira clearly hadn't wanted to wait that long. She seemed perpetually convinced that I was either leering or making fun of her. Usually it was neither. I just wasn't used to being around someone my own age any more. It didn't help that she was pretty either – way too pretty for me to be relaxed around her. Ferius said this might be a sign that I was developing a mental disorder and suggested I let her know if and when I noticed any additional symptoms.

But my discomfort around Seneira wasn't simply my usual awkwardness or even the fact that just talking to her made me feel oddly guilty about Nephenia. The real reason I was so troubled by Seneira was the markings around her eyes, so much like mine that even though it hurt to look at them, I couldn't stop myself.

'I could give you some of my *mesdet* paste,' I said, reaching back into my saddlebag. 'You could cover up the markings so you wouldn't need to wear that blindfold every time we pass through a village.'

She rolled her eyes – she did that a lot. 'Of course! Paste!

74

Why didn't I think of that? Oh, maybe because I *did*, of course.'

'So why—'

'It burns, that's why. Whenever I try to put paste on it, the skin starts to feel like it's on fire.'

I nodded. It never felt completely comfortable to cover over the markings, but it wasn't *that* bad. But Seneira, despite her plain clothing, looked and talked like she came from money. Probably she'd never had much hardship in her life before. Of course, neither had I until recently. 'Maybe you're just not used to it. Just try a little.'

'"Just try a *little*"?'

'I have seen the effects,' Rosie said, her voice calm as a warm breeze. 'They are . . . uncomfortable to behold. The child's shadowblack seems to seethe when anything is applied to it, and the pain is clearly considerable.'

'*Thank you*,' Seneira said.

'Though I confess she is unpleasant even at the best of times.'

'Maybe if you hadn't kidnapped m—'

'*Rescued*,' Rosie corrected.

'Wait,' I asked, turning to look at Seneira, suddenly concerned this situation wasn't at all what I'd thought. 'You said you were with her of your own free will.'

'It's complicated,' she replied, though her attitude seemed to soften towards me just a bit. 'I got into some trouble, and . . .' she hesitated, then smiled evilly as she said, '*Rosie*, helped me out.'

Rosie frowned. 'That's not my name. I am the Path of Thorns and—'

Seneira cut her off. 'No normal person refers to themselves

as "the path" of anything, so we can either go with Rosie or you can tell me your *real* name.'

The Argosi opened her mouth to say something, then closed it again. Finally she gave in. 'I suppose "Rosie" is as good as anything else.' She grimaced at Ferius, clearly blaming her for the nickname.

'Heh heh,' Reichis sniggered. 'I like having these two around. It's fun.'

'Anyway,' Seneira went on, 'I was being pursued by those insane Jan'Tep you met and Rosie fought them off. Then they kept coming and I knew I couldn't make it on my own. She offered to help protect me, only now she won't take me where I want to go.'

'The child ran away from home,' Rosie explained.

'I'm sixteen! When you're sixteen it's not called "running away", it's called, "going where you want to go".'

'Which you are free to do, but *I* am going north, to your city. So if you want my protection, that's where you'll go as well.'

'Wait,' I said to Rosie. 'If Seneira doesn't want to go home, why are *you* going there?'

It was Seneira who replied. Whatever goodwill I'd bought myself by my concern that she might be a prisoner had evidently been spent. 'How thick are you? I'm neither Jan'Tep nor am I a student of magic, but somehow I caught the shadowblack.' She pointed to Rosie and Ferius. 'These two weirdos are Argosi, which means anything strange happens in the world and they feel a burning need to go paint a card about it. Obviously they think the markings mean something.'

'They *do* mean something,' Rosie insisted.

'They *might*,' Ferius countered.

76

The two of them exchanged a look that seemed significant but meant nothing to me. Evidently I knew as little about the Argosi as I did about everything else in the world outside my home.

Having had enough of Seneira's disdain, I decided to change the subject. Ferius says that a good way to make people like you is to get them to talk about themselves. I know – it doesn't make sense to me either. Wouldn't someone want to hear about *your* good qualities in order to form a favourable opinion of you? Still, every once in a while she's onto something, so I asked Seneira, 'If you aren't studying to be a mage, what *are* you studying?'

It took a few seconds before she gave me an answer, and once she did, I understood her hesitation. 'I'm going to be a diplomat.'

It took a long time for Reichis to stop laughing.

11

The Face in the Sand

We stayed away from populated settlements as much as we could during that next week. Even when Seneira and I covered up our markings, even when nothing untoward happened, the people we encountered seemed uncomfortable around us. It was as if some small part of them could sense the shadowblack in their midst, like a breeze that makes the hairs on the back of your neck stand on end.

Avoiding towns suited me fine, since I wasn't exactly getting along with strangers lately. The only problem was it meant sleeping out in the desert every night, and the novelty of that experience wears off pretty quickly; hard ground, cold weather, occasional sandstorms, and the feeling of being exposed to a mean and angry world. It annoyed me no end that Seneira – whom I liked to think of as a privileged little princess – seemed to handle the outdoors better than I did.

'You're staring again,' she said, not even bothering to open her eyes from where she lay on her bedroll near the campfire. How did she *do* that?

'Sorry,' I said.

'Hey, Kellen,' Reichis chittered, 'ask her if she—'

'Don't start.'

The presence of a human female my age – and specifically my awkwardness around her – was a source of endless amusement for the squirrel cat. He'd suggest various elaborate mating rituals that I should perform for Seneira, insisting these were practised by 'reputable cultures' around the world, but which I was pretty sure he was inventing by himself. When I pointed out that there was already a girl I was interested in, he'd remind me that my chances of ever seeing Nephenia again during my almost certainly short life were slim to none.

'Well, you're even more boring than usual,' he said, then hopped down from my shoulder and wandered off into the darkness. 'I'm going to go murder something.'

'It's called *hunting*, you know.'

'Not the way I do it.'

I lay back down for the third time that night and tried to get some sleep. It only took a minute of shifting around uncomfortably to figure out that wasn't going to happen. It wasn't just the hard ground or the cold night air that bothered me – I felt a constant buzzing at the back of my skull that made me anxious all the time. Ever since that silk mage had shown me the spell warrant, I couldn't close my eyes without wondering who might be coming for me next.

What made it worse was that I couldn't talk to Ferius about my fears now that Rosie and Seneira were around. When we'd first left my homeland, whenever I got restless at night, Ferius would just start talking out of the blue, making up some story or going on about this plant or that insect and how strange it was that they'd got to this place and this time. But now she spent every night sitting across from Rosie, the two of them playing cards, hardly ever saying a word. Even *that* made me nervous.

Eventually I got into the habit of going for a walk into the desert whenever I couldn't sleep. The sand in this region was mostly blue in colour, which made it feel like wading out to sea. I liked it though – far enough from the fire, the breeze made the sand look like waves swirling all around me. If you stared long enough, you could almost imagine pictures in the sand: animals, ships, faces . . . they'd appear for a few seconds and then the wind would send them drifting away and a new image would emerge. Sometimes, when the breeze was soft enough, the shapes would remain and a face might almost seem to come alive, the eyes opening, the lips moving just a little.

The face I saw most often on my walks was that of my sister, Shalla. Sometimes if I squinted down at the sand just so, I could picture her, as if a western wind had come all the way here from the Jan'Tep territories to blow a million particles into the shape of her face, eyes deep in concentration, her customary frown letting me know I'd disappointed her once again. It was all just a trick of the mind of course: the dim light from the stars and the moon glinting on the sand could fool you into imagining you were seeing just about anything or anyone if you were tired enough. Still, I couldn't help but wonder what my sister would say to me if she were here.

Turned out there was no need to speculate.

'Finally,' said the image of Shalla swirling in the sand beneath me. 'I thought you'd never figure it out.'

12

The Messenger

I quickly ran through a series of possible explanations for my vision: another silk mage? Unlikely – there couldn't be *that* many of them wandering around the borderlands. Besides, now that I'd experienced what it was like when they got in your head, I was pretty sure I'd recognise the sensation. I could be crazy of course – that seemed like a pretty natural reaction to having people try to kill you over and over again. But somehow that felt too easy.

There was a third possibility of course, though that was even more troubling.

'It's me, dummy,' Shalla said, the particles of sand shifting to make her mouth assume a slight smirk.

'How . . . ? How are you doing this, Shalla?'

The smile shifted to become even more self-satisfied. 'Do you like it? I devised the spell myself. Well, I mean, there are precedents of course, but I'm fairly sure I'm the first mage to successfully project my image across this kind of distance.'

I'd been a pretty good student of magical theory, back when I was an initiate, so I couldn't help but try to figure out how she was doing it. At first I thought the fact that I was hearing her voice meant she was using silk magic to make the words appear in my mind, but silk spells don't travel well, and besides, Shalla sounded like she was whispering to me. 'Breath magic,' I said at last. 'You're using the wind to carry your image and voice to me.'

The face in the sand nodded. 'Breath *and* a touch of sand magic to deal with time of course. Otherwise there would be a delay whenever we spoke, and that would be annoying. Locating you was the hard part. Fortunately I found a bit of your dried blood on father's worktable, which meant I could key the spell to you.'

The casual way she spoke about the time my own parents had strapped me down to a table and permanently counterbanded me – forever denying me access to five of the six forms of magic – reminded me of one of the reasons why I'd left home in the first place. 'What is it you want, Shalla?'

'Don't be like that. It took me *ages* to make this spell work. It turns out the winds have to be moving just right, so I'm not sure how often I can do this.'

'Then why go to all the trouble?'

The sand shifted again, making my sister's image look oddly hurt by my words. 'I'm worried about you, Kellen. I need to know that you're okay.'

'I'm fine.'

Suddenly the wind picked up, and Shalla's voice became angry. 'You're not! Mother's been dosing herself with potions so that she can look for you with scrying spells – did you know that? She watched you getting beaten up by that boy. She cried for hours, threatening to leave if Father didn't go find you and bring you home.'

'And what did the great and noble Ke'heops say to that?'

A pause, and a shift in the breeze that made the image start

82

to fade. I thought the spell was broken, but a moment later the sands came together again. 'You know he can't risk leaving right now, Kellen. The council hasn't made him clan prince yet. He needs to be careful, bide his time until the other lords magi finally give our house the prestige and power it deserves.'

'Well, I wish him luck,' I said, knowing it would annoy Shalla. My people don't believe in luck.

The sand forming her eyebrows arched. 'Don't you care about us any more? You haven't asked how any of us are doing. Ra'meth is still alive, you know. He's weak, but he's still got friends on the council. Tennat and his brothers have sworn to destroy you and everyone who helped you.'

'Nephenia . . .' I hadn't meant to say her name aloud, but now I needed to ask, 'Is she all right?'

Shalla hesitated for a long while, and I knew she was contemplating what she might be able to make me do by threatening to withhold the information. But my sister is not nearly so cruel as she likes to pretend. 'Mouse girl is fine. Her name is Neph'aria now, remember?'

Neph'aria. I'd forgotten that she'd received her mage's name when she passed her trials. Now she could start her life, take care of her mother and be free of her father's rule.

I hope you find happiness, Neph, even if it'll never be with me.

Shalla must have sensed my weakness. 'She's seeing Pan'erath now, you know.'

'Pan?' Panahsi had been my best friend – my only friend really. But all that had changed when I'd sided with Ferius and uncovered the truth about our people. The Jan'Tep don't take betrayal lightly. Panhasi had been almost like a brother to me, but now he was Pan'erath: a loyal Jan'Tep mage, and I was a traitor.

'His family is more powerful than they were, and his grandmother has offered . . . protection to Neph'aria and her mother in exchange for a uniting of their two houses.'

'You're saying Nephenia's going to marry Pan?'

The image in the sand nodded. 'In a year's time . . . unless you do something about it.' The soft whisper of her voice became almost pleading. 'Come home, Kellen. It's not safe for you out there in the borderlands. Come back and serve your own people so we can protect you.'

That almost made me laugh. 'Protect me? How exactly are "my people" going to protect me when someone on the council of lords magi invoked a spell warrant on me?'

'What? That's not possible. No one would—'

'I saw the warrant myself, Shalla.'

'That . . .' The image in the sand seemed to waver. 'I'm going to find out what's going on, Kellen, I promise. If Ra'meth or one of his allies did this, then he's in violation of the council's edict against our two houses feuding. He'll be dismissed from the council.' A faint smile started to appear. 'In fact, if I can prove it, his entire family will be exiled from the Jan'Tep territories.'

'Shalla, don't do anything stupid. Ra'meth is dangerous. If he finds out you're looking into his affairs he might—'

She gave a faint snort, and grains of sand rose up from the ground as though carried on the breeze. 'I'm not afraid of Ra'meth, Kellen. After all, *you* beat him, didn't you?'

Without waiting for a reply, Shalla's image disappeared, leaving me standing alone like an idiot talking to the empty desert.

13

The Voices

Ferius and Rosie were *still* engrossed in their card games when I got back to our campsite. Reichis was off hunting – or *murdering*, as he liked to call it. Seneira was gone.

'Where is she?' I asked the two Argosi.

Ferius looked up from her cards. 'She ain't here?'

She started to get up but Rosie put a hand on her shoulder. 'The child sometimes prefers to be alone when the attacks come, as they inevitably do at night.'

'Attacks?' I asked. 'What attacks?'

Rosie tilted her head as she looked up at me. 'Do you not suffer symptoms from the shadowblack?'

I did of course, but once in a while, maybe every month or if I let myself get too angry – certainly not every night!

'Leave her be,' Rosie warned. 'This is something she must endure alone.'

The Argosi made suffering in solitude sound so obvious, so *noble*, but I hated having the shadowblack. The pain and the horrible visions I would suddenly see before me . . . The last thing I wanted when I was affected was to be by myself.

'Go on, kid,' Ferius said, staring down Rosie before she could stop me. 'Do what you think is best.'

I ran back to the campfire and traced Seneira's steps, following them into a copse of straggly desert trees until I could hear her breathing in the shadows. 'Seneira?'

'Go away,' she said, her voice rough, as though she'd been screaming for hours, though I would have heard her if she had.

'I just want to help.'

'How?' she asked. 'Can you make the episodes stop? Can you make the shadowblack go away? Can you make the markings stop hurting, even a little?'

I could make out her silhouette now, huddled by a tree. Very slowly I walked towards her. 'I'll go if you want, but you don't need to suffer through this alone. Why don't you come back to the fire where it's warm?'

'I don't want the others to see it,' she said.

'See what?'

I was close enough now that when she turned to me I could see her face in the dim light of the moon. The shadowblack markings around her eyes were swirling, shifting as if they had come alive.

Despite all my good intentions, I very nearly backed away. I'd had the condition longer than Seneira, but even during my worst episodes I'd never felt the markings twisting and turning like that. Worse, I could see that hers had grown, become a fraction longer, winding their way even further around her right eye. She'd told us that the shadowblack had first appeared a month ago, and yet it was progressing so much faster on her than on me.

'It hurts, Kellen,' she said. 'Why does it hurt so much?'

I swallowed my discomfort and knelt down next to her. She was holding a small oval object attached to a thin silver chain between her hands. 'Is that a charm?'

She shook her head and handed it to me, pressing a small button on the top that made it pop open into two halves. I had to hold it up to the moonlight to see that it held a tiny painting of a young boy. His features had enough in common with Seneira's that I guessed he must be her younger brother. 'Tyne saved up every penny he had for a year to get that made,' she said. 'He'll have turned seven since I've been gone. I'd promised him that for his birthday this year I'd make him one of me, so we could . . . It doesn't matter now.'

I gave her the locket and sat down beside her. 'How long does the pain last?'

She slid the chain back over her head. 'It's different each time. Sometimes just a few seconds, other times for hours.'

'A stabbing pain?' I asked. 'Like something burning inside your eye.'

She nodded, but then looked unsure. 'It's . . . It's hard to describe. It feels like someone's dripping acid on my skin, but it's what I feel inside that hurts the most.'

'The visions?' The worst part for me was the nightmarish images that came to me whenever the episodes took over – the way the whole world and everyone in it turned ugly. Cruel. It was as if all I could see was the very worst in people.

'I hear voices,' Seneira said. 'They say these awful things to me, Kellen. I can hear them laughing at me, taunting me, telling me they can make me do anything they want. It's like . . . It's like . . .'

'Like the demon wants you to know that one day it's going to take control of you?'

She nodded and looked at me as though she was waiting for me to say something that would make it better. When I didn't, she started to cry.

Not knowing what else to do, I took her hand. 'It's going to be—'

'Please don't,' she said. 'Don't lie to me.' She looked past the trees to where the campfire glimmered in the distance, a tiny speck of light in the dark. 'The Argosi, they act like everything is just . . . the way it is, like I need to make peace with whatever is happening to me. I can't. I *can't* pretend it's okay when I can feel in my soul that it's not. Whatever this is, I need to face it head on.'

There was a determination in Seneira that I couldn't help but admire. I leaned back against the tree, still holding her hand in mine. 'The shadowblack is awful,' I admitted. 'When the episodes come . . . it's pretty much the worst thing in the world. Don't let anyone tell you otherwise.'

'What do you do when the attacks come?'

I shrugged. 'Do my best to ignore the visions and wait for the pain to pass.'

She opened her mouth to speak, then suddenly doubled over as though someone had punched her in the stomach. 'Oh gods of sand and sky, it's back again! Make it stop!'

'Seneira,' I said, trying to make my voice as soothing as I could, 'just look at me, all right? Look at me.'

She looked up and I watched in horror as the markings began moving again. The green in her eyes disappeared as they filled with black. 'I hear them, Kellen. The things they're saying to me . . . the laughing . . . Please, make them stop!'

'Ignore them, all right? They aren't real. Try to think about good things. Think about your brother, about all the people you love or the places you enjoy the most.'

She squeezed her eyes shut and I could almost hear her

teeth grinding. Soft moans escaped her lips, becoming names. 'Tyne . . . Father . . . Revian . . . the Academy . . .'

She repeated the names over and over again, squeezing my hand so hard I could feel the bones pushing together, her nails biting into the flesh of my palm. I forced myself not to let go. 'I'm here,' I said, which sounded particularly useless, but somehow it must have made a difference because after a few seconds Seneira looked up at me. The markings around her eyes had stopped moving and the irises were green once again.

'Thank you . . . Kellen.'

The pain and the voices seemed to ease after another minute, then resumed again. It went on like that for an hour or so. Somewhere in there she asked, 'Will you wait with me? Just a little longer?'

The way she spoke . . . it was as if all her strength was slowly sinking away beneath the onslaught of pain and confusion, her resolve being drowned out by the terrifying voices taunting her. I felt her stiffen again as another attack began, and I looked out at the desert to the east of us, hoping to see the first sliver of morning appear over the horizon, but finding only darkness. Dawn was still hours away.

'I'll wait with you,' I said. 'As long as it takes.'

Seneira fell asleep after a while and lay against me, shivering from the cold, so exhausted that I wasn't able to rouse her to walk back to camp. I ended up carrying her, which wasn't easy – she wasn't especially heavy, but a lifetime of training to be a mage hadn't exactly made me particularly strong either. I was grateful when Rosie saw us approaching and came to carry her the rest of the way.

'Her skin is cold,' the Argosi said, setting her down on a bedroll by the fire. 'I take it the episode was somewhat pronounced?'

'"*Pronounced*"?' I repeated incredulously. 'That's what you call it? The shadowblack is *torturing* her!'

'Rosie doesn't mean to sound callous,' Ferius said, kneeling down to examine Seneira. 'She just can't help it. The Path of Thorns and Roses isn't big on sentiment.'

The other Argosi's eyes narrowed. 'I doubt her illness pays heed to sentimentality either. Or do you think bedtime stories and lullabies will ease the girl's suffering?'

Ferius stroked the damp, matted hair from Seneira's face. 'Couldn't hurt.'

'The Red Scream was not swayed by your soft words or kind heart, sister. Those afflicted by the plague would have been better served by a clean death than by your futile efforts to comfort them.'

The firelight reflected ominously on the skin of Ferius's cheeks as she locked eyes with the other Argosi. 'This *isn't* the Red Scream, Rosie, so just back off.'

The other woman showed no signs of being cowed. 'You dishonour my charge's courage with your coddling. If what she carries is some new form of magical plague, then we must prepare ourselves for the inevitable, and I fear you lack the —'

Reichis came padding out of the darkness. He sniffed at Seneira, then looked up at the two Argosi and hissed at them.

'Reichis?' I asked.

'The girl's only pretending to be asleep,' he growled. 'She's terrified and these two are just making it worse.'

No one but me knew what he was saying, but Ferius caught

my expression and soon figured it out. 'Morning's on its way. Best we all get some sleep and see where tomorrow takes us.'

Rosie nodded, conceding the point, but as she turned to move off she said, 'An Argosi follows the winds wherever they lead, sister, but never forget that the way of thunder follows close behind.'

Reichis glared after her. 'I am totally going to steal her stuff when she's not looking.'

I glanced down at Seneira. Her eyes were still closed but I could see the tears beginning to trickle down her cheeks. I was trying to think of something comforting to say when Reichis surprised me by nestling himself up against her neck, sharing his warmth with her.

I'd never known Reichis to be protective of another human being ... well, *any* human being, really, since most of the time he wasn't all that concerned with protecting *me*. But I didn't resent his instinct – if anything, I shared it. Seneira wasn't a mage or even one of my people, and yet the shadow-black was hurting her even more than it did me.

Something wasn't right. Reichis could sense it, and, even though he pretended not to like her, he felt a compulsion to guard her.

I guess I felt the same way.

Seneira's eyes remained closed, but her hand reached up and gently stroked his fur.

'Just so we're clear, Kellen,' the squirrel cat said as he closed his eyes, '*you* ever try petting me and I'll bite your hand off.'

14

Teleidos

By the next morning Ferius and Rosie had apparently come to some kind of agreement about following winds or breezes or some such Argosi nonsense because they were considerably more cordial as we continued our journey towards the city of Teleidos. I was glad to have the tension between them lessened, but one thing was still bothering me.

I let my horse fall behind the others and waited until Ferius joined me.

'Something on your mind, kid?' she asked.

'If Rosie thinks Seneira might have some kind of plague,' I began, keeping my voice low, 'then why are we going back to her city? Shouldn't we be keeping her away from populated areas?'

'First of all, none of us knows what's ailing the girl, so don't let Rosie get you all riled up. Second, magical plagues don't spread through the air or from bodily contact like normal diseases. And third, in case you haven't noticed, we're not letting her near anyone who hasn't already got a mite –' she gave me a smirk – '*too* close.'

I decided to pretend I didn't know what she was talking about.

Reichis did the squirrel-cat equivalent of chortling. 'See? I'm not the only one who thinks—'

'What about this "Red Scream"?' I asked Ferius. 'You and Rosie keep—'

'The Red Scream is ancient history, kid,' she replied, nudging her horse to ride on ahead of me. 'Leave it buried where it belongs.'

I couldn't get anything more out of her about magical plagues or why the Argosi would be so concerned about them. One look from Rosie told me she wasn't about to enlighten me either.

Seneira seemed better than she had the night before, though she didn't talk about what had happened. A kind of polite distance had settled itself between us, which felt odd after having spent hours together hand in hand while she fought through the attacks. I understood though: the shadowblack was something you lived with by pretending it didn't exist except when you had no choice. The pain was bad, but like Seneira had said, it was the voices – or in my case the visions – that made you feel sick even after the pain had passed.

But if Seneira didn't want to talk about her condition, she was more than happy to lecture us about the Seven Sands.

'The Daroman empire cut this road through the desert over two hundred years ago,' she explained. 'Not so they could take over the borderlands, you understand – just for convenience in case they had to go to war with one of the countries on the other side.'

'Why not just annex the Seven Sands into their own empire?' I asked.

'Because they can't be bothered,' she replied, and spread

her arms wide. 'Why concern yourself with the responsibility of governing a country when you can so conveniently manipulate it to your own ends?'

'I didn't think the borderlands *were* a country,' I said.

That turned out to be a mistake. Even Reichis sniffed the air and said, 'I think you just ticked her off, Kellen.'

'The Seven Sands *is* a country,' Seneira insisted. 'Just because the great powers use it as a kind of no-man's-land to keep from killing each other every day, doesn't mean we aren't a nation.'

Rosie nudged her horse closer to mine. 'The Daroman generals, the Berabesq viziers and the Jan'Tep clan princes rely on the Seven Sands staying ungovernable,' she explained. 'It helps keep the peace between their three nations to have it there right between them, and keeping it weak prevents it from becoming a threat to any of them.'

'That's not the only reason,' Seneira said angrily. 'The Berabesq use our citizens as go-betweens to trade goods with the Daroman and the Jan'Tep, so they never have to shake hands with the "infidels" they've sworn to destroy; for their part, the Daroman nobles hire mining guilds to extract gold, silver and iron for them from the mountain regions without ever having to take responsibility for the people who live there; the Jan'Tep . . .' She looked at me. 'Well, who knows what your people want, Kellen, but whatever it is, I promise you they'll take it from us without providing anything in return.'

She rode on ahead, leaving me with the peculiar feeling that I was somehow accountable for my country's misdeeds, despite the fact that, with one or two exceptions, my people wanted me dead.

After she was out of earshot, Rosie said quietly, 'Having

spent much time with this one, let me say that there are a great many subject that can make for diverting conversation. I suggest leaving the topics of the Seven Sands to one side.'

No kidding.

When Seneira had said she was a student, I'd assumed she meant at some backwater school of the variety one expects to see in a region like the Seven Sands: small, poor and with a barely literate teacher. What I *hadn't* expected was the Academy.

As a young Jan'Tep initiate, I'd heard passing references to a university that had risen up in the middle of the borderlands. Every couple of years a representative would come through our lands looking to recruit students, but they had scarce luck among the families of my clan: why would anyone want to go to a school that didn't teach magic? So, to me, Teleidos had been nothing more than a dot on a map until that afternoon as we entered a valley made fertile by a wide river, and saw for the first time the small but beautiful city that glistened like a jewel against the desert sand.

Most borderland towns consist of a bunch of shabby single-storey buildings cramped together along dusty dirt streets full of potholes. The shops and villas of Teleidos, by contrast, were built from smooth white sandstone that gleamed with blue and bronze accents, rising thirty feet high, adorning curved avenues that ran in concentric circles around the city. I counted eight boulevards radiating from the outskirts of the city to its centre, where a dozen large edifices that could have been palaces or courthouses stood sentry around a tower that stood taller than any building I'd ever seen.

'The Academy,' Seneira said with the reverence of a religious convert.

Even I wasn't immune to the sight. 'It must be a hundred feet tall.'

Ferius snorted. 'Kid, that tower is nearly *four hundred* feet tall. It's almost a hundred and fifty feet wide at the base.'

Four hundred feet. 'How do you even build something that high?' I asked.

'Same way you make any kind of monument: spend a lot of money. But the real question you ought to be askin' is *why* anyone builds something so fancy.'

'Okay, why?'

'Because you're a fool determined to make a statement to the world.' Ferius nudged her horse back into a slow walk, and so didn't see Seneira's outraged glare.

'The Academy is one of those big ideas folks sometimes get into their heads,' Ferius explained as we rode. 'The crazy fella that started it used his fortune to bribe the most famous teachers on the continent to come here. *That's* how they get all these rich foreign kids here. In Darome, in Gitabria, even across the water in the Tsehadi countries, everyone knows if you want to train a future bigwig, send them to the Academy.'

'You make it sound petty,' Seneira said, 'but you're wrong. The Academy isn't just a school, it's an idea – that people from all over can learn together and find common ground, that knowledge and art are more important than geography. And Beren Thrane isn't some "crazy fella"; he's a bold visionary who risked every coin he had to make something important, something that could make the world a better place.'

'All right, all right,' Ferius said, raising her hands in surrender. Then she raised one eyebrow and added, 'I don't suppose this "bold visionary" would happen to be a relative, would he?'

Seneira did not look pleased by that question, but conceded, 'He's my father.'

'Wait,' I said. 'Your father owns this town and you ran off? Why?'

'He doesn't *own* anything. He built the Academy and over the years the town grew and thrived around it. And why I ran off is *my* business and no one else's.'

'When she contracted the shadowblack, she feared it would trigger a panic, resulting in an exodus of students from the Academy,' Rosie explained. 'Thus her father's life's work would come to an abrupt end.'

Seneira scowled at her.

'Glower all you want, child, but I am Argosi; if your intent is to discomfit me, you would have better luck giving dirty looks to a pool of water.'

Seneira seemed willing to test that hypothesis, but I was more curious than ever. 'But where were you running off to?'

'Away.'

Rosie translated the terse reply. 'She thought she could travel to the Jan'Tep territories and find a cure.'

'Thanks a lot,' Seneira muttered. '*So* glad to know you keep secrets.'

'Secrets are not the Argosi way.'

Sure they aren't, I thought, wondering once again why Rosie had been so determined to travel to Seneira's city. *But I'm pretty sure secrets are a big part of the path of thorns and roses.*

15

Homecoming

Dusk was descending over the valley as we rode along the riverbank towards the city. Reichis kept crawling across my upper back, crouching on one shoulder then the other as he snarled at the black water and dark foliage that rippled as we passed by. 'What's the matter?' I asked.

'Swamps,' he replied, growling at the shadows.

'So?'

'So they're disgusting. Full of bugs, and I'll bet there're gods-damned crocodiles just waiting for us in the water.'

There aren't many animals Reichis is afraid of, but crocodiles are definitely the exception. 'Nothing but teeth and evil,' he added with a mutter.

When we finally reached the city gates, Ferius signalled for the rest of us to wait as she dismounted from her horse and went to the guardhouse to negotiate our entrance inside the walls. Argosi are surprisingly good at getting people to let them into places. Seneira put her blindfold back in place and pulled a hood over her head to reduce the chances of someone recognising her.

'Do a lot of people here know you?' I asked.

'I've lived here my whole life and my father's the headmaster of the Academy. What do you think?'

Before I could even think of a suitably caustic reply, she reached out a hand and touched my arm. 'I'm sorry, Kellen. I don't mean to be . . .'

'Grouchy? Bitchy? Annoying and stinky?' Reichis suggested.

I decided to forego his recommendations and instead asked, 'What's the matter?' It was only then that it occurred to me that maybe the shadowblack hadn't been the only reason Seneira had run away from Teleidos.

She hesitated, busying herself with adjusting the hood that was already hiding as much of her face as it possibly could. 'It feels like home,' she said finally, 'but I don't feel like the girl who used to live here.'

Before I could prompt her to say more, Ferius came out of the guardhouse and motioned for us to lead the horses through the city gates.

From a distance, Teleidos had looked like some kind of pristine palace, the smooth, almost polished look of its architecture and the serene geometry of its curved avenues lending it an almost spiritual tranquility. Inside, though, the city was a cacophony of lantern light and joyful laughter, of crowded avenues and buzzing businesses.

Everywhere I looked were signs of wealth and prosperity I'd not seen since coming to the borderlands. There were saloons and taverns, but also restaurants – places where people ate food that wasn't just there to get you to drink more liquor. Clothing stores exhibited their finest wares outside for passers-by, modelled by attractive young men and women. Artisans and craftspersons demonstrated their art, their skilled hands working tools upon wood and stone and canvas to the admiration of small crowds of people who'd stand around bidding on the pieces even before they were finished. Teleidos seemed to have everything, even bookstores. *Bookstores. Plural.*

Strangest of all, though, were the city's inhabitants. Most places I'd been in the borderlands, the only people walking around outside at night were either blind drunk or planning to rob you. But on the elegant sidewalks of Teleidos I saw men and women out walking, talking, eating and acting vaguely civilised. Odder still, a lot of them were around my age.

'Students of the Academy,' Seneira explained as we walked the horses past the crowds. The thin fabric of her blindfold allowed her to see reasonably well even as it hid her eyes from view. Still, anytime someone turned to take notice of the four of us, Seneira would duck her head and walk on the other side of her horse.

Reichis was barely able to contain his excitement. 'Look at them, Kellen! Have you ever seen so many targets all in one place?' He started to bunch his hind legs in preparation for jumping off the horse.

I grabbed him by the scruff of the neck – never a smart thing to do, but we couldn't afford an incident right now and my jaw still hurt from the last time he got me into trouble. 'Don't even think about it.'

He gave me a sad, whimpering expression, as if he were a poor, unloved puppy left out in the rain. 'Not even *one* pocket? I wouldn't have to take an entire wallet. Just a souvenir?'

In the four months since Reichis and I had formed our 'partnership', I'd learned that telling him he couldn't steal things just made him more determined, so instead I said,

'Just wait until we're on the way *out* of town this time before you incite a mob to chase us.'

He sniffed at my ear for a second and I flinched, expecting a sudden nasty bite, but then he said, 'Okay, but I can still steal from the Argosi, right?'

I turned to look at him. 'Rosie? Sure, knock yourself out.'

The muscles in a squirrel cat's face aren't really designed for smiling, but Reichis had taught himself to put on a sort of grin for occasions like these. It creeped me out.

'This way,' Seneira said, gesturing for us to head east along one of the circular avenues. Once we were away from the shops and crowds, she led us up a radiating street, turning again onto another curved avenue closer to the Academy. This area was made up of palatial villas which Seneira explained were given to the masters brought from other parts of the world to teach at the school.

'Where's your house?' I asked.

She didn't reply at first, but kept walking along the circular avenue until we reached a sparser area and a cul-de-sac with what looked like a pleasant but unusually modest two-storey house.

'*That's* where the headmaster of the Academy lives?' I asked.

Seneira nodded. 'It's the house my father grew up in, back when Teleidos was just a ramshackle little town. He says it was all he needed then, so why should he want more now?'

Reichis hopped down from my shoulder and stared up at the plain white building. 'Okay, so he's a moron. All that money and *this* is what he keeps for himself? I bet we won't find a single piece of silver or platinum in the entire house. What a dump.'

'Well,' Ferius said, tying her horse to a thin tree on the

101

side of the alley and removing her pack from the saddlebag. 'Let's not delay the joyous family reunion any more than we have to.'

She and Rosie started up the narrow path towards the house, but Seneira hesitated.

'What is it?' I asked.

She kept staring up at the house, but her gaze seemed even further away. I was surprised when I felt her hand slip into mine. 'I never told them I was going away. I just left a note on the table. What if my father—'

'He's family,' I said. 'Of course he'll be be happy to see you.' Well, I *supposed* that would be the case. My family works a bit differently. I thought about Shalla though, and added, 'Just think of your little brother. What's his name?'

'Tyne,' she said, and even the word seemed to coax a smile from her.

I took that as permission to pull her along with me up to the house. 'Think how thrilled Tyne will be to have his big sister back. I promise you, five minutes after you walk through that door it'll be like you never left.'

Turned out I should never have made that promise.

16

The Empty House

'Where are they?' Seneira asked for the third time as she went from one darkened room to another, her pace and her voice becoming increasingly frantic.

When we'd first found the place empty, I'd thought nothing of it, but then I noticed the way Ferius and Rosie moved slowly, methodically, through each part of the old house, their eyes catching on every sign that something here wasn't quite right. The first, and most obvious, was that there was food on the dining-room table. Reichis leaped up and sniffed at a plate of what looked to be some kind of poultry with vege-tables. The squirrel cat turned back to me, his mouth open the way it gets when he's smelled something rotten. 'Must be at least three days old,' he said, hopping back down. 'What a waste.'

On the floor where he landed I noticed a fork lying there, as if it had fallen and no one had bothered to pick it up. Somebody had left in a hurry.

Hearing Seneira's frenzied footsteps on the top floor, Reichis and I climbed the stairs and looked around. In addition to three bedrooms, a study and a small library, we found a large and well-appointed bathroom. I normally wouldn't have paid it much mind – other than to wonder when the last time was that I'd actually been properly clean – but then I saw the faint reflection of moonlight coming in through the window on the surface of the water that filled the ornate copper bathtub. It was room-temperature, of course, having been abandoned at the same time as the food downstairs. As I was walking away from the tub, my foot struck a wooden bucket. When I knocked it over, water spilled out. That was odd for two reasons: first, because the bathtub had a tap for running water that came through a kind of wood-stove furnace that would heat the water as it passed through. But the stove had no wood inside, nor any ashes, which meant the water in the tub had never been hot. The second strange thing was that when I reached down and felt the water that had poured from the bucket onto the floor, I noticed how cold it was.

'Stinks of magic,' Reichis said, coming over to sniff at it.

I picked up the bucket, and even in the dim light noticed the glyphs along the copper bands that held the wooden slats in place. 'It's got a cooling charm on it,' I said, looking back at the contents of the tub.

A cry from Seneira sent me running to the smallest of the three bedrooms. Though it was sparsely furnished, the cloth animals on the bed and the pair of wooden play swords mounted on the wall like trophies made it obvious that this was the room of a young boy. The bedsheets were in disarray and the blankets were strewn on the floor.

'They took them!' Seneira said, her hands squeezed tightly into fists.

'Who?' I asked.

'I don't know! My father has enemies, people who resent the idea of the Academy. It must be one of—'

'Your family was not taken,' Rosie said, coming into the room with Ferius close behind.

'You don't know that! You're just—'

'Look, child. Look all around you.'

Seneira did, and it amazed me that, despite being so clearly terrified for her father and brother, she was able to get herself under control. I'd have been climbing the walls. I followed her gaze, and noticed the signs all around us. There was a pile of extra sheets stacked on the floor next to the night table. The sheets on the bed weren't just in a messy tangle, they were soiled, which Reichis noticed immediately when he sauntered into the room. 'Piss and sweat,' he said, backing away.

I forced myself to examine the bedding more closely, and that's when I saw the ripped fabric on either side about halfway down – the kind you might get if the bed's occupant were clawing at the sheets repeatedly. It reminded me of the desperate, feverish reflex Seneira herself had shown when she'd practically broken my hand squeezing it during her last attack. The pieces that Rosie and Ferius had already put together finally made sense.

The sweat-soaked sheets, the discarded blankets – both of these pointed to someone with a fever. The extra sheets folded and piled up next to the bed meant the fever had been going on for some time. The half-eaten meal on the dining-room table suggested things had suddenly gotten worse. I imagined Seneira's father, hearing his son screaming for him and running up the stairs. So what does he find? The fever's worse than before, so he uses the bucket with the cooling charm to fill the tub with cold water and puts his son in there to bring the fever down, but the fever *doesn't* go down, so he

105

carries the boy in his arms and flees the house to find help. Judging from the rotting food in the dining room, that would have been at least three days ago.

I caught Seneira's horrified stare and knew that she'd worked it out too – had, in fact, gone one step further. 'Shadowblack,' she whispered. 'Tyne has the shadowblack.'

It was all any of us could do to keep Seneira from running out the front door in search of her brother. 'Father will have taken him to one of the hospitals,' she said, rushing down the stairs.

'Kid, wait a second,' Ferius called out, but Seneira ignored her.

Rosie was more direct. She leaped over the banister to the floor below, landing lightly on the balls of her feet with her knees bent before standing up to block Seneira's path. 'Your reckless urges serve no purpose, child. Listen to *all* the winds before—'

'Don't start with that Argosi nonsense! This is my *brother* we're talking about! If he's got the shadowblack then it means—'

Rosie put her hand on Seneira's cheek with a gentleness at such odds with her previous action that it reminded me of the name by which she called herself: the Path of Thorns and Roses. 'You assume it must be your fault, and yours is a kind and noble heart, one that cannot stand to be the cause of suffering for those you love. It is a good thing, this heart of yours, but you must temper it with wisdom and strength if you wish to help your brother.'

Seneira stared back at her, and I could see in her expression twin impulses fighting each other: an intense dislike of being

106

lectured warring against the desperate need to protect her family. 'Tell me what I need to do,' she said at last.

'First we need to figure out where your pa will have taken your brother,' Ferius said, coming down the stairs to join us. 'A regular hospital is too public. Too many people would have to know that your brother was sick, and word of the shadowblack tends to spread like wildfire on dry brush.' She gestured to the empty house. 'Since nobody's burned this place down yet, it's a safe bet nobody knows about your brother.'

'The Academy has a faculty of medicine,' Seneira said, her face lighting up with hope. 'My father could have snuck Tyne in through one of the maintenance passages in the bottom of the tower and stationed guards outside one of the private rooms.'

Rosie looked unconvinced. 'Such an elaborate plan would be foolhardy and require putting trust in too many people.'

'You never did understand people too well, sister,' Ferius countered. 'A man gets scared, he's going to want to go somewhere safe, somewhere he feels in control.'

'Very well, we will investigate this medical facility inside the Academy first.' She looked to Seneira. 'You must wait here, child, until we return.'

Seneira nodded, then walked right past Rosie and out the door, forcing the rest of us to follow.

Ferius chuckled as she walked by the stunned Argosi. 'See what I mean?'

17

The Great Tower

Up close the Academy was even more daunting than it had been when I'd first seen it from beyond the city walls. The tower itself was surrounded by a cobbled courtyard, lit by brass oil lanterns mounted on poles around the perimeter that allowed groups of students to sit on benches and read or talk or perhaps just stare up at the majesty of their school.

'Is it always this busy at night?' I asked. It was dark enough outside that we could probably reach the Academy without being noticed, but even from the shadows where we huddled I could see, through the massive open double doors, light and activity inside.

'The Academy never closes,' Seneira replied, the anxiety on her face increasing with each step, as though her desire to find her brother had to push against the fear that someone might discover that she had the shadowblack. Even with her blindfold on, there would be questions if one of her fellow students recognised her.

'You shouldn't have come,' Rosie told her, pointedly ignoring the warning glance Ferius shot her. 'Your presence only makes it more difficult for us to enter the medical facility unseen.'

'Really?' Seneira asked. 'And how long do you think you'll

be wandering around the tower trying to find it without me? Even if you can, why would my father or his guards trust a group of strangers just because they claim to know his daughter?'

A look passed across Rosie's features, just for a second, but it was enough for me to be pretty sure I'd just found one of the secrets that the Argosi had been keeping from us. I was about to say something when I caught the slightest flutter of Ferius's hand and saw that she was looking at me, signalling me to keep quiet for now. 'We need a distraction is all,' she said.

I knelt down to face Reichis, who'd made his fur go entirely black and was now almost invisible in the shadows except for his eyes. 'Well, partner?'

He looked back at me, twitching his whiskers. I could tell he was debating with himself whether to extort something from me in exchange, but I guess he remembered that I was currently broke on account of him having all my coins already. 'How big a distraction do you want?'

'Big enough that we can get inside that tower without anyone noticing us, but not so big you get the whole town chasing after us with torches.'

He gave me one of his creepy grins. 'Effective but discreet. Got it.'

'What's he sayin'?' Ferius asked.

I stood back up. 'That we should probably all make peace with our respective gods right about now.'

Reichis gave himself a shake, and his fur changed colour, going from pitch black to a kind of blazing red with silvery stripes. He took off at a run, growling his head off as he did and racing up one of the lamp posts before leaping off and gliding into the courtyard towards the head of one of the students innocently walking by. 'Beware the blood-red squirrel cat!' he declared, grabbing onto the young man's neck, seemingly unconcerned with the fact that no one but me could understand him. 'I crave human flesh tonight, and I will drain the blood of every skinbag I catch!'

The poor guy began screaming his head off, trying to grab at Reichis but having no luck as the squirrel cat kept shifting position. One particularly daring group of students came over to help, even as almost everyone else fled from the screeching animal. Reichis hopped from one would-be saviour to another, delivering a quick bite to an ear or nose before leaving them shouting in panic as he dropped to the cobblestones and raced into the tower.

So much for discreet, I thought, as the rest of us followed him inside.

We entered a massive open level with a thirty-foot ceiling and tiny shops arranged all around the inner wall. A pair of wide stone staircases spiralled up on either side of the tower, intersecting at mezzanines on each level. Rising through the centre was what appeared to be some kind of floating chamber attached to a complex system of weights and pulleys. Two attendants stood by, wearing gloves designed to help them work the cranks that would make the chamber go up and down the tower. They, like everyone else, were fixated on Reichis, who was now racing up the ropes, still screaming various threats that would have sounded ominous were anyone but me able to understand them.

'The medical wing is underground,' Seneira said, leading us down one side of the stairs.

I hesitated, looking back to make sure Reichis was okay. For the most part, people had stopped panicking and were now letting out appreciative oohs and aahs as the squirrel cat performed various acrobatic tricks, using the furry flaps that ran from his front paws to his back legs to glide down from the ceiling before skittering back up the ropes to repeat his performance. The little monster was loving all the attention.

'The squirrel cat's got it handled,' Ferius said, pushing me into motion.

Two floors below ground we came to a set of doors adorned with a stylised tree painted in red.

'That's the sign for healing in these parts,' Ferius explained.

It wasn't all that dissimilar to the first form of the Jan'Tep glyph for blood magic, except that our spells are used for torment as often as for healing.

Inside we found a network of hallways and rooms populated by men and women in white clothing. They each had the red tree symbol on the breast, but with varying quantities of branches. 'The number of branches indicates their rank within the profession,' Seneira explained, staying behind Ferius and Rosie to keep from being noticed. She quickly and confidently guided us down a series of corridors that became progressively less crowded. 'This wing is where the private rooms are,' she explained. 'They're usually only used for visiting dignitaries who don't want their illnesses to become public knowledge in their own countries.'

At the far end of a narrow hall, a man sat on a chair outside one of the rooms, a heavy mace resting across his lap. 'Looks like we need another distraction,' I said, reaching for a pinch of the powders at my side. I figured if I fired a blast the guard would have to leave his post to see what had happened. If we were lucky we could sneak by him and get down the hall and into the room before he returned.

Seneira stayed my hand. 'No more hiding. No more games.' Before any of us could stop her, she stepped out from behind Ferius and walked right up to the guard. 'Hello, Haight,' she said. 'I'd like to see my brother now.'

18

The Fever

The guard looked as if he'd just seen a spirit come to haunt him. 'Seneira?' He rose to his feet. 'We thought you were—'

She gave him a quick hug. 'I'm fine, Haight.'

He stared down at her, then at the rest of us, before his hand gripped his mace tighter. 'Why are you wearing a blindfold, Seneira?'

'Just a little eye trouble,' she replied. 'I need to see Tyne now. He's inside, isn't he?'

Haight hesitated, but I suppose he must have known Seneira wasn't going to be dissuaded. Reluctantly he stepped aside, watching Rosie, Ferius and myself as we passed by, no doubt evaluating how much of a threat each of us might be if he later needed to beat us into submission with that big mace of his.

Through the doors we were met by an expansive room in near pitch black except for a small lantern hanging over a narrow cot. In one corner, shrouded in shadow, a man sat slumped in a chair.

'Father?' Seneira said, a catch in her voice as if she wasn't sure whether to wake him.

The figure rose from the chair and turned to face us looking unsteady on his feet. He was between us and the light so I couldn't make out his features. For a few seconds he stood there, almost like a man drunk, then shuddered as if he had only then woken up. A wracking sob came from his throat. 'Seneira?'

He ran to her, and she had to hold him up as he nearly fell over trying to hug her. 'Father, I'm so sorry,' she said. 'I didn't mean—'

'You're back,' he said, the words barely more than a hoarse whisper, the sound of a man who'd already cried himself voiceless with grief. 'You're back.' He repeated the words over and over, his arms wrapped around his daughter and his head buried in her shoulder.

Rosie, Ferius and I remained at a polite distance, allowing father and daughter to share in their mixture of desperate relief and sorrow with as much dignity as possible. Unfortunately a scraping sound from a square iron grating overhead caught everyone's attention. 'Hey, somebody want to open this gods-damned thing up before I die of claustrophobia in here?' Reichis chittered angrily.

'What is that?' Seneira's father asked, looking up at the beady eyes peering through the grate.

'That's Reichis,' she replied. 'He's Kellen's . . .'

Don't say 'pet'. Don't say 'pet'. Oh, please, ancestors, don't let her say 'pet'.

'Friend,' she finished awkwardly.

Reichis gave a snort. 'Like I'd ever be friends with a skinbag.' Having evidently tired of waiting for us to free him, he managed to reach a paw through a gap in the iron grating and began fiddling with the latch until it popped open. He then leaped out, spreading his limbs and catching the air to

114

drift gracefully to the ground. He went over and briefly sniffed at Seneira's father before looking up at him and pronouncing, 'Cry baby.'

Reichis isn't big on expressions of grief.

'This is my father, Beren Thrane, headmaster of the Academy,' Seneira explained, and then began to introduce the rest of us. She'd barely opened her mouth before Beren ran over to Rosie and took her in a bear hug, practically lifting her off the ground. 'You did it! I . . . I'd given up hope, but I should've known that if anyone could find my daughter it would be an Argosi!'

Rosie appeared particularly uncomfortable at this sudden outpouring of gratitude, not least because she caught the enraged look on Seneira's face. '*Found* me? Father, you hired Rosie to search for me?'

Beren seemed confused as he turned to the Argosi. 'Rosie? I thought you were called the Path of Thorns and Roses.'

'*Not* the point,' Seneira said, glaring at the woman who she'd thought had come upon her by accident in the border-lands. 'You lied to me, Rosie. You said—'

'I did not lie, child. You simply made assumptions and I allowed you to reach your own—'

'Don't try to wriggle out of this! Whatever happened to "The Way of Water" and not taking advantage of other people?'

'I would hardly call saving your life "taking advantage",' Rosie replied.

Ferius jostled me with her elbow and said, 'Now you know why an Argosi usually travels alone.'

A quiet voice from the bed caught everyone's attention. 'Senny?'

Seneira ran to the bed. The light from the lantern illuminated

115

all the pain and fear in her expression as she looked at her younger brother. She leaned forward and hugged him to her, practically lifting him out of the bed. When she set him down again, the front of her shirt was damp with sweat.

The rest of us approached. Tyne looked very different from the joyful, almost mischievous little boy in the painting inside Seneira's locket; his face was pale, almost grey, except for the winding black marks around his right eye. He shook relentlessly as he lay on top of his sheets, uncovered except for linen underpants. For a second I thought he must be cold, but then I saw the redness of his skin, the sweat pouring off him. Reichis jumped up to perch at the head of the bed. 'This kid's burning up, Kellen.'

The boy reached out a hand, trying to pet Reichis, but his fingers hadn't even brushed the squirrel cat's fur before his eyelids flickered shut and his arm fell back to lie awkwardly across his chest.

'How did this happen?' Seneira asked her father.

'It was like with you, sweetheart,' he said, reaching out to gently lift his son's hand and set it at a more comfortable angle on the sheets. 'He woke up with a terrible fever one morning. When I went to his room, I found the markings around his eye. I tried to keep his fever down, but it just kept getting worse, day after day, until a few nights ago when he started screaming. I tried to cool him down, but nothing worked.' He looked at his son, his expression full of exhausted fearfulness. 'The attacks are so bad . . . They just keep coming and coming.'

'I don't understand,' Seneira said. 'I got the fever too, but it passed after a day, and the . . . attacks didn't start till weeks later.'

116

A sudden convulsion took the boy, his back arching as if someone had attached a chain to his belly and was suddenly yanking it up. His eyelids opened unnaturally wide, and oozing black tendrils filled the whites of his eyes. Seneira gave a cry and reached down to hold on to him while he shook and his arms flailed. When one of his hands caught in her hair, his fingers curled around and he began tearing at it. I ran over and grabbed his wrist, struggling to hold it in place so he wouldn't rip the hair from her head. 'Let him go,' Seneira said, tears streaming down her cheeks. 'You're hurting him.'

'I'm not,' I insisted, only to see the skin of his wrist looking red and cracked beneath my fingers.

Ferius grabbed part of the sheet and quickly wrapped it around her hand before taking hold of Tyne's forearm, holding on to him without having to squeeze into his flesh. I let go and stepped back. A second later the boy collapsed, sweat pouring from his forehead, a vein on the side of his neck pulsing far too fast.

'Senny?' he asked after a moment. 'Is that you?'

It was as if he'd no recollection of the past several minutes. Seneira leaned down and smiled at him through her tears. 'It's me, runt. When are you going to get out of that bed and clean your room?'

'I feel bad, Senny,' he said.

'It's just a cold. In a few days you'll be right as rain and we'll go kiting together.'

The boy's eyes began to clear, though the irises were still black. 'You went away.'

'Just for a while. I'm back now, and I'm going to make sure you get healthy.' She smoothed his damp hair from his

117

forehead. 'Nothing and nobody is going to stop us from making you better, you got that, runt?'

'You went away,' Tyne repeated, then closed his eyes as he whispered, 'You shouldn't have come back, Senny. That's what they wanted.'

19

Sleep

We couldn't get anything more out of Tyne that night, but in all likelihood his ominous warning was little more than the product of a fevered mind feeding him nightmares no child should have to endure. It didn't stop me from being completely creeped out, however.

'You okay, kid?' Ferius asked.

There were only two chairs in the room – which we'd left to Seneira and her father so they could sit on either side of Tyne's bed, each of them holding one of the boy's hands even as their eyes were focused on each other, on their relief at being together and the guilt that both clearly felt but neither deserved. Ferius and I sat on the floor, leaning against the hospital room's cold wall. I didn't particularly like the way my Argosi mentor was looking at me. 'Why are you asking?'

She gave a shrug, and for the third time started to reach into her waistcoat for a smoking reed only to remember it probably wasn't a good idea to smoke so close to a sick child. 'It's all right to be scared,' she said, dropping her hand into her lap. 'You're tired. You haven't slept in a proper bed in months. You've got your own people chasing you and the rest of the world ready to join in anytime they find out you've got the shadowblack.' A slight smirk came to her face as she gestured towards Seneira and said, more quietly, 'And now you meet this girl and she's got all kinds of problems, but anyone can see you fancy her anyway and you ain't sure how to—'

'Ferius?' I interrupted. 'Would you do something for me? Something important.'

'Yeah, kid?'

'Promise to never, ever give me romantic advice?'

Ferius chuckled. 'Afraid I can't do that.'

'Why not?'

She reached out a hand and patted me on the shoulder. 'Because anyone can see you're terrible at romance, kid.'

Reichis peeked his head up from a cabinet drawer he'd wormed his way into. 'The Argosi's right, Kellen; your mating technique needs a lot of work.'

'Go back to stealing medical supplies,' I told him, which was probably a mistake since I'd already had to get into a heated argument with him to keep him from taking one of the scalpels because it was 'shiny and pretty'. Reichis running around with a razor-sharp blade in his mouth was a problem the world didn't need.

'When is Rosie coming back?' I asked, mostly to keep Ferius and Reichis from fixating on the subjects I'd prefer be left alone. The other Argosi had made some vague noises about searching for signs of more victims of the shadowblack and then left the rest of us to share in Seneira's misery.

'Who knows?' Ferius said by way of reply. 'The path of thorns and roses tends to lead away from personal entangle-ments.'

'Wait . . . you mean she might have left for good? Just like that? Without even a goodbye?'

'Goodbyes ain't the Argosi way, kid.'

For some reason that sent a cold chill through me, and I wondered if one day I might wake up and find Ferius gone without so much as a word or a note. I was searching for a way to press her on that point that wouldn't make me sound like a needy child, when Seneira startled me. I hadn't even noticed her standing there.

'We're going to stay with Tyne tonight,' she said. 'You can sleep at the house if you want.'

Ferius gave me a raised eyebrow – her way of scolding me for being unobservant. 'We're fine right here for now. Go on back to your brother.'

Tyne had been falling in and out of consciousness for hours, his body convulsing uncontrollably every time one of the shadowblack seizures came upon him. Seneira and her father would hang on to the boy as if he were a fish on a line being yanked away by some unseen figure holding the pole. Seneira nodded and started to turn away, but then stopped. 'Are you . . . ? Will you be leaving town now that you've helped Rosie bring me home?'

Something softened in Ferius's expression, and when she spoke next it was with a more formal tone than I was used to from her. 'Rest easy, little sister. This is a weight too great even for a pair of shoulders as strong as yours. We will walk this road with you a while longer.'

'Thank you,' Seneira said. She gave us a grateful smile before returning to her brother's bedside.

'You sounded like Rosie just then,' I observed.

Ferius reached into her waistcoat for a fourth time, then

stopped herself and patted at the pocket as if that had been her intention all along. 'Don't talk nonsense, kid.'

'You did. Usually you talk like a drunken Daroman shepherd, but right there you spoke just like Rosie does.'

I waited for another denial, but none came.

'First thing you learn travelling the long roads, kid: language is as much in the way you speak as the words you choose.'

I thought about that. Most of the time, Ferius doesn't really want people to know what she's thinking – heck, sometimes I think she doesn't even want people to take her seriously – so she uses that frontier drawl of hers. But here she'd wanted Seneira to feel safe, to feel protected. Rosie had been the one keeping her from harm until now, so Ferius had spoken the way she would – the way in which Seneira could most easily believe it.

'You know, you make even simple things complicated,' I said.

Ferius smiled. 'Path of the Wild Daisy, kid.'

She pulled out one of her decks and dealt us out eight cards each, telling me the rules of a new game as she did. We played a few hands. I'd glance over at Seneira and her father every once in a while, then pay attention to the game again. After a while I heard Reichis snoring, passed out inside one of the drawers. It didn't seem like much time had passed, but at one point when I looked over, I saw Seneira and Beren slumped over on each side of Tyne's bed.

Figuring it was my turn to deal, I reached over to get the deck from Ferius, but the cards were strewn across the floor between us. I was going to chide her for dropping them, but her eyes were closed. That was unusual. Ferius never went to sleep until she'd secured whatever place we were holed up

122

in, whether by setting traps around a campsite or barring entrances when we were indoors. I considered jostling her awake, but my own eyes were so heavy I could barely keep them open.

Wait, I thought. *My eyes are already closed. Why can't I open them?*

There were, of course, any number of plausible explanations why I might be falling asleep. I was exhausted, bored and hadn't eaten in ages. But there was one particularly good reason for me to remain conscious: my utter terror of being attacked again.

Wake up, I told myself. The command had no effect. Something was preventing me from opening my eyes.

Fear. Reach for the fear.

I gave free rein to all my worst terrors of being killed in my sleep – visions I usually worked very hard to ignore. A cold sweat came over me, pushing through the somnolence as the overwhelming desire to flee fought against the urge to sleep. I'm not sure what it says about me that I can make myself so terrified that I was able to wake when Ferius, ever watchful, couldn't. My eyes finally blinked open, and that's when I saw him.

He was tall – well, taller than me anyway. The light shed from the lantern over the bed was enough for me to make out the swarthy, weather-worn look of his handsome features. The intruder wore black leather riding trousers with heavy boots and spurs. His shirt was soft white linen and a bracelet made from some kind of glistening black stone beads adorned his left wrist. On his head he wore a black Daroman frontier hat, which at first looked just like Ferius's, but then I noticed something odd: symbols etched in silver travelled all the way

123

around the band above the brim. Glyphs. The kinds of magical motifs I recognised because I'd been around them most of my life. That's when I noticed that the sleeves of his shirt were rolled up, and that there were three faded tattooed bands on each of his forearms.

Jan'Tep, I thought, as the last vestiges of whatever sleep spell he'd used faded away and I rose to my feet.

'Hello there, Kellen of the house of Ke,' he said, his hands loose at his sides, ready to cast another spell. 'Imagine finding you here.'

20

The Visitor

I still had about a dozen of Ferius's steel cards, so my first move was to yank one from my trouser pocket to fling at this new enemy. Thanks to a lack of practice, I managed to tear the cloth and then cut my own finger from gripping the card incorrectly.

'Whoa there, kid,' the Jan'Tep said, his hands already forming the somatic shape for an ember blast. With his sleeves rolled up, the faded tattooed band for ember on his right forearm began to glow. I didn't quite recognise the spell – it didn't look like fire or lightning – but most ember magic involves some kind of energy. And pain.

Out of the corner of my eye I saw something sail past me and hit the intruder in the face. It turned out to be Ferius's hat. It didn't do any damage, of course, but at least it broke his line of sight.

'What's goin' on, kid?' she asked, shaking her head furiously to wake herself up.

'Silk magic,' I said, tossing the steel cards at him but still too groggy for any of them to strike their targets with enough force to do any good.

'Actually, it's not a silk, just breath magic with a hint of—'

The intruder's words were cut off by Reichis leaping from inside the cabinet drawer onto the back of the mage's shoulders, immediately going for his neck. I ducked down low and threw myself at the man's legs, grabbing them as hard as I could and sending him tipping back to where he crashed into an examination table. He managed to throw Reichis off even as he freed one foot and kicked me hard in the side. I rolled with the momentum, making it hard for him to target me with his spell, and giving me the chance to free my hands to pull powder from the pouches at my belt so I could blast him back.

'What's happening?' Seneira demanded, stumbling towards us from her brother's bedside.

A clacking sound got my attention. Ferius had something in her hand that I hadn't seen before: a short metal tube about eight inches long. She flicked her wrist and suddenly another tube slid out in extension, and another, and another. It was now over two feet long. One end was at the intruder's neck. 'Now I know me and the kid might seem like trouble, but trust me, fella, you don't want to dance with the squirrel cat.'

The mage looked up to see Reichis now perched on the top of a glass medicine cabinet, his fur a perfect blood red, no stripes at all, looking very much as if he was trying to decide whether to tear out the man's throat first or his eyes. He let out a snarl for good measure.

The intruder's smile never left his face. 'Well now, haven't you all got a fine little circus act going? Even got yourself a performing animal.'

Reichis growled. 'I'm definitely eating his eyeballs. The rest of you can fight over his ears.'

The mage set his eyes on me. 'What do you reckon, Kellen,

126

son of Ke'heops? You think your Argosi friend can get to me with her steel rod or that squirrel cat can reach me with its claws before I get off one good spell on the lot of you?'

'A question for another day,' Rosie said, rising up behind him, the glint of a short, sharp needle attached to one finger-nail which she lightly pressed to the side of his throat. 'For now it would seem introductions are in order. I am the Path of Thorns and Roses.'

'Glad you decided to join us,' Ferius said.

The man stayed very, very still as he asked, 'Path of Thorns and Roses, eh? I'm guessing that needle would be the thorn part.'

'One of them,' Rosie replied, then leaned close to whisper almost intimately into the man's ear. 'I see no need to show you the rest, do you?'

Very slowly the intruder put up his hands. 'Okay, folks, let's nobody do anything reckless. After all, I was invited.'

'Invited?' I asked. 'You tried to—'

'Dexan?' Beren Thrane asked, walking groggily towards us. 'Dexan Videris?'

'One and the same,' the man said, adding a light chuckle to his answer as if this was all some big misunderstanding. 'Mind asking these folks to stand down?'

Beren looked aghast at the rest of us as if we'd been the cause of the commotion. 'Please, all of you, let him go. This man is here at my urging.'

Dexan snorted. 'If you call hiring four Daroman ex-marshals to drag a man out of his favourite saloon "urging".' He let his hands drop back to his side and added, 'Those fellas are fine, in case you're wondering, Mister Thrane. Didn't seem right

127

to kill a man just for doin' what he must to make a living.' To the rest of us he said, 'Sorry about that sleep spell, by the way. Wasn't sure what kind of situation I was walking into. Frankly I'm kind of surprised it worked. I've never been too good with slumber magic.'

The spell had been weak enough that it probably *shouldn't* have worked, only we'd all been so exhausted that we hadn't been able to resist. If the intruder had turned out to be the silk mage we'd fought a week ago, we'd all be dead.

'You're Jan'Tep?' Seneira asked Dexan. 'One of Kellen's people?'

'Same country, different clan.' He tipped his hat to her. 'Dexan Videris, ma'am. I guess I should say that, strictly speaking, neither Kellen nor I are really Jan'Tep any more.'

'You're an outcast?' I asked.

'Spellslinger,' he said proudly. 'I'm guessing you're one too, judging by the way your hands keep twitchin' for those pouches at your side.'

Reichis sniffed. 'He's a liar. He already knew you were a spellslinger, Kellen.'

'You gonna let that critter bite me?' Dexan asked Beren Thrane.

The headmaster, apparently having remembered this was his son's hospital room, and, in fact, his Academy, decided to take control. 'Right, now listen here. You, son, Kellen, I don't know what's in those pouches, but you drop your hands by your sides.' He turned to Ferius. 'And you, my lady, if you'd be so k—'

'I'm no lady,' she corrected him.

Reichis rolled his eyes. 'Ugh. This again.'

Beren took it in his stride however. I guess it must come

128

with dealing with people from all over the continent. 'Forgive me, madam, I meant no offence, but now I must ask that both you and the Path of Thorns and Roses remove your respective weapons from my guest's throat.'

Ferius did, and slapped a palm against one end of the metal stick, sending the cylinders sliding back inside each other. Rosie removed her hand and when I looked again, the needle was gone.

Beren turned a wary eye to where Reichis was perched on the cabinet. 'You as well, master squirrel cat.' The headmaster glanced over at me. 'Does he understand what people say?'

'When it suits him. Reichis, you can come down now.'

The squirrel cat did his usual showing off, leaping up and spreading his limbs so he could glide down the few feet to land on my shoulder. His fur changed to a mix of brown and orange, with just enough red in his stripes to remind everyone he might decide to turn violent at any time.

Beren now turned his attention to Dexan. 'And you, Master Videris, if you could—'

'*Mister*,' he said. 'Master means something else to folks like me.'

'Great,' Reichis muttered. 'Now they're both doing it.'

'*Mister* Videris,' Beren said, raising his voice to again try to take command, 'if you wouldn't mind explaining what happened here? You seem to have taken great pains to incite my daughter's friends.'

The other spellslinger gave a chuckle as if this had all been a night's fun for him. 'It's simple, Beren. Kellen here's a wanted man on account of . . . well, first rule of being a spellslinger is never to mess with another mage's business so I'll let him tell you himself if that's what he chooses.' He hesitated for a second. 'I will say that nothing he's being pursued for is his fault.'

That was kind of him, I thought. *Only . . . how does he know?*

'When I came in and said his name and house,' Dexan went on, 'well, he saw that I was also Jan'Tep, so he must've figured I was a hextracker come to get him.'

Beren Thrane looked at me with something approaching compassion in his eyes even as he put a protective arm around Seneira's shoulders. 'Well, I know something about young people being hunted for no good reason.'

'Now that we're all friends –' Ferius began, reaching into her waistcoat and this time not stopping before she pulled out a smoking reed. I noticed she didn't light it though – 'would someone mind telling me what's going on?'

Beren nodded, and an almost rapturous smile came to his face as he gestured towards Dexan. 'It took a great deal of effort and no small expense to find him, but I believe this is the man who can save my children from this blight called the shadowblack.'

'What?' I asked. 'How could . . . ?' I saw now that Dexan was staring right at me. He took a step closer and bent down. There, barely visible at all, was a kind of soft scar around his right eye. The skin had healed, but faint traces of the winding circular markings remained. 'Yeah,' he said, no doubt noticing the desperate look of hope on my face, 'I found a cure for the shadowblack.'

21

The Cure

We all stood around Tyne's bed, watching the spellslinger who called himself Dexan Videris as he examined the markings around the sleeping boy's eye.

'I apologise for sending those men to bring you,' Beren said, visibly uncomfortable that his son's life was in another's hands. 'I was desperate to find help for my boy, and when I heard the stories about you I couldn't take the chance that you might refuse to help us.'

'Well, can't say I appreciated those ex-marshals using man-catchers on me.' He reached up and rubbed at his neck. 'I can still feel those damned metal prongs.'

'Again, I can't tell you how sorry I—'

Dexan reached out a hand and patted him on the shoulder. 'You did what any father would do, I reckon, so no hard feelings. This time.' He went back to peering down at Tyne. 'I'm going to touch the markings now,' he said. 'It'll probably hurt, so I need someone to hold the boy down.'

Beren went to his son, but Dexan shook his head. 'Not you. I ain't asking a father to make his son suffer.' He looked at me. 'Want to help me out, Kellen? I reckon you should watch.'

I glanced at Ferius, then felt ashamed of myself for doing

so, and went to hold the boy down. He was so small and weak I didn't think it'd be much work, but once Dexan got started, it took all my strength.

Dexan reached into a pocket of his waistcoat and pulled out a small sliver of glistening black stone. 'Onyx,' he explained. 'Well, a special kind of onyx. Comes from around here actually.'

'Can it help him?' Seneira asked.

'Afraid not. Removing the shadowblack ain't an easy process. It'll take days, and that's only if the most important requirement is met.'

'If it's money . . .' Beren began.

'Oh, don't worry, you'll have to pay plenty for me to put myself through this again, but no, I'm talking about something else. Now, everybody shut up so I don't hurt the child more than necessary.'

Dexan gently reached down and pressed one edge of the sliver of onyx against the puffy black flesh around the boy's right eye. Suddenly Tyne bucked so hard I could barely hang onto him.

'Hold him,' Dexan ordered. I did, but part of me couldn't help but watch what was happening.

The black winding lines around Tyne's eye were . . . moving . . . slithering. The boy started screaming, so loudly and so horribly Seneira tried to pull Dexan away. 'Stop it! You're killing him!'

Dexan shrugged her off, continuing to press the onyx sliver even as he spoke a spell under his breath and formed a somatic shape I didn't recognise with his other hand. A kind of smoke – no, more like a thin black mist – rose up from the boy's eye.

'Damn it,' Dexan said, pulling away. He put the sliver of onyx back in his pocket. 'I'm sorry. I can't help him.'

132

Seneira went to her brother's side, grabbing a cloth and wiping some of the sweat from his forehead. 'What is it? Why can't you—'

Dexan turned to me. 'How much do you know about the shadowblack?'

I chose my words carefully. I wasn't sure how much of the dark part of our shared history had come out since the death of the dowager magus. I'd told the council, and Shalla knew, which meant my parents did too, but had they revealed the truth? Or did my people still glibly pretend we were a noble culture, seeking only to master the ways of magic to protect ourselves? 'I know it's connected to demon magic.'

'Close, but not quite. The shadowblack isn't a connection between the victim and some vague demonic energies. It's a direct link between the victim and an actual demon. That's why those afflicted suffer horrible visions and have urges to commit terrible acts of violence. It's the demon pulling at you, demanding subservience, trying to take control once and for all. They prefer mages because, well, mages can do the most harm.'

I shuddered involuntarily.

'Yeah,' Dexan said. 'Puts that particular curse in a whole other light, don't it?'

'Please,' Beren begged. 'Why can't you help my son?'

Dexan sighed. 'Because there's two parts to the curse.' He went back to Tyne's bedside and reached down a finger, almost but not quite touching the markings. 'This is one aspect, but the other is inside the person who cast it in the first place. Whoever did this to your son is a whole lot more powerful than I am. So long as the dirty rotten son of a bitch is alive, I can't break the hex. If I try, I'll just end up killing your boy.'

133

'What about Seneira?' I asked. 'Can you—'

Dexan shook his head. 'I don't need to torture the girl to tell you it's gonna be the same mage as the one that did her brother. I'm sorry, folks. I really am.' He walked away from the bed and towards the door.

'Wait!' I called out. 'What are you doing?'

Dexan stopped. 'I told you, the only way to help that child is to find the person who cast the curse on him and kill them.'

'Is that what you're going to do then? Find the mage who—'

'First rule of spellslinging, kid: don't mess with another mage's business.' He turned to look back at me and I saw something vaguely approaching humility on his face. 'I'm not like those Jan'Tep masters you knew back home, Kellen. I'm just a spellslinger, like you. All I got's a couple of spells and a few tricks up my sleeve.' He held up his forearms to show the faded tattooed bands. 'I've been away from my city's oasis for a long time now, my spells get weaker every year and I got people chasing me just like you do.' He looked back at Beren and Seneira. 'Sorry about the boy, and if you can find whoever did this to him and end them, well, I'll come back then and do what I can to fix him and his sister.'

He left the room, and Beren came to Ferius and me. It says something about how desperate he was that he looked to us – two strangers he'd only just met hours before – and dropped to his knees. 'Please,' he said, grabbing hold of our hands, 'help me find who did this to my son. Help me kill them.'

It says something about me too that, as I felt the itch on my own markings, I pulled my hand away and ran out the door to chase after Dexan Videris and the chance to cure myself.

134

22

The Deal

'Wait,' I shouted, pursuing him down the hallway.

He stopped. 'I wondered how long it would take you to come after me.'

'I . . . It's not like . . .'

'Relax, Kellen,' he said, and reached a finger up to tap at the scars around his eye. 'I've been through it, remember? I know what it's like. I know how bad it pulls at you, in the dark, in your dreams.'

'Can you get rid of it? Mine, I mean.'

He held my gaze a while before saying, 'No, I'm sorry.'

'What? What do you mean? The person who put it on me isn't alive! So why can't you—'

'It's all in the marks, kid. Yours are too perfect, too smooth. Somebody banded you in shadow, didn't they?'

I nodded. 'My grandmother.'

'Well, I don't know what she was thinking, but the procedure I discovered won't work on you. Not unless . . .' He trailed off.

'What? Unless what?'

'I don't know. Let me think.'

I waited, my heart pounding in my chest, praying to my

135

ancestors that he might be able to help me, to take away this damned curse and free me of it. I could go back – back to my home, back to Nephenia, back to my family. I might even be able to study magic again.

Dexan looked at me. 'Man, I know that look. You and me are a lot alike, I think.' Again he hesitated. 'I've got an idea, Kellen, but I need to do some research and try a few experiments.' He reached down and grabbed me by the collar. 'But listen up, kid: if I can do this, it's going to be hard, and it's going to be expensive, maybe more than you want to pay.'

He sounded like the price might include more than just money. It's not uncommon among my people to demand payment in the form of months of service or assistance with spells that put the participant at great risk. But the thought of getting rid of the shadowblack, of being able to return home . . . 'Just tell me what it takes,' I said. 'What do you want?'

'I'll need to think on that too. Give me a couple of days.' He let go of me and proceeded down the hallway.

'Wait!' I called out. 'How will I find you?'

He didn't bother to stop. 'I'll find *you*, when I'm good and ready. Trust me, kid, the messes you leave behind? You're not hard to find.'

I was going to go back into the room and see how I could help – really – but before I could, Ferius came out. She strode up to me like she was going to walk right through me. She stopped a foot away and she looked more disgusted than I'd ever seen her. She looked me up and down as if I was some kind of dirty stain she'd found on a new shirt. 'Is *this* who you are?'

136

'I was going to—'

'No, I really want to know, Kellen of the House of Ke – is *this* who you are?'

She almost never addressed me in the formal way of my people. 'Look, I wasn't—'

'Answer me!'

'Yes! All right? Yes, *this* is who I am. I'm a sixteen-year-old kid with nothing to my name but a bounty on my head and a curse that's going to turn me into a monster one day. So, yes, Ferius, who I am is somebody who needs to find a way to survive in the world before I can go around helping other people.'

'What about Seneira? A few nights ago you were all up in arms about how we needed to help her. Now you're ready to abandon these people just so you can chase after the snake-oil salesman who feeds you a line about having a cure for the shadowblack?'

'I . . .' There was a bad taste in my mouth. I guess it was guilt. 'Seneira's got *family*,' I said. 'Look at this place! She's got a father with money and influence to protect her. What do I have? People are trying to *kill* me, Ferius! And you won't even teach me the Argosi fighting ways so I can—'

She threw her hands up. 'I keep telling you, kid, there *ain't* no Argosi ways, not the kind you're looking for. It's a path – a path you find for yourself, not some set of tricks or spells you learn so you can feel strong by beating other people up.'

'Well, maybe I should find somebody who *can* teach me how to beat other people up,' I said, realising I was close to tears. 'Because I don't know what good it does me to have you spitting pointless nonsense at me all the time and then expecting me to help total strangers!'

'You mean like I helped you?'

My anger got the better of me then. 'Don't pretend you gave a damn about me, Ferius. You came to my city because the clan prince had died, and you wanted to . . . what's it called again? Follow "the way of the wind"? Hoping to find some "discordance" so you could paint another stupid card and show it to your Argosi friends?'

She stared at me for a long time, all kinds of expressions passing over her features so fast I couldn't make sense of them, but they seemed to come back to anger, the worst anger I'd ever seen on her. I could see her fists clenching.

'Are you going to hit me, Ferius?'

She closed her eyes for a moment. 'No, Kellen,' she replied, and then walked past me down the hall. 'I don't hit children.'

Beren found me waiting outside Tyne's room. I didn't really have any business being there, given what I'd done, but the truth was, I also had no other place to go. Reichis came with him, sauntering along behind. 'Seneira's staying with her brother for a while longer. Tyne woke for a few minutes.' Beren was almost beaming, despite the tears in his eyes. He pointed down to Reichis. 'Your squirrel cat leaped up in the air and glided down, doing all kinds of acrobatics and playing with him.' He hesitated for a moment, then asked, 'Does he . . . ? Is he intelligent? I've heard that the Jan'Tep familiars some-times—'

'He's not my familiar, but like I told you before, he under-stands what you're saying.'

Beren knelt down to face Reichis. 'Bless you, master squirrel cat, bless your kindness.'

'Sweet mouse meat!' Reichis groaned to me. 'Tell the skinbag to cut it out. Nothing's worse than watching grown creatures blubber.'

'What did he say?' Beren asked.

'He says it was his pleasure, and he'll be happy to come back and play with Tyne again if you'd like.'

'Oh, you arsehole,' Reichis growled. He leaped up and spread his glider flaps, covering my face like a furry bag, smothering me. 'Apologise before I choke you to death.'

'That's so sweet,' Beren said. 'He's hugging you.'

I prised Reichis off of me. 'Yeah, he's a delight.'

Beren looked uncomfortable about what he had to say next. 'After you left Tyne's room, your . . . mentor –'

'She's not my mentor.'

'Forgive me. Your *friend* Ferius offered to help me find the person responsible for my children's illness. She said you might be willing to help as well, though there might be a price.'

Great. Ferius had really hung me out to dry. Although I suppose since Dexan had made it clear he was going to want to be paid for helping me, she'd probably saved me from looking like an even bigger jerk when I asked for money later. Feeling about as rotten about myself as I'd ever thought possible, I said, 'I'll help. I'll do whatever I can. I promise.'

The relief on Beren's face made me feel even worse. 'Thank you. Thank you so much.' He led me down the hall towards the exit. 'Come stay at our home. We can put all of you up for as long as you want.'

'Thank you,' I said.

He patted me on the shoulder and sighed. 'Only one thing has kept me going during this terrible ordeal: the kindness of strangers like you.'

That made me feel worst of all.

23

The Bath

That night we stayed in some of the guest bedrooms in the Thrane residence. Beren cleaned up the mess he'd had to leave when he'd taken Tyne to the hospital, then insisted on feeding us until we were ready to explode. Once the meal was over, he went upstairs to light the small stove inside the bathroom that heated water going into the tub. He generously offered me the use of it, and by offered I mean practically shoved me into the bathing room, leaving behind a small plate of butter biscuits as inducement for me to take my time.

'You do stink a little,' Reichis said, after Beren had left. The squirrel cat gave me a sniff. 'Kind of like dead rat that's been eaten and then pooped out again.'

'Thanks.'

He sniffed again. 'Then it's like a blind buzzard with no sense of smell ate *that* and then *he* went and pooped—'

'I get it, all right?'

I removed my travel-stained clothes and hunted around the bathroom for a spot to put them where they wouldn't serve to dirty up the place. Eventually I settled for hanging them outside the window.

I dipped my toe in the water and found it hotter than I expected, but something about standing around naked in someone else's house felt unnatural to me, so I eased myself into the prodigiously large brass tub. First I made sure to balance the small plate of butter biscuits on the flat rim. It had been a long time since I'd eaten anything that hadn't either been picked off a tree or spent its final moments in a squirrel cat's jaws.

Once I got used to the heat, the experience became incredibly soothing. I hadn't realised how many aches and pains I'd accumulated in four months of hard living. *Sixteen years old and already I feel like an old man.*

'Hey, Kellen,' Reichis said.

I opened up an eye to see him balanced precariously on the edge of the tub. 'Yeah?'

'What's it like?'

'What's *what* like?'

He very carefully poked a furry foot into the water. 'This. Sitting there in a tub of hot water.'

'It's . . . nice, I guess.' Sometimes Reichis can tell what I'm feeling. I guess the squirrel cat was curious about my sudden sense of comfort.

He pointed a paw towards a short stool next to the tub. 'Put that in. The water's too deep for me.'

'Are you serious? You want to take a bath? I thought cats hated water.'

'I'm not a cat, moron. I'm a squirrel cat.'

I've learned it's best not to test Reichis's patience when it comes to issues of species, so I relented and reached over to grab the stool and set it down at the other end of the tub. The seat sat about five inches below the surface of the water.

141

'Okay,' Reichis said. 'I'm going in.' I think he was talking to himself more than me. He put one front paw then the other on the top of the stool, tipping his chin up to keep his nose above the water. He stayed like that for a moment, then hopped the rest of himself in. After a few minutes I was staring at a slightly wet and very confused squirrel-cat face.

'Are you okay?' I asked.

'I'm not sure. What's it supposed to feel like?'

'Warm.'

Reichis nodded. 'Yeah, it's warm.'

'Comfortable, I guess.'

He nodded again. 'Yeah . . . that's the word.' His gaze softened, the lids of his eyes half-closing. Then he settled himself on his back and stared up at the ceiling, the top of his muzzle and his feet sticking out of the water. 'Comfy . . .'

'You sure you're okay?'

He stuck out a front paw and gestured over to my edge of the tub. 'Gimme,' he said, sounding half asleep.

I wasn't sure what he was talking about at first, and then realised I'd left the plate there. 'Are you serious?'

'Gimme.'

Not knowing what else to do, I picked up one of the butter biscuits. I was going to put it in his paw, but he'd already stuck it back under the water, and instead opened up his fuzzy little mouth. I deposited the biscuit there and was soon treated to the sound of a squirrel cat nibbling on a butter biscuit while moaning rapturously. 'Oh yeah,' he mumbled, the words sounding garbled on account of all the chewing noises. 'This is how I want to spend my life from now on.'

'What about hunting . . . I mean, *murdering* rabbits?'

Reichis swallowed. 'Right now I just want to murder another one of those biscuits. Gimme.'

I really don't understand squirrel cats.

I must have fallen asleep because I woke to a knock at the bathroom door. 'Kellen?' Seneira asked.

'Just a second!'

I got myself out of the bath, managing not to kick over Reichis's stool in the process, which would have led to any number of bites and claw marks on my freshly cleaned skin. I grabbed hold of a towel and quickly dried myself off and then ran my fingers through my hair. There was a mirror above a small sink that reflected my newly washed features. *So that's what I look like.*

'Kellen? I just wanted to—' The handle started to turn.

'Don't come in!' I yelped, and wrapped the towel around my waist. Ferius had once told me that people in the border-lands aren't as concerned about nudity as the Jan'Tep, but I'd always suspected she was just setting me up to embarrass myself at some point in the future.

Satisfied that I was maintaining at least some small degree of propriety, I opened the door. Seneira was holding a bundle of clothes that I recognised as my other set. As a Jan'Tep initiate, I'd had all kinds of clothes: school clothes, casual clothes, formal clothes. An outlaw basically has two pairs of the same grubby travelling clothes and that's if they're lucky.

'My father's gone back to stay with Tyne. I cleaned up your spare garments as best I could,' Seneira said. 'They should be dry – I hung them by the fire.'

I considered apologising for having run out of Tyne's room before, but then it occurred to me that if Ferius had covered

143

for me with Beren, maybe Seneira had believed it too. I guess I just wasn't ready for her to know what a coward I was. 'Thanks,' I said, taking the bundle of clothes from her.

She seemed to be staring at my torso, which was lean and tanned from four months in the borderlands but still wasn't much to write home about. 'What's wrong?' I asked, self-consciously.

'You have scars,' she said.

'Doesn't everybody?' I grabbed at the shirt and put it on.

'Not when they're our age. Not as many as you, anyway.' She caught my eyes then, and I think she felt bad for me. 'I'm sorry, Kellen, I didn't mean to—'

'It's fine,' I said. It wasn't as if I'd spent my life getting beaten or anything, but I'd managed to get into enough scrapes over the past months that I was looking the worse for wear.

Seneira's gaze went past me then to where Reichis was still lying back on his stool. 'You bathe with your animal?'

When she said it like that, it sounded much worse than I'd thought. 'I . . . Not usually, he just—'

'Kellen,' Reichis growled, still lying back in the water, 'you tell that bitch that if she ruins this for me, I swear to all nine squirrel-cat gods I'm going to pull out her eyeballs and make her eat them.'

'What did he say?' Seneira asked.

'You really don't want to know.'

She nodded. 'I should let you get ready for bed. I was just hoping . . .'

I found myself profoundly aware of my lack of clothing and couldn't imagine any ending to that sentence for which I was prepared. 'What is it?'

'Ferius says you're going back to the Academy tomorrow. I . . . My father won't let me go there. He says there's too much chance of someone spotting me.' She held up a small cloth object in her hand. It took me a moment to figure out that it was a child's toy that looked vaguely like a horse. My people don't have dolls – they're too much like the kinds of sympathy figurines used by some mages to send pain to their enemies. 'Could you take this to Tyne? It was his favourite toy until a couple of years ago. He always says he's too old for toys now but . . . I don't know. Maybe I'm just being stupid.'

Okay, not what I expected.

I took the doll from her. 'I'll take it to him.'

'Thank you,' she said, and then caught my eyes. 'Tell him I love him, would you? I don't think he really understands what's happening. When I left the hospital, he thought I was running away again, leaving him behind. I never wanted him to think . . . I've made a mess of everything, Kellen.'

I started reaching for something comforting to say, but by then she had already gone, leaving me standing there in my towel. 'Come on, Reichis,' I said, as I started to put on the rest of my clothes. He gave me a dirty look but managed to rouse himself, hopping off the stool and onto the edge of the tub. 'Dry me,' he commanded, pointing to one of the spare towels.

'What's got into you?' I asked. 'One bath and you turn into a spoiled house pet?'

'Dry me –' he repeated, then got onto all fours and prepared to shake himself, an event that would almost certainly leave me completely soaked – 'or I'll dry myself.'

One thing I *do* know about squirrel cats? They can really be jerks sometimes.

145

24

The Seven Talents

Reichis tried his best to convince me that a second bath was in order, but I refused, and since nobody but me understands what he's saying, all his efforts to explain to Seneira what he wanted were interpreted as a desire to go outside. Eventually he gave up, though not before making it clear that unholy vengeance would be wreaked upon all those who'd stood between him and his newfound love of bathtubs and butter biscuits.

By the time I made my way to my bed, I found it so comfortable that I thought I'd pass out the instant I hit the pillow, but something stopped me. Maybe it was just having grown so used to the rituals of the road: the gathering of firewood, preparing the campsite, Ferius setting her traps and the three of us talking nonsense until the stars covered the sky. Or maybe it was because of how bad I felt. Ferius hadn't yelled at me or even been unfriendly, but we'd hardly spoken since the incident at the hospital. Reichis, on the other hand, slept (and snored) with the devotion of the truly righteous.

I tossed and turned for an hour or so, then found myself going out onto my room's shallow balcony, which looked over a beautifully landscaped garden. I'm not sure how long

I stood there before I noticed Rosie, moving so silently I couldn't hear her, practising some form of combat, almost as if she were sparring with an invisible opponent. There was an elegance to her movements, so profound that eventually I put on my clothes and went down to join her.

'What do you call that?' I asked.

'Eres trida,' she replied, without missing a beat, moving with effortless precision along the pebbled path of the back garden. 'A style of sand fighting.'

'Sand fighting?'

'Does one of those words confuse you?' Rosie made a quarter-turn, her back foot gliding smoothly along the uneven ground.

'I just . . .'

She stopped, though whether because she'd completed whatever routine she'd been practising or because I was annoying her, I didn't know. 'Sand fighting. Fighting in sand. Part of the second talent.'

'The second talent?'

Her eyes narrowed, and I got the distinct sense she thought I was mocking her. 'I don't know what that means,' I said. 'Honestly.'

'The second talent. *Eres.*' She said the word as if I should know it, then clarified with, 'Defence.'

'Oh.'

She came out of her combat stance and stood before me. 'Name the seven talents of the Argosi.'

That caught me off guard. 'I . . . I don't—'

'I thought you were learning the Argosi ways?'

'I thought so too.'

'Then name for me the seven talents!'

147

I felt annoyed at her for talking to me as though I was an idiot, and yet somehow didn't want to show myself ignorant of the things Ferius was supposed to have taught me. 'I . . . I guess swagger? Umm . . . dance, I think?'

'"Swagger"? "Dance"?' She shook her head and clicked her tongue with irritation. 'The seven talents of an Argosi wanderer are: Daring, to brave the world; Defence, to protect oneself and others; Eloquence, to communicate with strangers; Subtlety, to evade ensnarement; Resilience, to thrive anywhere; Persuasion, to compel right action; Perception, to see what others do not.'

'I . . . I didn't know any of that.'

Rosie's eyes softened, just a touch, and then she bowed her head briefly. 'Forgive me, this is my error. I assumed when I saw you with the Path of the Wild Daisy . . . with Ferius . . . that you were her teysan.'

'What's a teysan?'

'A student . . . an apprentice in the ways of the Argosi. I thought she was teaching you the seven talents in prepara-tion for you to take the next step towards your path. She and I were both trained by the same maetri – teacher – so I presumed . . .'

I felt my cheeks flush, both from embarrassment and a rush of anger. 'She said there *wasn't* any specific Argosi training. She said—'

Rosie raised her hands, palms up in front of her. 'Your pardon. In my foolishness and presumption, I have sown discord where none existed.'

Oh, it existed all right. I just never realised how much.

Rosie frowned. 'The way of the Argosi is the way of water,' she said. 'I would not wish for this to be an occasion where

I created disadvantage for another. Tell me, is there something I might do to restore the balance between us? I do not carry much with me, but I have certain mementoes from foreign lands. Perhaps one would—'

'I don't want you to give me your stuff!' The second the words were out of my lips I realised I'd overreacted. This wasn't her fault. She was just trying to make me feel better. 'Maybe . . . Maybe you could teach me some of those fighting techniques you were doing?'

Her expression looked troubled and then she bowed again. 'I apologise, but I cannot.'

'Why not? It's just—'

'Ferius has chosen not to train you, Kellen, and for this she must have her reasons. If I gainsay her in this, I break the balance between her and me, and that balance is already . . . precarious.'

'Great,' I said. 'Just perfect.'

Rosie came over and put a hand on my shoulder. 'The ways of the Argosi are . . . rigorous, Kellen. They are not for everyone. If the Path of the Wild Daisy has not welcomed you to it, then trust that this is not the life for you.'

'Sure, fine,' I said. 'I guess I'm not supposed to become an Argosi.'

Only what *am* I supposed to be?

25

The Academy

I slept late and woke up groggy and irritable. Even Reichis somehow knew to stay away from me. If it wasn't bad enough how quickly things had been falling apart for me lately, now I was going to look like some callous freeloader, eating the Thranes' food and sleeping till midday in their bed. I'd have to apologise, and then . . . what? What in the name of all my ancestors was I supposed to do?

I got dressed and went downstairs to find that events had kept on moving even without my presence.

Seneira, Ferius and Rosie were seated around a table.

'Saddle up, kid,' Ferius said when she saw me. 'We've got places to be.'

'What's—'

'I'll explain on the way.'

Reichis trotted down the stairs and Ferius immediately pointed a finger at him. 'Forget it, squirrel cat. You're staying here this time.'

Reichis looked over at me. 'Kellen, tell the Argosi that the next time she points her finger at me, she's going to have to dig it out of her—'

'Just . . . You don't want to come anyway, Reichis.'

'How do you know? She hasn't even told you what you're doing yet.'

'Because I'm fairly sure whatever it is doesn't involve stealing or killing.'

Reichis stared at me for a second, then turned and sauntered up the stairs. 'I'm going back to bed. Somebody wake me when this stops being boring.'

With that potential crisis averted, I barely had time to put on my belt that held the powders I use for my spell and get my boots on my feet before Ferius was ushering me out of the house. 'Wait a second. Where are we going?'

'The Academy. I want to see what we can learn about the place.'

I stopped at the door. 'Shouldn't Seneira come with us? She's the one who knows how the Academy works.'

'I can't,' Seneira said, her tone making it clear she was none too happy about the situation. 'If my classmates see me wearing a blindfold, they'll ask questions.' She pointed a finger to the markings around her eye. They looked a fraction longer than they had yesterday. 'If they see me without the blindfold, it'll be even worse.'

'Come on, kid,' Ferius said, grabbing me by the shoulder. 'Let's move.'

'Can I have a moment with Kellen before you go?' Seneira asked.

Ferius raised an eyebrow for a second, but then nodded and went outside to wait for me.

'What is it?' I asked.

'I have a favour to ask,' she said tentatively. 'There is someone I'm worried about, and I hoped you might enquire discreetly about their well-being.'

151

'I can try. Who?'

'His name is Revian,' she said. 'He's my . . . classmate.'

Revian. The name was familiar, though it took me a second to place it. 'You said his name the other night, when you were having the shadowblack attack.' *When I'd told her to think of the people she loved.*

Seneira looked half ashamed and half betrayed. 'Forget I asked. I shouldn't have—'

Ancestors, why am I so bad at dealing with people? 'What does he look like? I'll look out for him. Discreetly.'

She gave me a grateful smile, then proceeded to describe what sounded like a figure pulled straight out of a painting of one of the old gods of sun and sky. Then she went on to describe his kindness, compassion, dignity, courage and great sense of humour. Whoever Revian was, I hated him already.

As I was turning to leave, Seneira caught my arm. 'If you see him, tell him I . . .'

'Tell him what?'

She shook her head. 'I'm sorry. Just tell him that I miss him.'

Ferius and I rode the half-mile back to the Academy, then tethered our horses and made our way inside. 'First stop's on the twelfth floor,' she said.

Ferius walks surprisingly fast when she isn't making a show of walking especially slow, so I had to jog to keep up with her. 'What makes you think any of her teachers or classmates even want to talk to us?' I asked.

'Simple, kid: I'm going to charm her teachers, and you –' she stopped, and turned to muss my hair – 'you just try to be good-looking, okay?'

Wow. It really never takes Ferius very long to put me off. 'How exactly am I supposed to *try* to be good-looking?'

'You really want to know? As in, if I tell you, you'll actually listen for a change?'

I nodded.

'Right. First off, let's fix a few things.' She gently pushed me back against the wall. 'Make your butt, your shoulders and the back of your head touch the wall.'

'What's that going to—'

'Do you want to pester me with questions or learn how to be handsome?'

'Fine.' I leaned back.

'No, stand up straight. Remember: butt, shoulders, head.'

I contorted myself into an incredibly uncomfortable position.

'Good,' she said. 'Now, pretend you're completely at ease.' When I did, she said, 'No, don't start slouching again.'

I started to speak but she shut me up with a look. After a few more tries she seemed satisfied. 'Good, now, give me your best smile.'

I smiled.

She flinched.

'What?'

'Stop doing that with your mouth.'

'You said to smile.'

Ferius pointed to my eyes. 'Smile from here.'

'How the heck am I supposed to—'

'Hang on.' A girl around my age was walking up the stairs, pretty, with red hair that fell in curls to her shoulders. Ferius went over to her. 'Miss? You mind helping us out for a second here?'

Oh ancestors, you're doing this to torture me, aren't you?

153

Ferius had the girl stand on the other side of the wide staircase. I guessed classes must be in session because very few people were coming up or down. Those who did, however, smirked at the sight of me standing there like an idiot.

'Okay,' Ferius said, speaking to me in a quiet voice. 'That there is Hadina. I want you to look at Hadina and smile with your eyes.'

'I still don't know what that means.'

'It's all right, kid, I'm going to teach you.' She stepped out of the way, still staying close so she could talk to me without the girl . . . Hadina . . . hearing. 'Now, when you look at Hadina, I want you to look into her eyes – but don't just stare at her like she's a rock, and especially don't stare at her like she's some kind of food. Instead, I want you to look into her eyes and listen to what they're saying to you.'

'Listen? To her *eyes*?'

Ferius nodded. 'It's a dialogue. Just let her eyes say what they want to say. Listen to those eyes as if they're the most fascinating storytellers you've ever met.'

Listen to her eyes as if they're the most fascinating storytellers you've ever met. 'Okay, fine. For how long?'

'At least a second, maybe two, but no more than that. You stare at a stranger for more than two seconds and you're some weird kid looking for trouble.' She pushed my shoulders back. 'And stand up straight.'

So I did. I looked into the eyes of this girl I'd never met and tried to listen to them as if they had something to say to me. Of course, they *didn't* say anything to me. I had no idea what story her eyes had to tell. Strangely, though, something else happened: Hadina smiled at me – not a shy smile or embarrassed smile, but something else. Something . . . oddly flattering.

154

'Here endeth the lesson,' Ferius whispered, then went over to the girl and thanked her.

Hadina started up the stairs then stopped and came back down. 'My archimetry class ends in about an hour,' she said. 'I mean, if you want to practise your smile a bit more.'

'I—'

'He'd love to,' Ferius said, cutting me off. 'But he's got an appointment down at the hospital to look at a terrible rash on his . . . well, you know.'

Hadina – who'd known Ferius for all of a minute – somehow knew she was lying. Maybe she'd 'heard it in her eyes'. 'Well, maybe some other time,' she said, then added, 'I'm usually on the fourteenth floor on weekdays.'

After she'd left I found myself dumbfounded. 'What just happened?'

Ferius clapped me on the shoulder. 'You smiled at a girl, kid. Most natural thing in the world.'

'Only I didn't move my mouth.'

'Really?' She reached into her waistcoat, pulled out one of her shiny steel cards and held it up in front of me. I saw my reflection there, along with the slightest curve of a smile on my lips. It was odd, like staring at somebody else . . . somebody who was *almost* handsome.

'Quit admiring yourself, kid,' Ferius said, and carried on up the stairs. 'Let's get to work.'

'Wait,' I said, chasing after her. 'Does this work on all girls?'

She kept on upping her pace. 'Girls, boys, men. Sometimes it even works on women.'

We spent the rest of the afternoon talking to Seneira's teachers and classmates. I thought we'd have to come up with some explanation of why we were there, but I guess she'd been gone for a couple of weeks and they all figured she had an illness. Ferius said she was a distant relative, thinking about enrolling me in the school. The teachers looked dubious at first – apparently neither of us looked wealthy enough to afford the Academy – but sure enough, Ferius turned on the charm and they melted for her. They all seemed to think she was some kind of genius in their own fields, which wasn't possible, since they taught everything from how to build complex mechanical contraptions to the history of every country on the continent to strategic diplomacy (which, in my opinion, if Seneira wasn't failing then there was something seriously wrong with this school).

'Please,' Seneira's devices teacher begged as the conversation was winding down, 'won't you come and sit in on my seminar, Lady Ferius, you could—'

'Not "Lady", Master Westrien, just Ferius. I'm afraid I can't today.'

Ugh. Reichis was right. That 'don't call me lady' thing really did wear thin after a while.

Westrien looked a bit deflated. 'Well, I hope you'll reconsider some other time.'

She gave a small bow of her head. 'It would be an honour.'

I took note of her phrasing: it *would* be an honour. Ferius had a tendency to avoid lying and yet always managed to do so without the other person understanding what she really meant.

'Nice fella,' she said, after we'd left Master Westrien's seminar room. 'Couldn't understand a word of all that stuff he was going on about.'

I stared at her. 'But you were talking with him for, like, twenty minutes! About all kinds of stuff.'

156

'Nah, I wasn't talking, kid. I was helping him make music.'

'Music?'

She stopped. 'All those things he was saying, in every sentence there was a word that mattered, that meant something to him. Most of the time I was just asking him to elaborate on it, or inquiring how some other word he'd said affected his views about it, or wondered how Seneira was doing with that particular subject.'

'So you just kept prompting him and let him talk.'

'It's more than that. There are two parts to music, kid: the notes, and the silences. I let him play the notes . . .'

'And you played the silences. Okay, but other than getting an invitation to his seminar, what did you really accomplish?'

'I found out exactly what I wanted to know.'

'Which was?'

She shook her head. 'Sorry, kid, I don't want to influence your judgement.'

'My judgement of what?'

She steered me towards an open archway. 'According to Westrien, that's one of the study halls for Seneira's cohort. I want you to go in there and find out what you can about her and how she fits into this place.'

'Wait . . . Aren't you coming with me? You're the one that—'

'Can't, kid. I promised Rosie I'd go back and watch the house so she could do some investigating of her own.'

I suddenly felt stiff, awkward and, well, more than a little anxious. 'But I don't know any of those people! They're going to think I'm some kind of weird creep who –'

Ferius shoved me and I went stumbling into the classroom. 'Just remember to smile, kid.'

26

The Prodigies

'Do you think something's wrong with him?' a blond-haired guy about a year older than me asked, lounging on a curved windowsill at the opposite side of the room.

'He's not talking,' someone else said. 'He just keeps standing there. Maybe he's mute.'

A girl who looked maybe thirteen – too young to be in the same class as the rest of them, I would've thought – came up and stared at me through bespectacled green eyes. 'Why is he smiling like that? Maybe he's in one of the dramatism classes and this is his homework.'

Three perfectly sensible theories, I thought, standing frozen like an idiot. Somehow, in between Ferius's lesson on listening to other people's eyes and the moment when she shoved me into this room with people who all knew each other, all liked each other, all clearly thought they were important and interesting and that I was none of those things, I had developed a remarkably all-encompassing paralysis.

Say something, idiot. Move. At least just walk out the door.

Where I'm from, students are in the same class from the first time they walk into the oasis until the day they take their trials. It shouldn't have mattered – it's not like I'd never dealt with strangers before; it's just that normally I was running away from them because they were throwing things at me. Talking during those exchanges was strictly optional.

One of the students was waving at me now. 'Maybe he's blind?'

I shifted from trying to elegantly withdraw to deciding whether this was, in fact, the most embarrassingly stupid moment of my life.

It was.

Somehow that made me feel better. I had screwed Ferius's assignment up completely, leaving me only two options: skulk out of there with my tail between my legs and admit to Ferius that somehow, after having faced chaincasters and war mages, after fighting off my own best friend, after overcoming a lord magus – an actual lord magus – that somehow a group of (admittedly very cool-looking) teenagers was too much for me. The only other alternative was to try something different.

What the hell. If I'm going to blow this, I might as well use all the powder I've got.

I sought out someone at random, a girl with short, curly black hair sitting with a massive book in her lap. Like the others, she was staring at me, but she'd yet to speak. I let our eyes meet and listened, carefully counting the seconds in my head . . . one . . . two . . . I turned to the others and put a finger to my lips. 'Shh.'

'Did he just shush us?' the guy on the windowsill asked. 'Are you even a student here?'

'I'm studying right now,' I said.

The younger girl, the one with the spectacles and the green eyes, asked, 'What are you studying?'

I let my eyes drift back to the girl with the book, forced all the confidence and ease into myself that I could muster – and I swear, had there been a wall behind me, my butt, shoulders and head would have been touching it – and said, 'Art.'

A series of groans filled the room along with bursts of laughter. I let it all wash over me, not responding to it in the slightest. Instead I walked right up to the girl, gave a small bow and extended my hand. 'I'm Kellen,' I said.

She gave me a lopsided grin that said she thought everything about me was a bit ridiculous, but took my hand anyway. 'Cressia,' she said in a lilting Gitabrian accent. 'Are you always this weird, Kellen?'

Without missing a beat in the music, I said, 'Always, I promise.'

Someone clapped me on the back and whispered, loud enough for everyone to hear, 'You're on the wrong trail, if you're looking for love, friend. Cressia's not . . . inclined towards . . . us.'

It took me a few seconds to figure out what he meant, and by that time pretty much everyone was laughing, including Cressia. *Okay, note for future attempts at being charming: try not to hit on girls who prefer other girls.*

The guy at the windowsill held up his hand as though he was holding a glass. 'To . . . Kellen, was it? To Kellen, a man willing to make a daring and valiant effort, even if it came to a somewhat tragic ending.'

'To Kellen!' the others cheered.

I grinned and took several bows.

Things actually went not too badly from there. Having established my credentials as a slightly romantic fool, odd but not creepy, who nonetheless kept his cool, I became the object of some fascination. Following Ferius's method, I made sure to

160

answer most questions with a question of my own, letting others speak, picking up on the things they cared about and generally being the silence between the notes in the song we created together. After a while, I almost began to enjoy myself.

I kept up the ruse of being a distant relative of Seneira's, using their questions about her to glean as much information as I could about both her and her family. On the whole, they seemed to like her well enough, except that certain patterns came up again and again – a kind of refrain that saw only the mildest variations.

'Oh, I can't wait until she's back,' one of the girls said. 'I mean, she'll have missed a lot of school, but you just *know* she'll still be top of the class by the end of term.'

That earned a couple of chuckles – percussion to the music.

Another one came in, in perfect rhythm. 'Senny's an amazing student. It doesn't matter what subject, she always does well. It hardly even seems like she needs to study.'

Cressia, who I was starting to quite like, was the counterpoint to that melody. 'You guys are so transparent.' She pointed at me. 'Kellen's just being polite. You think he can't tell you're all being jerks to his . . . what was it again?'

'Third cousin,' I said. Cressia clearly didn't believe I was who I claimed to be. Another reason to admire her.

Toller, who seemed permanently attached to the windowsill, said, 'Come on, Cress, everybody knows Seneira's brilliant, but it's not like she doesn't have advantages.'

I could see the others looking at me, waiting to see how I'd react. My instinct was to go along with it, to agree and hope it made them like me. My instincts are usually crap. 'Advantages?' I said, and then proceeded to laugh as though he'd said the funniest thing in the world.

161

'What? What did I say?'

I didn't answer, instead just smiled at him.

'Oh . . . I get it.' He gestured to himself and the others. 'You mean because we're all . . .'

I nodded.

'Okay, that's fair.'

'What about you?' Lindy – the younger girl with the spectacles – asked. 'Are you going to join the Academy?'

I wasn't sure how to reply. I used to think of myself as a pretty good liar, but somehow I felt awkward about doing that here more than I had to. Thinking back to Ferius's reply to Master Westrien, I said sincerely, 'It would be an honour.'

Cressia set her book down on one of the tables with a loud thump and came over to me, walking around me as if I were a sculpture she was analysing. 'But what subject should our new friend Kellen study here, I wonder?'

'Devices,' Toller suggested. 'He's got that look – like he's always trying to figure out how things work.'

'Possible,' Cressia said, making another tour around me, 'but he's a romantic – we've seen proof of that.'

'Poetics,' Lindy said. 'He seems to like sounding clever.'

'Perhaps, perhaps, but he looks a bit road-worn for a poet or a rhetorician,' Cressia objected.

Various other subjects were called out, along with reasons why they made sense for me, or didn't. I waited patiently through it all, not letting them see that every possibility tugged at me, every subject was a possible path in life – to find something, to be someone.

Finally Cressia stopped in front of me. 'Well, Kellen, don't keep us in suspense. Who's right? What subject would you study, were you to be granted entry into the Academy?'

There was no particular answer that would gain me anything, so I gave the only one that could. 'The one you're thinking of,' I replied. 'The one no one else suggested.'

A hush descended on the classroom, and everyone waited with baited breath.

Damn, but I'm clever sometimes.

Cressia's smile lit up the room. 'I knew it!' She poked me in the chest. 'Ladies and gentlemen, we have a real live philosopher in our midst!'

Toller groaned. 'Oh, Martius, god of war, please don't make me have to be friends with a *philosophy* student.'

Lindy looked suspicious as she peered up at me. 'He's spent a lot of time out in the sun for a philosopher.'

'I'm more of a natural philosopher,' I said.

She stared up at my jaw. 'And he's got a bruise. Several actually.'

I wasn't sure how to explain that, so I didn't try. 'People like to hit me sometimes.'

Toller chortled. 'Hah! Okay, now I definitely believe he's a philosophy student.'

I laughed right along with the others, and for the next two hours I listened, told stories, listened, joked, listened some more and even made tentative plans with people I'd never met before – people my own age who lived and studied and had all kinds of futures planned out ahead of them. It would have been easy to forget why I was there, but eventually I realised I'd picked up everything I was going to learn. Also, I'd spotted Beren Thrane outside the classroom doing his best to be surreptitious. His best wasn't very good.

'I've got to go,' I said.

A couple of them made a face, and Lindy actually said, 'Boo!'

163

'But you're going to join the Academy, right?' Cressia asked. She tapped me on the chest. 'I believe my colleagues and I have decided that you're worthy to join our grand company, Philosopher Kellen. Of course, you'll have to promise to abide by one rule.'

'What rule is that?'

She leaned over and whispered in my ear. 'Don't ever use me as a prop in one of your little puppet shows again.'

27

The Eavesdroppers

'You seem to be making friends,' Beren said as he led me down the hall towards the grand staircase. He'd yet to tell me precisely why he'd sought me out or where we were going. 'What do you think of our students?'

The question was innocently phrased, but the narrowed eyes and intent gaze told me this wasn't idle curiosity. So was he trying to find out what I'd learned about their feelings towards Seneira? Or their feelings towards this school? I decided to play dumb – something I'd learned how to do without any of Ferius's tricks. 'They seem nice,' I said.

He looked a little disappointed in me, and I found myself hoping that he'd seen through my attempt to be vague if only because I didn't want him thinking I was an idiot. He stopped as we reached the bottom of the stairs and gestured to the throngs of students swirling around the large interior courtyard of the main floor. 'These young men and women are the future, Kellen.'

'The future of what?' I asked.

He pointed towards the high curved wall above the main entrance, where a mosaic made up of thousands of small tiles formed a colourful map of the continent. 'Tell me what you see, and what you don't see.'

Despite the artistic rendering, it was like any other map, except that the Seven Sands was set almost in the middle, though a little to the north-east, which allowed a white tower representing the Academy to sit dead centre. I supposed there was nothing inherently wrong with designing the map to make the school the focal point, though it was a bit ostentatious. Since I was assuming that *wasn't* what he wanted me to notice, I looked at the map more broadly until I saw what *wasn't* there: each of the major countries was labelled, from the Daroman empire to the Berabesq theocracy to the Jan'Tep arcanocracy, but the Seven Sands, sitting between them, was left unnamed.

'Every territory a sovereign nation,' Beren said, 'with its own culture, its own government. All except ours. The Seven Sands isn't even recognised by our neighbours as anything more than an empty desert to be looted as they see fit. They regard us as just one more part of the borderlands.' He walked over to stand near the wide open doors beneath the map and beckoned me to follow. 'Even in my own school I can't inscribe the name of my homeland on my own map for fear it might trigger a diplomatic incident.'

Seneira had told me something similar when we'd arrived in Teleidos. 'So what can you do about it?'

'Nothing,' he replied as a group of students walked past us, each nodding to him as they went by, paying deference to the Academy's headmaster. Beren caught my eye and smiled. 'But they can.'

We walked outside and he turned to gaze back up at the main tower, a look of wonder on his face as if he was seeing

166

it for the first time. 'The most powerful families on the continent send their best to study here, Kellen. Darome, Berabesq, Gitabria, even a few Jan'Tep . . . They may look down on my country, but they do not look down on my school!'

I couldn't imagine any of the great houses in my clan sending their children here, but I was starting to understand where Beren was going with this. 'And while those students are here, they don't just get to know each other, they get to know the people of the Seven Sands.'

Beren grinned and clapped a hand on my shoulder. 'Exactly. They come to realise that our children are not the unwashed backwoods hicks they've been told about, but individuals, like them – and just as capable of possessing remarkable intellectual and leadership qualities.'

All of a sudden Seneira's manner, her wit and intellect – even the way she could be as brusque and rude as any noblewoman – made perfect sense. 'Diplomacy,' I said.

He nodded. 'Diplomacy. The kind that could give my people a future, but only if . . .' His smile and easy manner faltered, revealing the sorrow and despair underneath. 'Please, Kellen, find whoever it is who's trying to kill my family.'

Beren begged me to come visit Tyne with him, insisting that there might be some sign or clue in the winding, twisting markings around the boy's eye that we'd missed before and that might help us understand the disease or at least find some way to ease its symptoms. The instant I entered Tyne's room in the Academy hospital I could see the shadowblack markings had grown since the day before, giving even greater contrast to the paleness of the surrounding skin. His forehead was hot and he looked a little feverish, but at least he was awake.

'Hello,' he said, his voice tentative. He glanced around self-consciously. I guess no one likes to meet strangers while wearing nothing but linen underpants and lying in a pool of their own sweat. Beren started fussing about there not being enough towels, then left in search of more, which only seemed to further embarrass the boy.

'I'm Kellen,' I said. 'We met yesterday, but you probably don't remember. The squirrel cat is my –' I took a perverse delight in finishing – 'pet. Reichis is my pet squirrel cat.'

'Is he here?' Tyne asked.

'No, but I'll try to bring him tomorrow.'

I reached into my pack and took out the cloth horse Seneira had asked me to bring. When I handed it to Tyne, he accepted it with both hands and nodded very seriously as if we'd just struck a bargain and the horse was intended to be a down payment on a squirrel cat.

'How are you feeling today?' I asked.

The boy shrugged. 'I get hot all the time and I sweat a lot.'

I pointed to the marks around his eye. 'Do those hurt?'

'Sometimes. Sometimes it wriggles around and it burns.'

Ancestors. The poor kid. 'When your eye hurts, do you . . . see anything strange?'

He shook his head.

'Or maybe you hear things?'

Another shake of his head, but then he leaned up on his elbows and whispered, 'Sometimes they listen.'

'Listen to what? To you?'

'No.' He glanced around as if to make sure no one else was in the room. 'I think they listen *through* me.'

'Are they listening now?'

Again he shook his head and tapped a finger on his eye.

'Only when it burns.' His lower lip started to tremble and he asked, 'Can you make it stop? I don't like it when they're listening.'

'Sure, Tyne, I'll . . .' I hesitated, remembering how Seneira hated being told everything was going to be okay when it wasn't. How much had it helped me to have my parents lie to me all those years about my own shadowblack? 'You're going to have to be brave for now, Tyne. I'm going to try and find out what's happening to you, but you'll have to be brave.'

The trembling in his lower lip got worse, but then he asked, 'Like Senny?'

I nodded. 'Just like her.'

'Okay,' he said.

I stood there a few minutes longer, not sure what else to say or do for him. Beren returned with a stack of towels and started placing them around Tyne. The boy looked up at me. 'Kellen?'

'Yeah?'

He started hugging himself and the first blush of fever gave a reddish glow to the skin on his cheeks and forehead. 'You'd better go now. I think they want to listen again.'

'Just ignore them, Tyne,' I said. 'Think of something else. Think of Senny.'

'You'd better go,' he repeated, his irises turning black as his eyes blinked over and over. Then he whispered, 'They can see you now, Kellen.'

28

The Hooded Figure

I left Tyne's room with those words echoing in my head: 'They can see you now, Kellen.' Why had he said it that way? As if . . . As if whatever demons were worming their way inside him through the shadowblack were somehow particularly interested in me.

Well, I keep wondering if my life could possibly get any worse. I guess it can.

I made my way through the hospital's maze of halls, suddenly feeling as if there were eyes following me everywhere, picking up the pace every time my lousy sense of direction made me take a wrong turn. By the time I found the exit I practically knocked over a doctor as I ran outside into the cool evening air.

Breathe, I told myself. *Just breathe and stop imagining demons on your trail.*

I started walking down the street, crossing over the circular avenues that ran around the Academy, unable to shake the eerie feeling of being watched. Of course, I suppose the fact that I *was* being followed didn't help.

Seneira's house was in the opposite direction from the centre of town, which meant I was walking down mostly empty streets. Even if I *could* find other people along the route, they might well be working with whoever was stalking me. I turned down first one alley then another until I found a darkened doorway I could duck into. Within seconds a hooded figure, male, about my height and build, rounded the corner, carrying what looked like an eighteen-inch iron rod.

'Two things you should know about me,' I said as I stepped out of the shadows.

He spun around to face me, raising the weapon to make it clear he could bash me with it if I made a move.

One thing I've learned from Ferius these past months: being afraid is often unavoidable, but *looking* afraid can be suicidal. I put on my best smile. 'First, I've had a pretty bad few months.'

'It could get a lot worse,' my pursuer warned, which helped because I could tell he was trying to make his voice deeper than it really was, which meant he almost certainly wasn't a bounty mage come to get me and probably not any kind of trained assassin either.

'The second thing you should know is that I'm not someone you want to get into a fight with.'

That last part was technically true: I tend to bleed on people a lot. Just ask Freckles.

I couldn't make out my pursuer's face, obscured as it was by shadows cast by the hood he wore, but the way he stood uncertainly, shifting his balance on his feet as if he expected me to rush him, told me I had, for once, successfully bluffed someone into thinking I was dangerous.

'You're a liar,' he said finally.

Well, that was true. 'What am I lying about?'

'You're not Seneira's second cousin.'

171

Okay, so he was either one of the students I'd talked to in the classroom or someone who'd been listening in. 'Third,' I said.

'You're not that either.' He raised the iron rod higher. 'Tell me who you really are or I'll—'

I'd already flipped open the tops of the pouches at my sides and now I let my fingers dip inside to pinch the powders. I was pretty sure I could take this guy out if it came to it, but I had a hunch that would turn out to be a bad idea. 'How about I tell you who *you* are instead?'

He did a bit of a double take. 'What are you talking about? You don't know me. You've never met me.'

'That's true,' I admitted. 'But I just spent the last few hours wandering around the Academy, talking to teachers and students who know Seneira. Want to know what I found out?'

He hesitated, probably figuring this could be some kind of trick but not sure what it might be. 'What?'

'Nobody particularly likes her. Oh, they respect her intelligence, but mostly they think she's privileged, stuck up and pompous.'

His grip on the iron bar tightened. 'You don't know what you're talking about! Seneira's nothing like that. She's—'

'Relax, Revian.'

He froze, suddenly glancing around in case anyone was nearby. I guess wealthy Academy students aren't supposed to accost people with iron bars. 'How did you know?' he asked, sounding defeated. His voice now had a somewhat higher and distinctly more natural pitch.

'I exaggerated about Seneira's classmates. They like her fine, just not enough to make more than a cursory enquiry as to how my "third cousin" was doing when she's been absent

172

from school for weeks. Nobody even asked what illness she has, and no one asked if they could come visit her. You, on the other hand, apparently spent an hour spying on me and then came after me with an iron bar on the off-chance I might mean her harm.'

'Do you? Because if—'

'I'm a friend,' I said. 'Well, not much of one, I guess. But I am trying to help her. That part's true.'

Revian stared at me a long time before lowering his weapon. 'You've seen her?' he asked. 'I mean, is she okay?'

He sounded anxious and sad . . . no, not sad, *despairing*. He knew about Seneira's shadowblack. 'She's unharmed, other than the . . . illness of course.'

He nodded. 'We talked before she left town. I begged her to stay, but she said she had to protect her family. When I heard you pretending to be her cousin, I thought . . . Not everyone here likes her or her father.'

'But you do?'

He took a step forward, trying, I think, to intimidate me. He didn't do a very good job of it because I could see he was shaking. It felt good for someone to actually be afraid of me for a change. 'She's my betrothed,' he said suddenly.

The air went out of me faster than if he'd punched me in the gut. 'You're marrying Seneira?'

He nodded. 'It's been arranged since we were children. Our families believe that uniting our houses through marriage could be beneficial to both.' He must have seen something in my expression, because he added, 'I *do* love her, and even if we weren't meant to be wed, I'd still do terrible things to the person who hurt her.'

His sincerity and loyalty shouldn't have bothered me, except

173

I'd heard it in Seneira's voice when she'd described Revian too. *So what?* I asked myself. Who was Seneira to me? Some girl I'd met on the road who'd brought me nothing but annoyance and more than my share of trouble. Besides, I still had feelings for Nephenia, even if she'd had to move on without me.

I guess I'd better get used to being alone.

I shouldn't have cared about any of this; the Academy, the Seven Sands, Seneira . . . none of it had anything to do with me. Whatever happened, once it was all done, Ferius, Reichis and I would ride out of town back onto the long roads, camping out at night, setting up traps and hoping that the next hextracker who hunted me down wouldn't be the one who finished the job. *The way of the Argosi is the way of wind,* I thought ruefully.

'Do the . . . markings around her eyes still trouble her?' Revian asked, suddenly desperate now that he figured I might know something. 'Please, it's been weeks since I saw her.'

'If you want to know so bad, why didn't you just –'

I stopped. I'd been about to ask why he hadn't gone to see her instead of stalking me in the halls of the Academy. Then a few things fell into place: the fact that he hadn't been in class; the fact that he hadn't gone straight to her house; and, most of all, the hood he had pulled down low enough that I couldn't see much of his face.

'Take off the hood, Revian.'

He shook his head.

'You might as well do it,' I said. 'I already know what I'm going to see.'

Slowly he reached up with shaking hands and removed the hood.

Revian was every bit as handsome as Seneira had described,

with hair like spun gold and smooth, perfect skin over finely chiselled features. He really *did* look like something out of a painting. Well, except for the twisting black markings that circled around his right eye.

'Please,' Revian said, still sincere but somehow not quite so noble in my estimation now his question had taken on a second meaning. 'Tell me she's all right.'

29

The House Mage

Revian walked with me partway back to Seneira's house and told me his story.

'It began a few days ago,' he said, pulling his hood back on to hide his face. 'I woke up soaking in sweat with a searing pain in my right eye. When I crawled out of bed and went into the bathroom to splash water on my face, I saw the markings.'

'Do you have visions?' I asked. 'When the attacks come, I mean.'

He shook his head. 'Mostly just pain. Sometimes I hear things . . . Voices.'

So, more like Seneira's than mine.

'You're Jan'Tep,' Revian commented. 'I've made a study of your people and culture. My father wants me to become a diplomat one day, to build bridges between the Daroman empire and the Jan'Tep arcanocracy.'

Good luck with that.

Then he really surprised me. 'You're a spellslinger, aren't you?'

The question sounded oddly desperate. I fumbled for an answer, and ended up stumbling on the truth. 'I guess so. Still trying to figure that out.'

'Is that why you're here? To cure Seneira?' He reached up a finger to touch the markings around his eye. 'Can you cure me?'

'What? Of course not. I can't even cure . . .' I stopped myself when I remembered the paste covering my own shadowblack. 'I can't even cure a cold,' I recovered.

Revian didn't seem to notice. 'My parents tried to hire a man – a spellslinger like you – because they believed he might be able to help me, but he said we have to find the mage who cast the curse in the first place.'

'Do you have any enemies? Particularly ones who might also have a problem with Seneira or her family.'

He gave a terse, bitter laugh, and gestured in the direction of the Academy. 'Take your pick. You think those people you met today were being nice to you because they want to be your friends?' He decided to answer his own question. 'They're the sons and daughters of wealthy and powerful families from across the continent, Kellen. In their own countries they live in palaces, and when they return home they will become politicians and courtiers and military leaders. To them, you're nothing more than a novelty, or perhaps a tool that they can use for their own ends.'

'You don't sound as if you have much faith in Beren's vision of the Seven Sands becoming a country.'

'The Academy is a noble idea, but a foolishly optimistic one. For all the prestige Seneira's father has been able to buy for his school, there are many who want to see it crumble.'

I pointed at the markings around his eye. 'Bad enough to start a plague?'

He hesitated for moment, then nodded. 'Do you know what a whisper witch is?'

177

I had no idea. For the most part, the Jan'Tep have neither time nor respect for any other culture's ideas about magic. On the other hand, I didn't know Revian particularly well and didn't feel like revealing my ignorance, so I played it the way Ferius had with the masters at the Academy. 'You're saying there's a whisper witch in Teleidos?'

He nodded. 'In the wild swamps outside the city. Nobody's seen her in years, but the locals say her name is Mamma Whispers, and if you're willing to pay the price, if you want it badly enough, she can summon spirits to help you . . . or demons to curse your enemies.'

Demons. That would do it.

'Revian,' a voice called out.

I turned and saw two men coming down the alley towards us. They wore long cloaks over their coats with hoods that hid their faces. I started reaching for my powders again but Revian stopped me. 'It's all right. They're house mages. They work for my parents.'

Well, that explained why I hadn't heard them coming. One of them must have sparked his breath band, like me, only he was clearly better at quieting spells than I was. I glanced back at Revian, suddenly keenly aware of just how wealthy and influential his family must be. Proper Jan'Tep mages don't work for foreigners unless the client has enough political or military power to be valuable to the clan.

'You were told to remain within the house,' the taller of the men said. He was watching me closely.

'It's all right, Ler'danet,' Revian insisted. 'Kellen's a friend of Seneira's.' He glanced at me a little hopefully. 'And my friend as well.'

'He is not a friend of your family,' the shorter one clarified.

He too was staring daggers at me. 'In fact, Kellen of the House of Ke has no friends at all.'

Okay, this wasn't looking good for me. 'Sorry, masters. I was just leaving.'

Revian gave a chuckle. 'Come on, Kellen, I promise, you don't need to be scared of—'

'*Sethaten*,' Ler'danet, the tall mage, whispered, pairing the word with a gesture of his right hand. Revian went out like a snuffed candle.

Great. A silk mage. Because I haven't had enough trouble with those lately.

The shorter one caught Revian before he landed and invoked the third foundational form of breath magic. '*Fessandi*,' he said, and Revian began to float on his back as though propped up by the air itself.

'Take the boy home,' Ler'danet commanded.

The other house mage walked away with Revian floating along beside him, and soon it was just the two of us standing there.

'Revian is going to be pretty pissed off when he wakes up,' I noted. 'Especially if he finds out you killed his friend.'

Ler'danet smiled in that way people do when they find the very sight of you distasteful. 'Bad enough I am forced to work for the boy's Daroman parents. I do not take commands from *him*.'

I started to reach for my powders, but for some reason my hands kept missing the pouches. Then I saw the smirk on Ler'danet's face. *Damned silk magic.*

Usually in a situation like this I wait for Ferius to say something clever that has a slim chance of getting us out of trouble. Unfortunately she wasn't here and nothing particularly brilliant was coming to my mind.

179

'First rule of house mages and house pets,' a voice said, emerging from the shadows of the alleyway behind us.

Just how many people are going to sneak up on me today?

I turned to see Dexan Videris grinning at us both. 'If you're going to let them out of the house, keep them on a short leash.'

'*Exile*,' Ler'danet said, the word dripping with disgust. I guess he wasn't fond of Jan'Tep outcasts in general. 'Shouldn't you be running away now? That is your way, isn't it?'

'Most days, sure, but Kellen here is a spellslinger like me, and, well, the fifth rule of spellslinging is . . .'

Please let it be 'Always help a fellow spellslinger in need.'

'There's always profit to be found in having a fellow spellslinger owe you a favour.'

Okay, that'll work.

Suddenly Dexan clapped his palms together and a flash of blue-white light lit the alley. Ler'danet raised an arm up to protect his eyes even as his other hand formed the somatic shape for a new spell. '*Shupal derveis*,' he shouted, and all of a sudden both Dexan and I were sent flying backwards. I hit my back against an unlit lamp post and struggled to get to my feet.

Dexan recovered faster than I did. 'Aw, come on now, Ler'danet. Don't insult me with that old cantrip.' He reached up and pulled something from the band around his frontier hat and tossed it up high. It gave off a small, almost insignificant explosion, but then yellow dust started falling all around us. 'Best hold your breath, kid.'

I tried, but as soon as the dust touched my skin I started feeling off somehow – dizzy, almost sleepy. I couldn't quite find my balance and yet didn't seem to mind much at all. Ler'danet was stumbling around, struggling to stay on his feet.

'First thing I learned to love about the territories,' Dexan said, walking towards Ler'danet. 'They got all kinds of ways of having a good time. Now *our* people, of course, well, we don't usually have much use for liquor or other such amusements. That's why we can't cast spells worth a damn when we're drunk.' He held up his right hand, bright sparks of ember magic swirling around his fingers. ''Less you practise getting drunk a whole lot, that is.' He extended his arm and thin crackles of lightning whipped through the air, digging into Ler'danet like dozens of tiny needles.

For a second it looked as if the house mage was going to fall, but then he reached inside his cloak and a thin three-foot length of chain whipped out. At first I thought it must have a shielding charm on it, but the blue sparks of Dexan's spell didn't dissipate – instead they began to shimmer and dance around the length of the chain.

'Darn it,' Dexan said, backing away, dragging me with him by the collar. 'Now where did you get yourself a siphon chain, Ler'danet?'

The other mage burped awkwardly, but nonetheless began to stalk towards us, whipping the chain back and forth, sending sparks flying from it. 'Unlike you, *exile*, I despise this place. It's filthy, backwards and full of vermin.' He grinned. 'But at least no one minds when you kill a few rats.'

My head was starting to clear, but not nearly enough to be able to cast a spell. Dexan's smirk had disappeared and he was concentrating now on staying out of the way of the chain before it killed him with his own spell. Ler'danet whipped the chain with more and more force as he recovered from the yellow dust. I thought about jumping at him, but I'd only get killed faster that way. Instead I surreptitiously reached into my pocket and extracted some of Ferius's steel throwing cards. I figured I'd only have one chance at this, because the instant Ler'danet saw them he'd use the chain on me and I'd be dead. So I watched as the chain swung back and forth, back and forth, trying to get a feel for the timing.

'Kid?' Dexan said. 'Don't suppose you—'

Now! I threw one of the cards, more by instinct than aim. It sailed towards Ler'danet, the steel surface shimmering blue as it flew under the sparking chain. The house mage screamed in pain as the card bit into his cheek. He dropped the chain and instantly the lightning spell faded from it. Ler'danet reached back into his cloak, but by then I was already running at him.

'Go low, kid!' Dexan shouted.

I dived for the house mage's legs, wrapping my arms around them and making him stumble. Just as he was falling, I looked up and saw Dexan leap over me, slamming Ler'danet to the ground and knocking the wind out of him. The house mage's throat rattled as he tried to suck air into his lungs. Dexan dropped something small and light, like a tiny green leaf, into the mage's mouth. Ler'danet's eyes went wide. He began frantically clawing at the inside of his mouth even as he struggled for breath.

'He's choking!' I said, mindful of the – to my way of thinking entirely unfair – Argosi admonition against killing defeated enemies. I crawled over to him and tried to help, but the mage pushed me away.

'Well, normally I'd say that's just tough,' Dexan said, rising to his feet and dusting himself off, 'but old Ler'danet's going to be fine. He's just upset because by now he's figured out that I made him swallow addleweed.'

The mage took in a long, wheezing gasp, then his breathing

began to settle. He looked up, his eyes not seeming to recognise me, looking very confused by the world around him.

'Yeah,' Dexan said, standing over him. 'Ler'danet here won't be casting any spells for the next few weeks. Or doing much arithmetic.'

We dragged Ler'danet away from the middle of the alley and left him under the awning of what looked like an abandoned shop. Dexan figured his partner would come looking for him soon enough and get him back to Revian's parents' home, where he'd receive medical care – likely followed by getting fired.

'Teleidos is a civilised place,' Dexan explained. 'Folks don't like it much when house mages go around trying to kill people.'

'Tell that to Ler'danet,' I said, rubbing at the spot on my back where I'd struck the lamp post.

Dexan clapped a hand on my shoulder. 'Just be thankful I was looking for you, kid. Guys like you and me are none too popular with the Jan'Tep these days.'

'How did you know where I'd be?' I asked.

He chuckled. 'I told you, Kellen, you're not hard to find.'

There were any number of Jan'Tep tracking spells, so I was curious to know which one he'd used.

'Second rule of being a spellslinger . . .' he began.

'Let me guess: "Don't share your secrets." I get it. Have you found a way to help Seneira and her brother?'

He stopped walking. 'Sorry, kid. Until we find the mage that cursed them and put an end to him, there's nothing I can do.' He must've seen from my expression what my next question was going to be. 'Forget it. I told you before – first rule of being a spellslinger is never mess in another spellslinger's business.

183

Once whoever started this rash of shadowblack cursing is dead, I'll help cure the girl and her brother, but until then, I'm staying out of it.'

I told Dexan about the whisper witch Revian had mentioned. Even before I was done he was shaking his head. 'Stay away from Mamma Whispers, kid. You don't mess with her unless you're ready to kill her. Are you ready to do that, Kellen? Murder someone in cold blood?'

I didn't have an answer to that.

Dexan noticed my hesitation. 'Want some free advice?'

'Sure, I guess.'

He pointed up the road towards Seneira's house. 'Those folks you're trying to help? They're nice people, but they're not *your* people. When this whole mess is done and over with? Well –' he tapped a finger on my left cheek just below the paste covering up the black marks that wound around my eye – 'they won't want some exiled Jan'Tep with the shadowblack hanging around.'

Somehow that thought – the idea of everyone else being cured, but me still being stuck with this curse, with the pain, with the visions – was too much. That thing that always happens a few minutes after nearly dying? The incredible cold, the uncontrollable shaking? The worst part is that it's sometimes accompanied by pathetic crying.

'Hey, kid,' Dexan said, putting a hand on my shoulder. 'It's rough, I know.' He took away his hand and added, 'But it's not all bad news.'

A sudden spark of hope lit up inside me. 'You've found a cure? For *my* shadowblack?'

'I can't make it go away permanently, not when your grand-mother banded you in shadow. But I think I've found a set

184

of spells – three of them – that, if I do them right, will make it harder for hextrackers to use the spell warrant to track you. More importantly, I'm pretty sure the technique will also reduce the frequency of your shadowblack attacks and stop the visions from being quite so bad.'

'How does it –' Dexan's grin stopped me. 'Oh, right. Never share your secrets. So what's the price?'

His expression changed, becoming more serious. 'The thing is, it's not a one-off spell. I'd have to cast it repeatedly, probably every week or so.'

'But then—'

'That's the price. You'd need to stick with me. We'd be partners.'

'You'd *want* me as a partner?'

'Why not? You and me did pretty good together back there against old Ler'danet, didn't we? Besides –' he leaned back against the fence of a small house and stuck his thumbs in his belt – 'being a spellslinger is a dangerous business. I've spent a lot of years on the run. Having someone to watch my back . . . well, that wouldn't be so bad.' He gave me a thoughtful look. 'I could teach you a lot, you know. I left our people when I was about your age, and I've spent the last fifteen years learning things. Things that could help you survive in that big bad world out there.'

He started telling me about some of his adventures travelling the continent. For all the danger, he made it sound . . . exciting. A spellslinger was a valuable commodity to a lot of people. Traders carrying expensive cargo, families looking for someone to track down a loved one, even governments sometimes wanted the services of a mage who wasn't beholden to the Jan'Tep arcanocracy.

185

'You'd have to say goodbye to your Argosi friend,' he warned. 'I don't plan on travelling down her road.'

I was surprised by the sudden sick feeling in the pit of my stomach. It's not as if Ferius and I had been getting along, and she showed no signs of wanting to teach me how to fight or keep myself alive out there. Learning to 'smile' had been kind of fun, but smiling wasn't going to help me fend off a bounty hunter.

'Can I think about it?' I asked.

'Of course, but don't take too long to decide.' He glanced around the empty street. 'This town's got bad vibrations to it – and I say that as a guy who never sparked his silk band and isn't superstitious. I figure it's time to make for someplace that doesn't feel like it's going to seven kinds of hell any time soon.' He extended a hand towards me. Not knowing what else to do, I shook it. He had a firm grip that made me wince. 'I'll give you a day to sort yourself out, kid, but after that I'm out of here.'

I nodded, rubbing at my hand that now ached. Maybe Reichis is right and I need to put on some muscle. 'When I decide, how should I—'

Dexan laughed again as he walked off into the night. 'I keep telling you, kid: I'll find you.'

30

The Betrothed

It was fully dark by the time I got back to Seneira's house, and she was there by herself. Rosie and Ferius were off doing their own investigating, and apparently Beren had been summoned to the home of Revian's parents. It seemed they were no longer quite so keen on their precious son marrying the girl who they now suspected had given him the shadowblack.

'Do you love him?' I asked, as we stepped outside to the garden.

All through our conversation and my informing her of Revian's condition, I'd tried to come up with ways of asking how she felt that *wouldn't* make me sound like a jealous idiot. This was not one of the variations I'd practised in my head.

'Do you love him?' What a moron!

Seneira had been stuck here since we arrived in Teleidos, suffering from a condition she didn't understand, unable to return to her normal life or even see her sick brother again. The last thing she needed was a bunch of stupid questions about the person she was supposed to marry – assuming the shadowblack didn't take her first.

Reichis sauntered over to inspect a flower bed he was considering as a possible toilet. "'Do you love him?'" he repeated, doing the best impression one can expect from a squirrel cat of a hopeless, lovesick youth. 'When did you become part rabbit?'

Seneira was staring at me, eyes narrowed; I half expected her to slap me. Instead she said, 'I'm sorry, Kellen, I should have told you Revian and I were betrothed. Our families . . . The agreement was made when we were children.'

In fact there was no reason in the world why she should have mentioned her marital plans to me. I'd only known her a few days and, really, other than the shadowblack, what did we have in common?

'It's not . . .' She hesitated. 'Revian and I, it's not like . . .'

'Not like what?'

She shook her head. 'I'm sorry, that's between Revian and me. I shouldn't have said anything.'

Reichis lifted up his head, looking as though he'd caught a scent in the air, then wandered over to Seneira and sniffed at her. 'Kiss her,' he said finally.

'What?'

He looked up at me through beady squirrel-cat eyes. 'She wants you to kiss her.'

'I doubt it. She's . . .' I stopped myself, mostly on account of the fact that Seneira was watching me.

'Kellen?' she asked.

'Yeah?'

'Please tell me you and your squirrel cat aren't talking about me.'

'Just kiss her already,' Reichis said, sitting back on his haunches as if Seneira wasn't even there. 'Trust me: she likes you. Obviously if she's supposed to mate with this other idiot then she can't *tell* you that, so she's waiting for *you* to kiss *her*.'

188

'You don't know that,' I said.

Seneira looked confused, thinking I'd spoken to her. 'Of course I don't *know* what it is you imagine the animal is saying to you.'

Reichis tapped his snout. 'I call it like I smell it.'

One of the skills I was going to have to learn one day (in addition to escaping chokeholds, taking a punch and *not* asking girls I had no business falling for whether or not they loved their betrothed) was how to simultaneously have a conversation with Reichis and whoever else was around who *didn't* happen to speak squirrel cat.

'I'm sorry,' I said to Seneira. 'I never should have brought it up.'

If I'd been hoping that Revian's affections for Seneira might be unrequited – or that taking romantic advice from a squirrel cat made any sense at all – I was disabused of that notion by the look of concern on Seneira's face. 'The shadowblack . . . it must be awful for him. I thought that by running I could protect the people I loved, but all I did was bring even more suffering into their lives.' She reached up a hand to the black markings around her eye, wincing as she touched them. 'I wish . . . I wish you'd met me before all this happened, Kellen.'

I felt like this was one of those pauses in the music that Ferius talks about, so I asked, 'What were you like?'

A trace of defiance broke through the sadness and self-doubt. 'I was a fighter. I never sat around crying or waiting for other people to save me.'

'Maybe you're still a fighter,' I said. 'Maybe you're just waiting for the right moment.'

'When will that be, Kellen? And who am I supposed to fight?'

189

There was such desperate need in her voice, in the way she looked up at me, as if somehow I could give her the answers, but I couldn't. I had no idea what was happening to the people of this town, and right now the only thought that kept going through my head was Dexan's offer: *They're nice people, but they're not your people.*

I don't know if Seneira was just tired of standing there waiting for me to say or do something, or if maybe she could sense what I was thinking, because a moment later she gave me a sad smile, said goodnight and left me in the garden.

Reichis started to follow her inside, then stopped just long enough to turn back around and say, 'Should've kissed her like I told you. Moron.'

31

The Warning

I turned in for the night, stopping by the bathroom just long enough to wash my face. I felt oddly nauseous for some reason, and found myself staring at the drops of water that remained in the basin as they slowly slid down the sides. The droplets came together in places, forming shapes and then coming apart again. The sight was strangely compelling, and as more of the droplets coalesced in the basin, I found I couldn't turn my head away. That's when I realised what was going on.

'Son of a bitch, Shalla! Seriously?'

The image in the basin took on the shape of her eyes, her nose, her mouth – which displayed not the slightest sign of contrition. 'What?' she asked, in a voice that sounded faintly, well, watery. 'I couldn't find you through the sands, and the only options other than this were the bathtub or the toilet.'

Not a thought I wanted in my head. 'What do you want, Shalla?'

The droplets of water slipped and slid, and her expression grew concerned. 'I had to reach you again, Kellen. You need to get out of there.'

'Out of where?' I asked.

'Don't play dumb with me. I know you're near that disgusting place – the Academy or whatever it is they call it.'

'Disgusting? It's a school.'

'It's a monument to vanity and futility.'

Shalla has this habit sometimes of using my father's words as though they were her own. The fact that I can tell when she's doing it is maybe one of the only things I have over her. 'So Ke'heops doesn't approve?'

'No one approves, Kellen. The Seven Sands isn't a country. It will *never* be a country. And you need to get out of there.' The eyes formed by the water moved slightly, as if Shalla were trying to see into the room. 'Are you with the girl?'

'Which girl?'

A slight sneer formed. 'The one with the shadowblack plague, of course. What else would you be doing in that barbaric place?'

Her use of the word 'plague' troubled me. 'What do you know, Shalla?'

'I . . . Not much, only that the council of lords magi has forbidden any Jan'Tep from travelling into the Seven Sands until further notice. The councils from the other clans are doing the same.' The drops of water forming her eyes took on a less confident and more concerned shape. 'Something bad is happening in Teleidos, Kellen. Please, just get away from there. Come home.'

'Did you find out about the death warrant?' I asked. 'Do you know who—'

The water shape shook, almost coming apart. 'No one's talking, and I don't think anyone outside the council knows. Even Father won't talk to me about it.'

192

'Then why would I come home, Shalla? Chances are whoever put that warrant out for me will want to see me dead the second I set foot back in our city.'

'I'll protect you!' she said. 'I won't let anyone harm you, Kellen. You're my brother.'

She would too. Shalla had a loyalty that was almost painful sometimes – when she wasn't doing our father's bidding. No matter how much she cared about me though, the strands that connected us would always be weaker than the ones she shared with Ke'heops. More and more that was becoming the defining quality of my life: every relationship was tenuous. Reichis was supposed to be my partner, but mostly he just got me into trouble. Ferius was supposed to be my mentor, but it turned out she had no intention of teaching me the ways of the Argosi. Nephenia had cared about me, for a time, but the further away I travelled from our homeland and the Jan'Tep way of life, the weaker that connection became. And Seneira? Well, she was betrothed to Revian.

'Kellen?' Shalla asked, her voice more distant now.

So what was I left with? A little breath magic, some exploding powders and a spell warrant that said any mage who crossed my path would get a nice payment for killing me. In the metal of the sink, the reflection of the black markings around my eye were distorted, almost mocking. I was so sick of the shadowblack, of the way it destroyed not only my life but that of everyone else around me. More than that, I suddenly realised I couldn't stomach the idea that someone would inflict this on another human being. I thought about the voices Seneira talked about during her attacks and the way they laughed at her, at the pain they caused her and Tyne and even Revian.

193

Shalla and Dexan had each offered me a way out – a chance at a better life – but the price of either was leaving Seneira and her family and maybe the whole Seven Sands to suffer whatever horrors were stalking them.

'Kellen, just come home,' Shalla said, her words barely more than drips of water tapping against the sink.

I picked up the hand towel from the side of the sink. 'I love you, little sister. Stay safe.'

Before she could say anything else, I wiped the last drops of water from the basin and put the towel back on its hook.

WAY of THUNDER

The way of the Argosi is the way of thunder.

The thunder comes rarely, but when it does, it strikes without hesitation or remorse. An Argosi seeks not to impose themselves on others, but neither will they allow harm or enslavement of the innocent. When the balance of water has been broken by those who would force others to their will, then does an Argosi restore the equilibrium. Like the thunder, they do so swiftly, boldly and, sometimes, mercilessly.

32

The Whispers

'Have I mentioned that crocodiles just love places like this?'
Reichis asked, sitting on my shoulder and peering out into
the swamp ahead of us.

'A few times.' I started walking again, as quietly as I could,
yet somehow my every footstep seemed to set off leaves
crunching, insects buzzing.

'I mean, this is a *really* stupid idea, Kellen.'

'You said that already, too.'

Reichis is usually perfectly happy to go wandering around
dark places in the middle of the night, but something about
this particular swampy forest had us both on edge. It didn't
help that we were hunting for someone who had the power
to summon spirits or demons or whatever else it was to kill
us or destroy our souls or maybe just eat us alive.

'If you'd just kissed that girl like I told you—'

'What good would that have done?'

He gave a snort. 'She'd have got so angry she'd have slapped
you into next week! That girl would've hit you so hard,
Kellen, you wouldn't even *think* of risking our lives going
after some crazy whisper witch – you'd be too busy trying
to find someone to cast an ice spell so you could get the

swelling down on your face!' He started giggling uncontrollably and had to dig his claws into my shoulder to keep from falling off.

'You little bastard. I *knew* you were setting me up!'

It took him a while to settle. Then he said, 'But seriously, you should kiss her next time.'

I would have picked him up and thrown him into a tree if it wasn't for the fact that he'd just glide back down again to land on my head.

A crackling behind us caused me to spin around, almost dislodging Reichis. I saw nothing, however.

'Just the wind,' he said. 'It's picking up the leaves and making them—'

'I know how wind works.'

'I still think we should have waited for Ferius.'

Yeah, I thought as another gust of wind sent the leaves spinning around us. *Me too*. 'Ferius wouldn't have let us come,' I said, as much to myself as to Reichis. 'She'd say something stupid like, "Never listen to rumours about hedge wizards and whisper witches, kid . . . they's just a bunch a hogwash."'

Reichis chuckled. 'Yeah, and then Rosie would be like, "My . . . sister . . . has a certain unwarranted empathy for . . . recluses."' For a talking animal, he does pretty good impressions of humans.

'Then Ferius would say, "Sister, them's wrastlin' words!"'

'Oh, oh, and then Rosie would come back with, "You have lost the way, Path of Farting Daisies. Now we must fight to the death . . . or perhaps just play cards and stare at each other again."'

I started laughing so hard I had to hold on to a tree to keep from falling over. Reichis and I went back and forth like that as we made our way deeper into the swamp, knowing we should stop but somehow unable to.

Eventually Reichis asked, 'You know why this is such a stupid idea?'

'You said that already. Like, twelve times.'

'Yeah, but do you know *why* it's a stupid idea?'

I stopped. 'Why?'

Reichis shivered on my shoulder. 'Because this place is giving me the creeps, and I'm a squirrel cat – normally we're the ones giving *other* people the creeps.'

A light laugh came at us, the sound of wind chimes in a soft breeze, dancing around us as though each note were being carried on the back of an insect darting this way and that.

'Who's there?' I asked, my hands already dipping into the pouches at my belt.

'Didn't no one tell you, mister spellslinger? It's dangerous to mess with Mamma Whispers in her own place of business.'

Reichis growled, sniffing at the air. 'I can't see her.'

'Who are you?' I asked, then closed my eyes so that I could figure out where the reply was coming from.

'Why you askin', Jan'Tep?' She stretched the word out, making it sound like 'Jaahhn-Tehep'. 'Maybe you trying to trick Mamma Whispers? Maybe you come to do a bit of murder?'

'We're not here to murder anyone,' I said.

'We're not?' Reichis asked. He sounded distinctly disappointed.

My attempts to locate her from the sound of her voice failed miserably. It was as if she were flying through the underbrush all around us. Reichis wasn't having any better luck with her scent. 'Something's not right,' he said.

201

'My spirits, they don't want you tracking me, spellslinger. They make the air move for me. The spirits always help out Mamma Whispers.'

'Then why are you afraid to show yourself?' I asked. 'Do you prefer to do your work unseen? Infecting innocent people with the shadowblack?'

'Shadowblack?' She spat the word. 'You shouldn't be sayin' such things around here, spellslinger.'

The sound of leaves and soft underbrush crunching crackled in the night air. 'You want to see Mamma Whispers? Be careful what you wish for.'

The figure that emerged from the trees was not at all what I'd expected. I'd imagined a woman, maybe in her forties or fifties, large and powerful. Instead what I saw was a girl of no more than ten or eleven, barefoot and wearing a simple peasant dress that hung to the ground. Her hair was long and black, topped by a hat that might have been worn by a wealthy gentleman were it not battered and threadbare.

'You're a kid,' I said aloud. Probably not the best idea.

'I am what you see, spellslinger, and what you *don't* see too.'

Reichis gave a low growl. 'I already don't like her.'

The girl took another step towards us, and her presence made me more uncomfortable the closer she came, as if she belonged here but we didn't. 'Stay back,' I said.

'Or what?' she asked, her voice young but the way she spoke that of a much older woman. 'You going to burn me with your magic? Go ahead, spellslinger, show Mamma Whispers what you got.'

I had no intention of blasting a little girl, even if she *wasn't* really that young. 'I'm not here to fight you. I just have questions.'

The girl grinned. 'But what if I'm here to fight you?'

Okay, so much for the gentle approach. I lifted my hands up, each one holding enough powder to make an impression once I cast the spell. I wasn't intending to aim it at her, just to fire off a warning shot, but as I hurled the powders into the air, I saw her lips move and heard a whispering sound. Suddenly the powders flew out of my hands, swirling up high, only to come right towards me and Reichis. I ducked down low just in time for the powders to pass overhead, clashing together and setting off an explosion of red and black glimmer that would have given me a nasty burn if they'd touched me.

'My spirits don't appreciate your kind of magic, spellslinger. You shouldn't have come to mess with Mamma Whispers. They don't like that, no they don't.'

'I told you, I didn't come here to fight!'

The girl came closer again, still seeming like no kind of threat at all, and looked up at me through wide, seemingly innocent eyes. 'Maybe. Maybe not. We see what my spirits say.'

Again I watched in fascination as her lips moved just a fraction and I could hear the wind moving in response. Soon it picked up in force, swirling all around us, and other voices appeared . . . ones I recognised.

'Last chance to walk away, Kellen,' the first one said. It was Tennat, the words those he'd spoken at our initiates' duel months ago.

The wind picked up. 'A Jan'Tep must be strong,' my father said from somewhere behind me.

I spun around but he wasn't there. 'What's going on?' I demanded.

A new voice appeared, off to my right. 'These are the questions of a child, Kellen.' Mer'esan, the night she first summoned me to the palace.

More and more voices appeared, falling on top of one another, coming and going in the breeze, all voices I recognised, all words that had been spoken months before. Over and over they called out to me: Shalla, my parents, Nephenia, Panahsi, Ra'meth, Abydos ... The swirl of sound became maddening and I was about to cover my ears to block out the noise when suddenly they all stopped, all except for one voice. It was Master Osia'phest, on my last night in my city, reading from the slip of paper upon which I'd written my answer to the fourth trial: 'There's no amount of magic in the world that's worth the price of a man's conscience.'

Everything went silent, until finally Mamma Whispers said, 'Well now, aren't you a fascination?'

Reichis bristled on my shoulder. 'Can I kill her now?'

'Maybe later. How did you do that?' I asked the girl.

She shrugged. 'I didn't do nothing. My spirits though, they can be powerful useful when they're of a mind to be.'

She'd certainly proved that to be true. To my people, the words 'spirit' and 'demon' were pretty much interchangeable. 'What else can your spirits do?' I asked.

The girl gave me a sour look. 'They don't put the shadow-black on innocents, if that's what you came to find out.'

Reichis leaned forward on my shoulder and sniffed the air. 'Hard to tell with all the crazy smells around here, but I think she's telling the truth.'

I felt tired then, as if all my anger, all my fear, all my brave words about fighting to protect Seneira and her family, were just that – *words*. 'I'm sorry,' I said, to the strange girl

204

standing in front of me, and to all the people I couldn't seem to help.

The girl whispered something into the night air, and suddenly the winds swirled around me again, murmuring snatches of conversations from the last few days. *Mage plague . . . The Academy . . . Laughter . . . They're watching you now, Kellen.* The sounds stopped abruptly, and Mamma Whispers said, 'You're being played, spellslinger, listenin' to the wrong voices, following the wrong path.'

'Then what is the *right* path?' I demanded. 'What am I supposed to *do*?'

She laughed in response. 'That's a big question, boy.' She lifted a thin arm and pointed a thin finger to the sky. 'Look at all of those stars. Why you need to pick just one to follow?'

'That's not what I mean, damn it! Who's behind all of this? You keep talking about your spirits, telling me I'm following the wrong trail. Fine, then ask your spirits who *is* causing the shadowblack plague!'

I half expected her to run off into the forest, or maybe attack me with some kind of spirit spell, but instead she nodded, and whispered into the darkness behind her. At first there was nothing. Then the wind picked up again. 'They see threads, my spirits do,' she said. 'Threads here, in the Seven Sands, stretching far, spellslinger, from Teleidos all the way to . . .' She started turning round and round in a circle, as if she really were just a child spinning to make herself dizzy. Suddenly she stopped, her arm pointing due west. 'Some of the threads go there.'

'Where? That's just more forest and, past that, more desert.'
'Further.'

There was only one place further west than the desert. 'The Jan'Tep lands . . .'

She started backing away in slow, languorous steps. 'I wouldn't know, spellslinger. My spirits, they see far, but they don't like to leave this place.'

'And you?' I asked. 'Do you ever leave here?'

She smiled as if I'd said something entirely stupid and kept walking backwards until her small form blended into the darkness. 'I'm Mamma Whispers, spellslinger. Why would I want to?'

33

The Warring Paths

We made our way back to Seneira's house, to find everyone had gone to bed except for Ferius and Rosie who'd returned and were – much to Reichis's amusement – playing cards. I told them about Revian and his family's house mages, and about my encounter with Mamma Whispers. I'd expected some kind of reaction, maybe even a tongue-lashing for having recklessly sought out a potential killer, but they just kept passing cards back and forth.

'You never look like you're having fun,' I remarked.

Rosie shot me a raised eyebrow that reminded me way too much of Shalla. 'Fun?'

'You're playing cards. *Playing*. Shouldn't it be . . . enjoyable?'

The Argosi turned her withering stare on Ferius, who shrugged. 'Give Rosie enough time and you'll find she can take the fun out of just about anything.'

Somehow that set the other woman off. 'Jokes? Is that all you have to offer the boy? You take him from his home, let him believe he can be your teysan, yet you teach him nothing. He cannot even *name* the seven talents, let alone—'

Ferius smirked. 'Words? Is that what troubles you, sister?' She gestured to me. 'Go ahead, tell him all the important words you like, if that's what you think it means to be an Argosi.'

'Do not play the fool with me, sister, even if that *does* seem to be the path of the wild daisy. You know how few of us there are left. As a maetri you have a duty to search for those who could learn our ways.'

Ferius let out a barking laugh. 'First you tell me I don't know how to teach and then you say I have a duty to do so? It seems the path of thorns and roses winds in circles, sister.'

Rosie slammed a fist on the table before pointing at me. '*He* is not your teysan. I would teach him myself, but anyone can see he is too unfocused, self-centred . . .' She paused then turned to me. 'Forgive me – my words are harsh and none of this is your fault. I'm sure you will one day become a fine . . . mage or spellslinger or whatever it is you are.'

Well, that made me feel so much better.

'Hey, are we going to fight?' Reichis said, making for the stairs. 'Because I was kind of hoping to have a bath, but if I'm going to get blood on my fur I can wait.'

I gave him a look intended to tell him to go upstairs. He gave the squirrel-cat equivalent of a shrug and settled down on a step to watch.

Ferius and Rosie stared at each other a long time, saying nothing, not making a move. After a while Ferius said, 'Best you leave this be, sister.'

The other Argosi stood, letting her cards fall to the table. 'I think not, sister.'

'Is today the day then, *sister*?' Ferius asked. 'You *really* want to wrastle me, what with everything that's goin' on around here?'

'What's "going on", sister, is a plague – one you and I are duty-bound to put an end to, and yet the Path of the Wild Daisy would prevent me from doing what must be done.'

Now it was Ferius's turn to rise, her right hand sliding into the inside pocket of her waistcoat. 'You put a hand on that girl or anyone else, *sister*, and your path will lead you to five different countries looking for your fingers.'

Rosie reached behind her and I could tell she too had some kind of weapon in the folds of her travelling clothes.

'Wait,' I said, suddenly worried they might try to kill each other right there and then. 'What are you talking about?'

Neither of them answered. Then Ferius brought her hand back out of her waistcoat and held it up to show it was empty. The other woman did likewise. 'A disagreement,' Rosie said, 'over what it means to be Argosi.' She left the table and walked out, pausing at the door to say, 'I've been tracing stories of other victims of the shadowblack, sister. I am close to finding the evidence that will require me to follow the way of thunder. Best that you leave this place before that happens.'

I waited until Ferius looked calm before I brought up my encounter with the strange girl who called herself Mamma Whispers a second time. Even then, Ferius had nothing to say until I pressed her on the issue. 'Well?'

'Well, what?'

'These "threads" Mamma Whispers told me about. If they really lead back to my people then—'

'How many times do I have to tell you not to keep getting distracted by nonsense, kid?'

That took me aback. 'I told you about what she did to me,

209

right? Making me hear things that had happened to me in the past? Her magic is real.'

Ferius leaned back and pulled a smoking reed from her waistcoat, then lit it using a candle from the table. 'Never said it wasn't real, only that it was nonsense.'

'You keep doing that,' I said, irritated. 'You talk about magic like it's a joke, but it's not. Magic is *power*, Ferius.'

'Kid, one day, if you live long enough, you're gonna figure out that power is the biggest joke of all.'

I didn't know how to answer that. What do you say to somebody who is both impossibly dense and yet somehow always seems to come out on top? I felt a stab of resentment towards Ferius – for how she could outwit the whole world in ways that would just get me killed. 'Dexan offered to make me his partner,' I said.

Reichis looked down from the upstairs banister, something small and shiny and almost certainly stolen in his mouth. 'Wait, what's this now?'

'Us,' I corrected myself, hoping to assuage the squirrel cat's concern before it resulted in future bite marks. 'He says he can help me fight off the shadowblack and teach us how to survive in the borderlands.'

Ferius didn't even bother to look at me, just let out a smoke-filled breath that became a circle in the air in front of her. 'Sounds like a good deal, kid.'

'He says I'd have to leave with him tomorrow.'

Another smoke ring. 'Best get packing then, I guess.'

'Don't you care? Doesn't it matter to you that I'd be gone and you'd probably never see me again?'

Before she could answer, Reichis padded down the stairs

and sniffed at her. 'She cares all right. She's going to start bawling any minute now.'

Ferius waved him away and put out her smoking reed on the plate holding the candle. 'Kellen, I'm sorry.'

I thought she was going to say something else, but when she didn't I asked, 'Sorry for what?'

She sighed. 'I know you're scared, kid, and you've got good reason to be. You want to do the right thing, but your fear makes you look for ways to protect yourself. So you look for more magic, or charms, or for someone to teach you how to fight – someone to show you how to take that anger and channel it, just like you do the explosive powders when you cast those spells of yours.'

'Is it so wrong to be afraid of the people trying to kill me? To want to be able to defend myself?'

'Fear and anger.' She leaned back against the chair and rubbed at her eyes as though she was exhausted. 'Nothing wrong with fear and anger, kid. It's just not the path of the wild daisy.'

'Then what is?' I asked.

She held my gaze for a long time, neither smiling nor smirking. 'Joy.'

'Joy?' I had to laugh. 'How is it "joy" when you let a man three times your size take a swing at you that could leave you crippled or worse? How is it "joy" when you take out those steel cards of yours and face off against mages who could burn you alive with a spell? How is it—'

Abruptly she rose from her chair. 'Come on,' she said, and headed for the door.

'What? Where?'

211

She stopped, but didn't turn around. 'You keep asking questions, kid, and I keep answering them, but that never seems to work for you. Rosie reckons it's because I don't think you're worth teaching, so let me ask you straight as can be: do you want to learn the path of the wild daisy, Kellen?'

'I . . . I want to at least understand what it is.'

'Close enough,' she said, and opened the door and stepped out into the night. 'Come follow the path with me.'

34

The Dancing Lesson

We rode a few miles out of town, far from the lights and people, far from all the trappings of civilisation. The night air was cool and made me shiver. I was uncomfortably aware of just how quickly I'd got used to hot meals and a soft bed. Of course, not everyone is as easily shamed by an attachment to luxury.

'I want a bath,' Reichis grumbled, clambering from my right shoulder to my left and back again as if that would somehow convince us to turn back.

'What's he moanin' about?' Ferius asked.

'You don't want to know,' I said, trying to spare Reichis the embarrassment. I needn't have bothered.

'I want a damned bath,' he repeated. 'Oh, and butter biscuits. *Lots* of butter biscuits. And tell Seneira's father not to short us this time.'

'You do realise they're *their* butter biscuits, don't you? I thought squirrel cats were supposed to be thieves and murderers, not spoiled brats.'

Reichis went dead silent, and I realised I'd made a huge mistake. He hopped from my shoulder to the front of the saddle and turned to stare at me, his eyes full of deadly intent and his fur suddenly black as night save for menacing grey stripes. 'Say that again,' he said in a soft growl. 'Say it twice, just so I can be sure I heard you right.'

This was not going to end well. 'I didn't mean—'

'Hey, kid,' Ferius said, catching my eye. Normally she ignores Reichis when he gets like this, but now she was grinning, 'Want to see something funny?'

'Um . . . I *really* don't think you should—'

Reichis turned and snarled at her. She ignored him. Well, not exactly *ignored*.

'My, oh my,' she said, gazing across from her horse. 'Will you look at that fur? So sleek and shiny. Why, it's like watching molten silver flow along a mighty river.'

'Well, obviously,' he said, now suddenly engrossed in inspecting the claws of his right forepaw.

'And those claws! Each one like a deadly blade forged by a master Berabesq swordsmith!'

Reichis's hackles had all but settled down now as he lifted his chin and his whiskers twitched. 'Well, at least she's not entirely blind. Guess she can keep her eyeballs for now.'

But Ferius wasn't done. 'And what muscles. Just look at those haunches! Why, I bet you turn the eye of every female in the world when you go by.'

Reichis seemed a trifle uncomfortable at the insistent praise. 'Fine, fine. I'm beautiful. Kellen, tell the Argosi to give it a rest now.'

But she didn't. 'And don't even get me started on that muzzle.' She leaned over, peering at him. 'Like a lion, only more handsome. Noble, courageous . . .'

Reichis gave a twitch and shook himself. I noticed something odd happening to his fur. The black becoming paler, the silver stripes fading away. 'Okay, make her shut up now, Kellen.'

'See those eyes? Full of intelligence. You can see it. And wisdom too. They're like deep pools of captured moonlight, beautiful as any gemstone. Diamonds really – that's what those are.'

Reichis's fur was shifting colour, the pale grey becoming white, then the white something else . . . a kind of rosy pink that bloomed all over him. 'Damn it!' he swore.

Ferius broke out laughing. 'Works every time.'

'What did you do to him?' I asked.

She pointed at his coat, which was now almost entirely pink. 'They can make their fur change colour to match their surroundings, but it also reacts to their moods. This is what squirrel cats look like when you make them blush.'

'Hell!' Reichis growled, nearly falling off the horse as he kept shifting around to examine his coat. His face was scrunched in deep concentration. He looked like he was desperately trying to go to the bathroom. 'Go back to black, damn it!' He glanced back at the still-pink fur on his flanks. 'I'm iron. I'm a monster. I'm the darkness of endless night!' He looked up at me helplessly. 'It's changing back, right?'

I considered how best to answer, then remembered that in the months since Reichis had reluctantly agreed to become my 'business partner', he'd taken every opportunity to mock me, steal from me and, on more than one occasion, bite me. 'You're still kind of pink,' I said.

As Reichis frantically tried to make his fur change back, Ferius said, 'Here endeth the lesson, kid.'

'Lesson in what?'

She pulled her horse to a stop and dismounted smoothly.

215

'You said you wanted to learn the way I walk the Argosi path.'

I got off my horse and pointed at Reichis. '*That? That's* the path of the wild daisy?'

'Yep.'

'So, when somebody decides they want to kill me, I should just compliment them into submission?'

She grinned. 'Well, that or dance with them.' She lit a small campfire and then set off for a flat patch in the desert and motioned for me to join her. 'Come on, kid. Time to learn the second talent.'

'Rosie said the second talent of the Argosi was *defence*.'

'Words, kid. You really want to get hung up on words?'

Okay, that made an odd kind of sense to me. Ferius never did seem to like using the language of violence, so maybe she just had her own terms for the seven talents of the Argosi, the same as she did for things like the 'way of water' and the 'way of thunder'.

I went over to join her and got into what I figured was a decent enough fighting stance, excited that I was finally going to learn Argosi fighting. Then I saw the smirk on her face and my optimism turned to panic. 'Wait . . . You did mean "dance" as a metaphor, right? As in, "Hey, fella, you dance with me, you dance with death"?'

'I mean "dance" as in *dance*, kid.'

'But . . .' Here's something most people don't know about the Jan'Tep: we don't dance. Not ever. There isn't a single form of dance practised in our culture. A mage has no use for dancing. Besides, it's unseemly.

Reichis shot me an evil grin, delighted that now it was *my* turn to be embarrassed. 'Oh, this is going to be good.'

Ferius gestured for me to take her hand in mine and put my other on her waist. 'Now, you can find hundreds of styles of dance among the different folks on this continent, but they all boil down to one of seventeen basic forms. We're going to start with the easiest, which is the chadelle.'

Her proximity made me uncomfortable. The only time one Jan'Tep adult gets this close to another is if they're about to be intimate. Ferius was probably twenty years older than me and, well, just thinking about this dancing thing was making me exceedingly nervous. I was about to back away when Reichis chittered, 'He's going to chicken out!'

'Shut up,' I said, and clasped Ferius's hand tighter. There was no way I was going to lose face in front of an animal that greets other members of its species by sniffing their butts. 'What do I do now?' I asked Ferius.

'Just follow the music.'

'What music?'

Ferius gave a whistle, just a single, clear note at first, like a flute player testing their instrument. Then without warning she went into a tune, each note playing up and down a scale that was unfamiliar to me as she steered me around the dusty desert ground. The Jan'Tep have music, of course, but it's mostly for funerals or court events or things like that. This tune was different. Faster, almost jaunty. I was just starting to make sense of it when I felt myself fumbling and Ferius had to hold me up until I got my feet back under control. 'Can't we go slower?' I asked.

'This *is* slow, kid.' She kept dancing even as she paused in her whistling, forcing me to imagine the tune was still playing in my head. 'Just relax,' she went on. 'Let your feet find the movements on their own. The Argosi believe that every dance exists in the body of all living things, just waiting to be allowed out.'

Reichis chittered gleefully. 'Hey, Kellen, the only dance I see in your body looks a lot like the death spasm of the long-tailed sand mole!'

'Shh,' Ferius warned him. She couldn't have known what he said, but I guess he's got a certain tone to him when he's mocking me. 'One more sound out of you and I'll tell you a squirrel cat story that'll make your fur go pink for a month.'

My furry nemesis temporarily chastened, I turned my attention back to the dance. The problem wasn't just the movements, but catching the rhythm. I'd always thought of my people as graceful; even as kids we're taught to stand and walk with perfect elegance, to weave our hands fluidly through the air when we cast our spells. Whenever my friends and I had seen the Daroman or Gitabrian traders who passed through our city dancing outside their caravans at night, we'd always mocked their barbaric gyrations. Panahsi used to joke that we ought to call the healers because our guests were having seizures. But out here? Under the starry sky in a wild and untamed country-side? *I* was the ungainly one. The dance felt right. Natural. I was just terrible at it.

'I can't do this,' I said, pulling away.

Ferius refused to let go. 'You'll find the flow soon enough, you just need to let it come to you. It's probably no different than those funny gestures you make with your hands when you work that Jan'Tep magic of yours.'

'It's not the same at all. Somatic shapes let you cast spells.'

She grinned and gave me a sly wink. 'Let me tell you

something, kid – there's no better spell a man can learn than how to dance proper.'

I'm not stupid. I got that she was implying that women like a man who knows how to dance. No doubt in the countries outside my homeland that mattered, but it didn't do me any good. The only girl I cared about 'dancing' with was Nephenia, and she was back in my city, betrothed to my former best friend, learning to become a mage, living the life I'd hoped for myself, probably forgetting about me in the process.

I pulled away from Ferius and ended up stumbling back several steps before I finally caught my balance. 'This is dumb.'

'What's the problem, kid?'

I didn't want to answer. I didn't want to tell her that my legs were already tired and my face hurt where Freckles had punched me. I didn't want her to know that my hands were starting to shake and any minute now I was going to start bawling like a two-year-old who can't go to sleep because he's afraid of the dark.

Except, I *was* afraid of the dark. I was afraid of who might be waiting for me out there. 'People are trying to kill me – do you not get that? I don't need to learn how to dance. I need to learn how to fight!'

'Hit me.'

'What?'

She took off her hat and set it on the ground. 'Come on, kid. Hit me.'

Reichis trotted over. 'This I've got to see.'

'Forget it,' I said. 'You've trained in fighting your whole life. You don't think I know you'll just toss me aside?'

'True enough, but I ain't gonna do anything you haven't

done this past hour.' As if to prove it, she put one hand up at shoulder height, palm facing in, and the other just above her hip like she was dancing with an invisible partner.

I was angry enough to take a run at her, but I kept my cool. Instead of rushing in like the clumsy oaf she was planning on turning me into, I pretended. At the last instant, I shuffled to the right, going for her unprotected side.

Ferius sent me flying like an empty grain sack.

She was still dancing with her invisible partner when I got back up, whistling that cheerful tune of hers and twirling around by herself. I made myself stop and watch for a few seconds until I could recognise the pattern of her movements. This time when I attacked, I didn't go for where she was, but where she was going to be.

I felt the air rush by my cheeks as she sent me sailing past her a second time. When I turned back she still looked as if she was dancing by herself. This didn't seem like any kind of martial art. Hell, it didn't even look particularly graceful. 'How are you doing this?' I asked.

'Come on, kid. One more try.'

Fine. But this time you're in for a surprise.

The problem was that I kept trying to play by her rules, but she had the advantage of all her training and experience, so I decided it was time to cheat. As I got to my feet, I scooped up a handful of sand. When I made my run for her this time, I held out my left hand as if I was going to make a grab for her, but at the last second I threw the sand from my other hand right at her face. *It's going to work this time*, I thought. The instant the sand hit her, she'd be thrown off and I could then push her with my other hand. Not hard of course, just a light touch to show I'd outsmarted her.

I was so focused on her movements that I saw every detail play out before me. The sand flew from my outstretched hand towards her face, but somehow she was already leaning back as if her phantom partner were dipping her as part of the dance. The sand went right over her head with barely a grain touching her cheek. I was still trying to figure out how that was possible when I felt her hand take mine as she turned. I hadn't even realised how off balance I was from tossing the sand and now she was using that against me.

As I went tumbling again, I caught a glimpse of her face. She was smiling. It wasn't a mean-spirited smile or the grim smirk of someone engaged in combat even as an exercise. I wasn't an enemy or even a student to her. Ferius really was just dancing with me, no different than we had been before.

I was still marvelling at this when I landed flat on my back a few feet away. I had no clue how she'd beaten me, so I leaned up on my elbows and just watched her. She made it look so easy, so effortless. I would have felt incredibly stupid if it weren't for the sight of Reichis a few yards away, standing up on his hind legs and awkwardly mimicking Ferius's movements. When he caught me staring he went down on all fours and his fur rose up in deep black hackles with blood-red stripes. 'What? What? I wasn't doing anything. You tell anyone about this and I'll—'

'Who the hell would I tell?' I asked. Reichis is remarkably vain, considering he sometimes likes to keep bits of rabbit meat in his cheeks just in case he gets hungry later. 'Better settle down or your fur might go pink again.'

He glanced down at his coat worriedly, but then grinned, evidently happy at the fearsome colours he'd taken on.

'Well, kid?' Ferius asked. 'You believe me now?'

221

I got back on my feet and nodded. There was no doubt this dancing of hers could be useful in a fight, and that meant it was a skill I had to master.

Ferius stopped and gave me an odd look. She sighed. 'You're still not getting it.'

'What do you mean? I'm not—'

'You can't learn the ways of the dance until you find the joy in it.'

Joy. How much joy was I supposed to have out here in the borderlands with my life in danger at every turn? Everything I'd ever known was hundreds of miles away. There was no place for me in this rugged frontier any more than there was among my own people. I was alone, and probably would be for the rest of my life.

Ferius gestured for me to join her. I did, and once again found myself in the uncomfortable half-embrace of the chadelle. 'I need you to listen to me, Kellen.'

I nodded.

'This isn't fighting. It's not something you push at or try to control like you do with your Jan'Tep magic. Don't try to find it; let it find you.'

'How?'

'Just be open to it. I'm not your opponent, I'm not your lover, I'm not even a woman.'

'You're not?'

'Nope. I'm just another body, moving freely in the warm night air.' She tilted me back a bit. 'Look up at that sky.'

I tilted my head back and gazed at the stars. You couldn't see them half so well in the city of my birth, where glow-glass lanterns cast a dim gleam over everything, but here, it was as if the sky itself was no more than a foot above me, like I could just reach up and poke it with my finger.

'This desert,' Ferius said. 'Right now. Here. It's the most beautiful place on earth, isn't it?'

It was. I don't know how or why, but somehow we were standing on the most beautiful spot I'd ever been. It wasn't like it was my first night out in the borderlands. This was different though. I couldn't stop staring up at those stars. It was as if they were moving now, rotating above me, dancing themselves to sleep.

'You're not Kellen, son of Ke'heops,' Ferius said. 'You're not the Jan'Tep outcast. You're a free spirit, not a single chain binding you.'

I was barely paying attention to her words, but the meaning came through nonetheless. I hadn't felt anything like this in a long time. The closest sensation I could think of was the way a spell felt when you had it all perfectly in your mind, held motionless until the words came out of your mouth, and in that instant you let go of it completely.

'I think I'm ready to dance now,' I said. But when I looked back at Ferius I saw the landscape moving around us. We were already dancing, and probably had been for a while.

Very slowly, Ferius brought us to a stop. 'Here endeth the lesson, kid,' she said for the second time that night.

'But we only just started. I only just got the—'

Ferius let go of my hand and gestured towards the fire. 'Look.'

The flames had almost completely died out now, the wood mostly ash. Reichis was curled up into a ball sleeping next to it, his fur having settled into a dusky brown colour that matched the ground.

'How long?' I asked.

'A while,' Ferius replied gently. 'But now we need to stop. Time to let the dance go.'

'Why?'

'Because there are bad things happening out there to good people, and even those of us who follow the path of the wild daisy have to travel in darkness sometimes.'

35

The Numbness

I had no idea what time it was when we got back, but I fell onto my bed without even removing my clothes. For one blissful hour I slept like the dead, only to be woken by a stabbing pain in my left eye, accompanied by horrific visions that made me reach for my powders. Fortunately Reichis bit me before I got to them. 'Wake up, Kellen!' he chittered. 'You're sleep— What do you call it when someone tries to perform a spell in their sleep? Sleepcasting?'

'I don't know,' I said, pressing the heel of my hand into my left eye. Ancestors, but it hurt. Suddenly I felt another pain, this time on my other hand, which now sported the marks of squirrel cat teeth. 'What the hell?'

Reichis looked up at me. 'I thought maybe if I bit you it would take your mind off the pain in your eye. Did it work?'

I shook my head and got up from the bed, stumbling towards the door of the room. Everywhere I looked I saw blood, and the woodgrain of the walls seemed to twist and contort itself as if something were trying to claw its way through.

'Where are you going?' Reichis asked.

'Outside . . .' I said, barely able to speak. 'Got to get outside.'

I heard him jump down from the bed to follow me. 'No,' I said. 'Stay here.'

I think he might have been a bit hurt by that.

By the time I made my way out to the back garden, the pain had started to ease and the visions began to subside. The trees looked like trees rather than twisting, grinding monsters struggling to free themselves of the bonds at their feet. The sky was black rather than red, and the smooth pebbles beneath my feet felt soft and welcoming instead of like a field of razor blades. I was so relieved that it took me a moment to realise I wasn't alone.

'You too, huh?' Seneira asked.

She was crouching down next to a patch of blue and yellow flowers, hugging her knees and rocking back and forth.

'Bad?' she asked.

I nodded. 'You?'

'Yeah, pretty bad.'

I sat down beside her and leaned back on my elbows, looking up at the sky to make sure the stars were still stars and not thousands of angry bees coming to sting me. I felt exhausted – one more gift the shadowblack brought with it.

'You know the worst part?' Seneira asked. 'It's not even the pain, or the voices – though those make me want to scream until I can drown them out. But the worst part is that, when it's all over, I can't feel anything any more.'

'What do you mean?'

She gave a small shrug and shook her head. 'I feel nothing. I'm not happy. I'm not sad. When I think about my friends or my father, or even Tyne, it's like . . . it's like they're strangers,

226

like I don't even have a family.' She turned to looked at me. 'Does that happen to you?'

I didn't answer, mostly because I couldn't. I never felt like I had a family any more, so how could I could tell if the shadowblack made it any worse?

'I pinched myself,' Seneira went on, showing me her wrist. It was too dark for me to see if there was a bruise there or not. 'Really hard, just to see if I felt it.'

'Did you?'

'No. I mean, I felt the pain, but it just didn't seem to matter.'

'How long does it last?' I asked. 'The not feeling anything, I mean.'

She lay back beside me. 'An hour maybe. Sometimes more. Even then I don't . . . Life just seems . . . dulled somehow, like I can't see colours the way I used to. Food tastes . . . okay, I guess.' She took my hand and made my fingers brush against her palm. 'Even this. I feel it, but it's like it's happening to someone else.'

The sound of squirrel-cat paws padding against the floor from inside the house reached my ears just before Reichis's fuzzy face appeared at the back door. 'Kiss her,' he said.

'Forget it.'

'Forget what?' Seneira asked.

'Nothing.'

She glanced over to where Reichis sat on his haunches on the back step. 'Oh, your . . . business partner.'

'Kiss her, Kellen,' the squirrel cat chittered, sniffing at the air. 'I'm not kidding this time. Some part of her wants you to.'

'What did he say?'

'Nothing, he just . . .' A thought occurred to me.

I got back to my feet and extended a hand down towards

227

her. She took it and I pulled her up. 'What is it?' she asked.

I took her right hand in my left, and put my other hand around to the small of her back. 'Dancing.'

'Dancing?'

I nodded, then realised I should probably have asked before grabbing at her. 'Do you . . . ?'

She shrugged. 'Can't hurt, I suppose.'

We had no music, and I'm pretty sure I am, by any standard, a terrible dancer – a fact Reichis seemed exceedingly comfortable pointing out repeatedly, despite his own preposterous-looking attempts. Somehow, though, as Seneira and I spun and stepped across the back garden over the next few minutes, I felt something change in her. At first I thought she was stiffening, becoming uncomfortable, but when I went to stop, she shook her head and started pulling me along. I realised then that I'd only thought she'd been tensing up because, for the first few minutes, she'd been almost lifeless. Now she seemed alive again, moving with a kind of purpose and determination as if the two of us were going into battle together. It wasn't happiness, but rather a kind of staunch resolve to *feel* happy.

After a while she changed again, seeming lighter, freer. Sometimes we'd lose the rhythm and either she'd stumble or I'd step on her feet, and when it happened she'd laugh and we'd start again. I'm not sure how long we danced for, but the first blush of dawn was appearing on the horizon when she stopped, and abruptly pulled me into a hug that she held for a long time. 'Thank you, Kellen,' she said, then let go of me and ran back into the house.

I stood there by myself, until Reichis came over to me and asked, 'Walking the path of the wild daisy, are we?'

'Maybe,' I replied. 'A step or two, anyway.'

36

The Warded House

I slept through the morning and afternoon, dreaming of dancing. At first my mind conjured joyous visions, but when the music stopped, Seneira wasn't there and I saw myself standing all alone in the desert, and wondered if that, too, might be an aspect of the path of the wild daisy.

I awoke in pain again, though this time the source wasn't my left eye; it was the palm of my right hand. When I looked down, I saw a slightly raised circular area about a half-inch in diameter, right in the centre of my palm, as if a coin had been embedded under the skin and someone had attached a string to it and was tugging at it. I rose out of bed, jostling Reichis, who swore several times before returning to the snoring cacophony he calls 'napping'.

The raised area on my palm still pulled. When I followed the tugging sensation, it led me to the window. After a few seconds of moving around the room and discerning the different sensations, I had a theory about what was happening. I put on my clothes and headed down the stairs and out the door.

The tugging led me away from Seneira's house and down the street, through alleyways and across a bridge. After about ten minutes of this, I found the source of the pull: Dexan

Videris was waiting for me, sitting on a bench in the middle of a small public garden.

'Thought you said you'd find me,' I said.

He shrugged. 'This is easier.'

I looked down at the skin on my palm. 'You did something to me. Yesterday when we shook hands, you pressed some kind of charm into my palm.'

'It's just temporary,' he said. 'Should fade away on its own in a couple of days.'

'Nice trick,' I said, wondering how it worked.

Dexan grinned. 'Just one of the many skills I have to impart to you, my young apprentice.'

'Dexan, I . . .'

The grin faded. 'You're not coming?' He rose up from the bench. 'Damn it, Kellen, this is a good offer!'

'I know it is,' I said, keenly aware of how much better my life would be if he could help me ward off the shadowblack attacks, teach me more tricks and ways to survive in the borderlands. The problem, though, was that I couldn't bring myself to abandon Seneira. Who was going to help with *her* attacks?

'Ah, hell,' Dexan said, seeing my expression. 'I can tell from that dumb look on your face that nobody ever taught you the third rule of spellslinging.'

'What's that?'

'Never let love make you stupid.'

'Is there a kind of love that *doesn't* make you stupid?' I asked.

Dexan chuckled. 'Guess not.' He put a hand on my shoulder. 'All right. Listen, kid, if you're going to try to help that girl, there's something you should probably know.'

'What's that?'

He looked uncomfortable. 'I'm breaking my own rule here, but that kid, Revian? The guy that girl you're all nutty over is *actually* supposed to be with?'

'What about him?'

'Stay away from him. More importantly, stay away from his family.'

'Why?'

'Because they're up to something big.' He nodded towards the north end of town. 'That mansion they live in, up on the hill? After Ler'danet tried to end you and me, I decided to go see if I could put a little hurt on them back, only that place is surrounded with some of the most powerful wards I've ever seen. Somebody like you or me ends up in there? Our magic won't be worth spit. I doubt even Ler'danet or the other house mage can cast spells in there.'

'That doesn't mean—'

'Come on, kid, don't be dumb. Nobody in the borderlands buys that much protection against mages when they've already got their own working for them, unless they've got a real reason to worry about magic.'

'So you think they're the target?'

Dexan shook his head. 'No, don't you get it? I think they're the ones that hired whoever put the shadowblack on the girl and her brother, only they figured they wouldn't have to pay since they were protected, so now whoever did the girl infected her fiancé too, because *that* was the only way to force the parents to pay up.'

'But then . . .' I grabbed at his arm. 'You could help us. If we find out who they hired, we can—'

Dexan shrugged me off. 'I told you before, kid, never mess with another spellslinger's livelihood. Especially if

231

they're more powerful than you; it tends to get you killed.'

'All right,' I said. 'But what if . . . if I find a way to deal with whoever cast the curse, will you stay and remove the shadowblack from Seneira and her brother . . . and Revian too?'

Dexan looked uncertain, then glanced at the setting sun. 'I'll make you a deal, kid. I've still got some packing to do, so if you can get this mess sorted out before tomorrow night, I'll stick around and help the girl and whoever else I can.' He stuck out his hand. 'Deal?'

I started to shake his hand, and to ask, 'Okay, but how will I find you if—'

The sudden sharp sensation in my palm answered the question.

'Just follow the pain in your hand, kid,' Dexan said as he walked away. 'It's like I always say: love hurts.'

By the time I got to Seneira's house, everything had changed. Rosie was back, and for once she and Ferius didn't look like they were about to kill each other. Apparently she had followed the trail of other victims and discovered something none of us expected.

'This isn't the first time the Seven Sands has seen an unexplained outbreak of the shadowblack,' Rosie explained. 'It's been happening for several years, here and there, rarely in the same town or village. Always far enough apart to keep anyone from looking too closely.'

'Until now,' I said.

Ferius nodded. 'The question is, why?' She looked over at me. 'You trust this Dexan fella? The oldest scam in history is to make somebody sick and then offer the cure.'

232

'Well, I never trusted him,' Reichis said, coming down the stairs with some kind of silver ring stuck around one paw.

'*That* belongs to me,' Rosie said.

Reichis shook his paw repeatedly until it flew off and bounced across the floor. 'Tell the Argosi she can have it. Feels way less comfortable than it looks.'

She gave him a scathing look. He hissed at her. They went back and forth wordlessly while I considered the matter of Dexan Videris. The man had saved my life and invited me to become his partner, but Ferius was right: if someone had been going around infecting people with the shadowblack, wouldn't the first person we should suspect be the guy claiming he could cure it? Only . . . 'It doesn't make sense. If Dexan's been doing this for years, why would he suddenly become so sloppy? Why target Seneira's family and then say he *can't* cure Tyne?'

'The paths of thieves and deceivers twist and turn in unusual ways,' Rosie said, pocketing the silver ring she'd retrieved from the floor.

'There's something else too,' I said. 'Mamma Whispers said the threads pulling at whatever's been happening here go all the way back to the Jan'Tep lands. Dexan's been on the run from our people for years.'

Ferius rubbed at her eyes. I wondered if she'd been sleeping much lately. 'So that brings us back to Revian's family, with their Jan'Tep house mages and this mansion you say is warded against spells.'

'Your thoughts go in circles, sister,' Rosie said. 'We must investigate further into these older incidents of the shadowblack and determine if –'

The front door burst open and Beren came inside looking exhausted and terrified. 'Where's Seneira? Is she back yet?'

233

Rosie went to him. 'Breathe deeply, brother, and calm yourself. Tell us what's happened.'

'It's Tyne. He's got sicker and he keeps asking for Senny.'

I only realised then I hadn't seen her since last night. 'Where is she?'

Beren looked at me. 'So she hasn't come back? She promised me she'd—'

'Back from where?' I asked.

'Revian's family sent a carriage this morning and a messenger saying he was terribly sick, that he was begging to see Seneira. They said they could get her there without anyone seeing, and we didn't know Tyne was doing worse . . .' He turned and started for the door. 'I have to go get her! She needs to be with her brother, not –'

Rosie grabbed his arms, squeezing so tightly I was worried she might actually hurt him. 'Go be with your boy.' She looked back to Ferius and me. 'We will retrieve your daughter.'

37

The Unexpected Mage

The four of us made our way in the darkness to the home of Revian's parents. Rosie took the lead, and Ferius, Reichis and I followed. Soon enough we'd snuck over the tall iron fence and were inside the grounds. The house was massive, larger and more grandiose than Seneira's family home. I wondered if Revian was ever lonely here, with so many empty rooms all around him.

'There,' Rosie said, pointing to one of the exterior walls.

I followed the line of her finger and saw the first of what proved to be a great many silver warding glyphs. When they'd built this place, they'd made damn sure nothing magical could get to them inside.

'What's the plan?' I asked.

Rosie turned to me. 'We will be very quiet, and very careful. Do nothing that could draw attention to—'

A sudden scream from inside the house made me turn. Blue and red light gleamed through the windows, almost blinding us before disappearing, followed by another scream, a man's voice this time. Someone was being hurt very badly.

'Okay,' Ferius said, 'new plan.' She took off at a run towards the front door.

The screams continued, sounding increasingly tormented as we got closer. Ferius kicked the door near the lock, but it held. Rosie pushed her aside. 'You never were very conscientious in your study of the physical arts, sister.' The kick she delivered would have broken bone, but it still didn't open the door. 'A few more strikes should suffice,' she insisted.

It was Ferius's turn to push her out of the way. She gestured to me. 'Kid, do your thing.'

I pulled powder from the pouches at my belt, tossed it in the air and made the somatic shapes with my hands as I said, '*Carath.*' The blast took out the door and half the frame. Sometimes I get a little excited.

We ran inside, into a large open foyer. What we saw there made my stomach go cold.

Revian was in the centre of the room, his arms outstretched, floating two feet in the air. Ler'danet and the other house mage were lying in heaps, the skin burned from their faces, their hands even in death forming the somatic shapes for shielding spells. Nearby, a man and a woman – I assumed they were Revian's mother and father – lay on the ground in pools of blood, their own flesh torn from them. Around Revian's right eye, the winding lines of the shadowblack seemed to burn and glow like a star that shed only darkness. Seneira was standing in front of him, her expression flat, almost numb, waiting for her own death.

'Kellen?' Revian said, seeing me. He seemed to be in a daze.

I pulled powder again, not inclined to let him do to me what he'd done to the others and what he seemed intent on doing to Seneira. 'Let go of whatever magic you're drawing to you, Revian. I won't warn you a second time.'

He stared back at me, his expression almost pleading. 'How

is this happening, Kellen? I'm not a mage. I don't know any spells.'

I could almost feel the force of ember magic radiating from him, building in a crescendo, ready to be cast in a spell that surely couldn't be good for any of us. Then I realised something: Revian's hands weren't forming any somatic shapes. He wasn't speaking any of the incantations. His eyes were so wild there was no way he was holding the necessary envisioning for a spell.

'Kellen, he's talking to me.'

'Who's talking to you, Revian?'

'I don't know . . . He's . . . He wants to say something . . .' Revian's mouth contorted in a twisted surge of agony. The voice that spoke next was his, but the words, the diction, were completely different. 'Watch carefully, little spellslinger, watch what we do to this girl, and know that we can do the same to you, should you continue to interfere in our affairs.'

'What's he talking about?' Reichis asked, his claws digging into my shoulder.

'I don't . . .' I glanced over and saw his fur was rising up of its own accord, the air was filled with static like the instant after you hear the thunder, just before . . . 'Oh hell,' I said, turning to Ferius and Rosie. 'Get Seneira out of here, now!'

Revian caught my eye and I could see tears streaming down his cheeks. 'They're going to make me do it, Kellen. Please . . . make them stop!'

'You've got to hold them back, Revian. Don't be their slave.'

'They're too strong, Kellen! Tell me what to do!'

'Fight them! Think of someone you care about . . .' Like an idiot, I hesitated. 'Think of Seneira. Think of how much you love each other. You can be strong for her, Revian, I know you can.'

He looked down at her and I could see the agony in his face even as the black marks around his eye swirled angrily, faster and faster. 'I'm trying, Kellen. I'm trying so hard.'

'You can hold them back, Revian. I promise you can! Just keep—'

Three things happened then, seemingly all at once. The first was that Rosie ran past me and scooped up Seneira in her arms, leaping towards one of the tall windows and turning in mid-air so that her back struck the glass, shattering it as the two of them went through. Something grabbed at me, hauling me back to the front door even as I took hold of Reichis before he could fall off my shoulder. Revian watched me go, his face a mask of terrible sorrow as he fought the forces that sought to control him. I could see on his face that his will was breaking. The strain of resisting the magic burning inside him must have been unimaginable, and he'd held it back so courageously it made me wish I'd known him longer, that in these last seconds I could have been a better friend to him. He looked so . . . ashamed. When he caught my eye, he said, 'Tell her I –'

There was just time to see the first blush of multicoloured fire manifesting from Revian's hands, his mouth and his eyes, as the flames began to reach out for all of us. Then the air went out of me and I realised Ferius had thrown me to the ground outside the house. I was still holding on to Reichis, and for an instant the two of us were staring up at the sky as if we'd come to lie on the grass and talk nonsense like we sometimes did. Then Ferius dropped on top of us, shielding us from the explosion.

The sound was deafening, and for several seconds I couldn't see or hear anything. Then Ferius rolled off me. I could see she was dazed. Rosie and Seneira came around to us, the Argosi covered in cuts and lacerations from the broken glass. Seneira looked unharmed, save for the fact that the man she'd always known she would marry, who would be her partner in life, had somehow been incinerated by ember magic in a house warded against spellcraft.

I got up from the grass and looked at the remains of Revian's home. There wasn't much of it left.

38

The Question

For the next few minutes we did the things you do in these situations. Ferius shook off the effects of the explosion faster than the rest of us and, after she had checked Seneira and me over, went to tend to Rosie's wounds. We were all in shock, I think, even Reichis, whose eyes glanced around slower than usual, as if he was having trouble focusing. He wasn't saying anything.

I waited until the smoke had cleared and then went inside. Soon there would be people coming to see what had happened, which meant we didn't have much time. Even through the dull haze and the throbbing in my head, there was something I had to see for myself; the house had been warded against magic, and yet I recognised the spell Revian had cast.

'What are you looking for?' Seneira asked. She looked confused, as if she'd only just remembered how to speak.

I walked over to the centre of the room, now covered in rubble, where Revian had been floating just minutes before. 'Stay back, Seneira.'

'Surely the body will be destroyed from the blast,' Rosie said, glancing around at the charred interior. It was as if a dozen bolts of lightning had all struck at once.

'Not necessarily.'

She, Ferius and I pushed slabs of broken sandstone and pieces of shattered furniture out of the way. Eventually we found Revian. He was dead of course, but not from lightning.

'How is this possible?' Seneira asked. She wasn't crying or shouting. It was as if she'd forgotten how to feel.

'An ember spell protects the caster from its effects.'

'But the boy is dead,' Rosie said.

'Well, drop a ton of debris on a person and they die regardless of what spell they're casting.'

'What's this?' Ferius asked.

I knelt down to examine what she'd found, but the first thing I noticed was Revian's face. His eyes were still wide open, as if he was pondering something inexplicable. So was I: the markings around his eye were completely gone. On the ground next to his head was a tiny pile of ash. It wasn't like the charred debris around us; this was made of distinct particles like grains of black sand. 'Ancestors . . . I should have known.'

'What is it?' Ferius asked.

I pointed to the markings around my eye. 'This – what you see – it's part of me. It's in my skin. Nothing could remove it.'

'But that fella, Dexan –' Ferius began.

I shook my head. 'He had scars. Look at Revian's face. The skin is perfectly smooth.'

'So then . . .'

I reached out a hand to close Revian's eyes. I'd barely known him, and yet, in that last moment before he died, he'd looked at me as if I was a friend come to save him, who might be able to tell him what had happened to him. Unfortunately

241

I'd figured it out too late – the reason why none of this made sense, why people who weren't Jan'Tep were suddenly getting a disease that only affected mages.

'It's not the shadowblack,' I said, looking up at Seneira.

'Then what is it?'

'I don't know, but whatever it is, it doesn't just torment the victims. It's allowing someone to use them as anchors, to cast spells in places protected by magical wards.' I turned to Ferius. 'Someone used Revian to murder his parents. And whoever did it? I know one more thing about them: they're Jan'Tep mages.'

When I was a kid, I used to wonder why my people didn't rule the world. I mean, the Jan'Tep are by far the most powerful mages on the continent. Whatever paltry spiritual forces the Berabesq viziers believe their many-headed god provides them, whatever mystical artefacts the Daroman generals scrounge up to supplement their military forces, none of those things could hold a candle to the power of a true master mage.

Sometimes I'd ask my mother and father, but they'd just make some remark about how I should probably spend my time learning to *become* a mage and then I wouldn't need to ask them the question. Shalla – whom I hadn't asked but who'd eavesdropped on the conversation – told me it was because our people were merciful. 'And besides,' she'd added cynically, 'what would be the point of being the greatest nation in the world if there were no others to compare ourselves to?'

It was Osia'phest, my old spellmaster, who'd given me the closest thing to an answer. 'Our magic is powerful, yes,' he'd said, shuffling about among the shelves of books in his dusty sanctum, 'but our flesh is no different than that of other men. What does it matter that a war mage's lightning is more powerful than a sword or a crossbow if his blood already spills from the wound left by the enemy's blade or bolt? Further, magic, like all of nature, follows rules. As a shield can protect its wielder from an arrow, so too can a warded house protect its owner from spells.'

That, I'd come to understand, was why my people didn't simply assassinate our rivals' leaders and take over their countries. The other nations had found ways to protect their palaces from our spells.

Only, what if you *could* get past their wards?

What if the mage could send an anchor into a warded building and channel the magic through them? Since the actual spell was originating from far away, the magic would simply appear through the victim, and the wards would be ineffectual.

'Something about this is not right,' Rosie said, mounting her horse.

No kidding.

'You got an itch?' Ferius asked.

Rosie nodded. 'Those previous victims I was looking into – one family lives in a town not far from here.'

'All right,' Ferius said. 'Kellen, best you and I take Seneira to the Academy hospital. Her father needs to know what happened here.' I noticed she was careful not to mention Tyne's worsening condition.

I knelt down to check on Reichis. 'You all right, partner?' I asked.

He stared at me blankly, and I worried that something had happened to break the connection we shared, but after a few seconds he shook himself off. 'I really need to kill whoever did this.'

'I need you to do something for me first.'

'What?'

'Go with Ferius and Seneira. Keep an eye on them for me, okay?'

He gave a quiet growl that was his way of agreeing while letting me know he wasn't happy about it.

'Where are you going, kid?' Ferius asked.

I looked out past the open door towards the desert in the distance. 'There's someone I need to speak to.'

I sat cross-legged on the ground, staring at my patch of sand. Teleidos is fairly heavily developed, full of large buildings and sidewalks and even small, elegantly designed public gardens. So I'd had to walk almost to the edge of town before I found undisturbed sand where there weren't people all around so that I could attempt the invocation.

The big problem, of course, was that whatever spell Shalla had cast to communicate with me was far too complicated for someone of my limited abilities to attempt. Also, since I'd never sparked the tattooed metallic band for sand magic – and never would, thanks to the counter-glyphs my father had permanently etched into the skin of my forearm – there were parts of the spell that would always be denied me. My only option was to try something simpler and hope I got lucky.

For once in my life.

From what I understood of Shalla's explanation, the spell she'd used had many components to it – bits and pieces of different forms of magic to handle individual tasks, working together almost like a clock or some other contraption. If that were true, then the spell might still be active, like a warrant, just waiting to be reawakened. Since Shalla had mentioned breath magic as a key requirement, and since that was the only kind of Jan'Tep magic I could do, that's where I had to start.

'*Tuvan-eh-savan-teh-beranth*,' I intoned, hoping I remembered the incantation correctly. Nothing happened, but that could be due to any number of factors. A Jan'Tep spell requires five components: the words, perfectly spoken; the envisioning, held in the mind with total clarity; the somatic shapes made with the hands; the anchoring, for which I was using the sand and the breeze; and, finally, dominion: the will of the mage. I was always weakest at that last part.

'*Tuvan-eh-savan-teh-beranth*,' I repeated, making extra sure I was holding the somatic shape correctly. When it again didn't work, I tried going through each component of the spell yet again, searching for my mistake. Of course, there might not *be* any mistake. I might just not be strong enough.

My anxiety broke my concentration, which meant my envisioning of the spell fell apart. I became frustrated, knowing full well that Shalla could have done this in her sleep. I could just imagine her, standing there, staring at me with that perpetually amused yet disappointed expression on her face, her oh-so-flawless features and bright golden hair so different from the dark mop that adorned my head. Most of all, it was her voice that always irritated me: more mature than any thirteen-year-old's voice had a right to me, the diction so perfect, each syllable like a note of music. I didn't know why I was even bothering to try to contact Shalla – it was like she was already here anyway.

Oh.

'*Tuvan-eh-savan-teh-beranth*,' I said for the final time.

I hadn't noticed the wind picking up until a few grains of sand flew into my eyes, making them water. When I looked back down at the ground, the particles were swirling from the breeze. 'Kellen?' Shalla's face said to me.

'Shalla?'

The image frowned. 'How did you . . . ?' I was about to explain how I'd made the spell work when the image shifted again. 'Oh, of course. I forgot to close off the spell, so I suppose when you did that amateurish breath invocation, my own casting must have been inadvertently awakened.'

'Sure,' I said, not wanting to get into a fight. I needed information. 'Shalla, who in our clan could—'

She cut me off, the shapes of her eyes in the sand suddenly shifting around. 'Ancestors, Kellen, are you still in Teleidos?'

'I am. There's something—'

'Get out of there!' she shouted, the swirling wind picking up in response to the increased magical forces. 'I told you to leave that place!'

'You did,' I said, my own voice quiet. 'You seemed to know exactly when I should leave.'

A subtle back and forth in the sand told me she was shaking her head. 'It's not like that, Kellen. Just . . . please, just trust me, you don't want to be there.'

'Why, Shalla? Because there is no shadowblack plague? Because our own people are behind this?'

'This has *nothing* to do with you, Kellen. Get away from that awful place!'

This was getting me nowhere, and Shalla had always been more stubborn than I was. 'Tell me what you know, and maybe I will.'

246

She hesitated, the tiny particles of sand oddly still now, despite the breeze. 'I don't know much, Kellen, but when I tried my own scrying spells to find the source of the shadowblack, I couldn't make any sense of what I was seeing.'

'What do you mean?'

'There were . . . the only word I can think of to describe it is *strands*, Kellen. Thin strands of ethereal forces stretching all the way from the Jan'Tep territories to the Seven Sands. Then, when I tried to push further . . .'

'What? What happened?'

Shalla's image in the sand took on a strange expression, one I wasn't used to seeing on my sister's face: fear. 'Someone pushed me out of the ethereal plane and knocked me unconscious, Kellen. Someone much more powerful than I am.'

The mere fact that Shalla had acknowledged that anyone might be more powerful than her told me just how serious this was.

The sands shifted again, and her face began to dissolve. 'The spells I created to make it possible for us to communicate are fading, and I can't risk casting them again in case it draws attention from whoever is behind this. I don't know when we'll be able to speak next, Kellen, but now you know everything I know, so do what you promised and leave Teleidos tonight.'

I didn't bother mentioning that I hadn't actually promised anything. Instead I wiped the sand clear with my hand. 'Stay safe, sister.'

247

39

The Witness

It was early morning by the time I returned to Seneira's house. I'd expected to find myself alone since she and Ferius were at the hospital with her family and Rosie was off who knew where. The whole way back I'd been thinking about Revian's death, and what I could possibly do or say to make it any easier on Seneira.

It turned out I needn't have worried about that, because when I got to the house, she and her father were already there, seated at the kitchen table, and something even worse had happened.

'He's dead,' Beren said, his skin pale as a ghost's as he clung to his daughter, and she in turn clutched a child's cloth horse. Flickering light from the hanging lantern above cast shadows all around them. 'My boy is dead.'

A great, wracking sob escaped his lips. He buried his face in his daughter's hair.

Seneira sat quietly, reaching out her free hand to pet Reichis, staring off into a distance I couldn't see and looking for all the world as if she had no idea any of us were there.

The sound of the door opening caught my attention and

248

I turned to see Rosie enter. She gave Ferius a nod before going back out.

I felt Ferius's hand on my shoulder. 'Come on, kid. Let's give them time to grieve.'

Outside we found Rosie standing next to a horse pulling a small, plain cart. A young woman stood nervously nearby, holding the hand of a small boy who looked to be about five years old. 'She calls herself Adella,' Rosie said.

The boy looked up at Rosie as if waiting for her to give his name. When she didn't, he said, 'My name is Yerek Farssus. My father's name was Junius Farssus, but he doesn't live with us any more. My sister's name—'

'Always this obsession with names,' Rosie said, looking weary. To Ferius she added, 'Last night I followed a trail of rumours to the town of Lastreida, about twelve miles from here, where these two live. Just over a year ago, the boy began suffering from a terrible fever, followed by the appearance of dark, winding markings around his right eye.'

I knelt down to peer at the boy's face. There was nothing there – no markings, not even any scars like Dexan had. Yerek stared at me wide-eyed, and it took a second to realise he was staring at Reichis, who had come out of the house and hopped up to my shoulder. 'Kitty cat!' he said excitedly.

Oh, Ancestors, I swore silently as I grabbed hold of Reichis and stood up before he could maul the boy. He sometimes forgets that children aren't just short adults and thus fair game for biting when they give offence.

'What was it like when you got sick?' Ferius asked the boy.

'I got all sweaty and it hurt a lot,' Yerek replied, nodding his head vigorously as if he needed to make sure we believed the story. 'I heard a demon talking. It wasn't very nice.'

'We searched everywhere for a cure,' Adella said, putting a protective arm around Yerek. 'Nothing worked . . . No, it was more insidious than that – everything we tried only made him worse.'

'Almost as if the disease could sense someone trying to interfere with it,' Rosie said, but she was looking at Ferius.

'Go on,' Ferius encouraged Adella. 'Tell us the rest.'

The young woman nodded. 'The symptoms were so severe we started to think Yerek might . . .' She looked down at her son. 'We feared the worst.' A smile appeared on her face. 'But then a man came to see us, said he'd heard we were looking for a doctor who could cure the shadowblack. I mean, I didn't even know that's what it was called, but when he described it, well, it was just what Yerek had.'

'What was his name?' I asked.

'Soredan,' she replied. 'Doctor Soredan.'

'Soredan?'

Ferius asked, 'This Doctor Soredan, was he a tall drink of water, dark hair, quick smile?' She pointed to her head. 'Wears a hat kind of like mine?'

Adella nodded. 'Only his had symbols around it.'

'Dexan,' I said. 'It was Dexan.'

Rosie rolled her eyes as if my statement had been too obvious to warrant saying aloud.

Over the next few minutes, Ferius patiently got the rest of the story from Adella, with Yerek chiming in every few seconds to make sure we didn't forget he was the one who'd gone through it all. Dexan, in his guise as this Doctor Soredan, had said the procedure was dangerous and expensive. At first he'd

250

been unspecific about how much it would cost, but after Adella had worked out how much she could get from selling everything of value she had and borrowing what her family could afford, the next day Soredan turned up with a price that was almost exactly that much. A few days later they got the money together and Soredan performed the 'procedure' – which sounded a lot like a ritual spell to me. The next morning Yerek was cured.

'Times are hard now,' she said. 'We had to sell our shop and now I do laundry work for wealthier folks in town, but it was worth it.' She pulled Yerek closer. 'Worth every penny.'

'I'm glad it worked out,' Ferius said, her voice calm and light even though I knew she must be as angry as I was. She knelt down and stared at Yerek. 'Yep. Looks like a regular kid to me. Kinda funny-looking though.'

'You should talk!' Yerek giggled enthusiastically, reaching out a hand to grab at the white forelock of Ferius's otherwise red hair.

Adella gestured to the house. 'Do you think . . . I asked your friend to bring us because I'd heard there were others suffering the same illness. I thought maybe they'd want to hear it from me that there's hope. Maybe they could find Doctor Soredan and—'

'I think they've found him,' Ferius said, glancing back at the house, 'but it might not be the best time to visit.'

Adella nodded as if she understood. 'We'll go then, but your friend here knows where to find us if there's anything we can do to help.'

She picked up Yerek and set him on the seat at the front of the horse cart, then mounted up herself and took the reins. She gave us a brief wave before giving the horse a gentle

251

slap on the hindquarters and setting it into a slow walk, pulling the cart around and back down to the street.

'Convenient how the disease shows up, and a few days later so does the cure,' Ferius said.

'But didn't Dexan say that Beren had sent men to grab him up? He didn't exactly show up at their door.'

'He's getting smarter, that's all.' She nodded to the horse cart headed away from us. 'You keep pulling the same scam the same way, pretty soon someone will figure it out. So instead he pays a few people to spread the word around town of a spellslinger who can cure the shadowblack. Somebody like Beren, with money and connections, well, he isn't going to wait around.'

'So Dexan just sits tight and waits to be found.'

She nodded. 'Better money when you don't make it so easy.'

I looked back at Seneira's house. 'But why not cure Tyne? Why let him die like that?'

'Could be the boy's condition spread too fast,' Ferius replied. An edge came to her voice when she added, 'Could be that a dead boy only makes a grieving father willing to pay even more to save his daughter.' She turned to face Rosie and I saw now that Ferius's anger wasn't reserved just for Dexan. 'Guess that's that, ain't it?'

Rosie nodded. It was only then that I noticed her horse was saddled nearby and she was carrying her pack.

'Wait,' I said. 'What's going on?'

'There is no plague here,' she replied. 'Whatever machinations are at play, whatever tragedies are yet to befall these people, it is no plague.'

'So, what . . . you're just going to leave?'

'I am.'

'You can't be serious! You're going to abandon Seneira and her father? The other kids at the Academy? They—'

'Whatever is happening to them, it is about them, not the wider world. An Argosi—'

'Don't,' Ferius warned. 'He won't understand.'

'Understand what?' I asked her. 'That the Argosi don't give a damn unless the "wider world" is about to fall apart?'

'It ain't like that, kid.'

'You coddle him,' Rosie said. She turned to face me, not showing a trace of remorse in her eyes. 'The way of thunder is not to strike at every source of sorrow or suffering. An Argosi must choose carefully in what matters they will interfere. To do otherwise is to court even greater sorrows.'

There was a sort of cold logic to it: the Argosi didn't just go around doing good deeds. They looked for events that could change the course of history for the whole world. A plague could do that. A conspiracy to hurt a few teenagers or their families, or even bring down the Academy, couldn't. 'Is that what you believe too?' I asked Ferius.

'The Path of the Wild Daisy has never seen the world quite the way the rest of us do,' Rosie said. 'She is ... prone to interfere.'

'I am at that,' Ferius said.

The two women stared at each other for a long time. I didn't see hostility there, or even disappointment, just a strange kind of shared uncertainty, as if, despite all the years they must have known each other, they just couldn't understand the other's way of thinking.

Eventually Rosie put a foot in the stirrup and mounted her horse. 'Goodbye, Kellen of the Jan'Tep,' she said to me. 'I hope you find a path that suits you one day.'

253

I watched as she nudged her horse into a slow trot and made her way down the road.

'Well, now I don't feel so bad,' Reichis said, still perched on my shoulder.

'Bad? For what?'

'I kinda stole a bunch of her stuff.' He must have been expecting me to berate him, because he immediately added, 'Not a lot. Just a couple of coins, a miniature carved elephant that looked kind of cool, oh, and that tiny jar of weakweed she kept with her. Never know when that'll come in handy.'

'What's he on about?' Ferius asked.

I translated, and I guess my utter lack of guilt over his thieving must have come through. 'No point in hating her,' Ferius said.

'Yeah? Why not?'

She sighed. 'Because hate gets you nowhere. Because it's not Rosie's fault. Because she might, in the end, be right about these things.' Ferius turned and headed back towards the house. 'But mainly because most days I can hate her enough for the both of us.'

40

The Kiss

That night I awoke to the sound of crying outside the door to my room, so quiet I thought at first I'd dreamed it, but eventually wakefulness took hold of me and I knew it wasn't my imagination. I moved Reichis as gently as I could so that I could get out of bed, and then put on my shirt and trousers. When I opened the door, I found Seneira outside, sitting there, arms wrapped around her knees.

'Seneira?'

'I'm sorry,' she said, seven kinds of pain filling her voice. 'It hurts so bad right now.'

I knelt down next to her. 'The markings?'

She nodded, and even in the near-darkness I saw the black lines swirling beneath the skin surrounding her eyes. 'I didn't know what to do,' she sobbed. 'I came to ask you for help, but then I couldn't seem to bring myself to knock, and I couldn't leave either. I don't know what's wrong with me. Why did this happen to us, Kellen? Why did they kill Tyne and Revian? What did I do to—'

'It's not you,' I said, anger rising up in me. I forced it back down. Anger made my own attacks worse, so it wasn't likely to help Seneira. *But I'm coming after you, Dexan, and I'm going to make you talk.*

'Are you hearing the voices?' I asked more calmly.

Again she nodded. 'They're so loud, Kellen. They just keep laughing at me. They . . . They like hurting me. I can't shut them out. It's like . . . It's like they're playing with me. I can feel them, like their fingers are scraping at the insides of my mind.' Her fingers clenched, hard, and I had to prise them apart to keep her nails from digging into her palms. 'Make them stop, Kellen, please!'

'I don't know how,' I said, feeling more useless now than I ever had in my life.

'Please!'

'I'm sorry, Seneira! I'm so sorry but there's nothing I can—'

'Kiss her,' Reichis said.

I turned and saw him sitting on his haunches behind me, his eyes glinting in the half-light. 'Not now!' I yelled at him.

'I'm serious this time, Kellen. Whatever's happening to her, you need to break the connection, shake whoever's digging around inside her before—'

'What do you know about magic?' I demanded. 'Nothing. You're a damned squirrel cat. All you know is killing and thieving and—'

'Listen to me,' Reichis growled, his hackles rising. 'I'm telling you, I can *smell* them on her. It's the markings around her eye. They're using them to get to her, feeding on her misery and her fear. You need to shake her out of it.'

'I'm not going to k—' I stopped myself just in time.

'What's he saying?' Seneira asked, her fingers digging into her hair now.

'Nothing. He's an idiot. Just try to relax.'

256

'I can't,' she said, rocking back and forth now. 'Please, if there's anything you can do . . . some spell or trick . . . I need to make it stop!'

I glanced back at Reichis. I knew he was serious about what he'd told me because for once he wasn't threatening retaliation for me insulting him. Reluctantly I told Seneira what he'd said.

'Is this . . . ? Is this some kind of . . . No, you wouldn't joke about that. You're not like that.' She doubled over again as the attack worsened. 'Oh gods of earth and air . . .'

Suddenly she reached out with both hands and grabbed my face, pulling me close until our lips came together, too hard and too fast to be sensuous, too anguished to be anything but dire need.

I fell into that kiss, holding on as best I could, trying to find a way to give her some tiny shred of solace from the sickness that assailed her. I could feel the tension in the muscles of her face, the clenching of her jaw. It was an odd way to experience what was, in fact, only the second real kiss of my entire life.

Slowly, very slowly, the pressure eased a little, and the shaking stopped. I tried to pull away, to ask if the pain was subsiding and the voices fading. Seneira hung on though, her hands still on the sides of my face, my arms around her waist.

I heard Reichis wander off, leaving us alone.

Seneira looked at me, and I saw the markings around her eyes had stopped moving and the lines in her brow had smoothed. I saw something else in her face too, something I knew was mirrored on my own. We kissed again, this time for a very different reason than we had before.

What had started in despair and anguish became something new, and for the next few hours we just sat there together on the hallway floor, sometimes kissing, sometimes talking about the people she'd lost and what they'd meant to her. Sometimes we just held on to each other, bound together by the strange black markings around our eyes, by pain and heartache and the desperate need to find something to replace them.

Together.

41

The Spellslinger

The next morning in my room, Ferius and I argued over how to deal with Dexan while Seneira tried to keep the peace. It didn't go well.

'Kid, we can't just run in there with fists flying! We've got to think this through. Wait until we—'

'There isn't time!' I shouted, which was a bad idea since I was in the middle of refilling the pouches I use to hold the powders for my spell – not a task you want to get sloppy with. 'Dexan said he'd be leaving tonight, so we have to get him now before he figures out that we're on to his scheme and makes a run for it.'

'How will you even find him?' Seneira asked.

'Yeah, kid,' Ferius said. 'This town's big enough to—'

I held out the palm of my right hand. Even now I could feel the charm he'd managed to force into my skin pulling at me. 'He wanted me to be his partner, remember? This will lead us right to him.'

'And then what?' Ferius asked, gesturing towards my pouches. 'You going to out-magic him? He's been at this a lot longer than you, Kellen.'

'Yeah, but I've got a surprise for him.' I turned to Seneira.

'Do you have any gloves that might fit my hands?' I asked. 'Maybe your father has some or . . .'

She nodded and left the room.

'What's going on, kid?' Ferius asked.

By way of reply, I went over to the velvet pouch where Reichis kept his stolen treasures.

'Hey!' the squirrel cat said, somewhat in disbelief that I'd rifle through his things.

'Just need this,' I said, and pulled out the small jar of weakweed he'd stolen from Rosie. 'I don't plan to let Dexan cast any spells.'

Once it got dark, Ferius, Reichis and I followed the tug of the charm embedded under the skin of my palm. It led us on a winding route through the city into an area with almost no oil lanterns or other sources of light on the street. There, in what looked from the outside to be an abandoned building, we found Dexan getting ready to leave town.

'You lied to me,' I said when we confronted him.

'Yeah? About what, kid?'

'About everything.'

Without giving him any warning, I punched him in the face. Generally I don't favour punching, since it's not good for the hands and I kind of rely on them for somatic shapes, but I was pretty angry and, besides, I'd taken precautions.

Dexan rubbed at his face. 'Really, kid? Resorting to fisticuffs like some backwoods hick?'

'Guess the Seven Sands are rubbing off on me. Speaking of which, you'll want to rub that stuff off your face at some point.'

He reached up a hand to his cheek, and then his eyes went

to the gloves on my hands. 'Damn, kid, clocking a fellow spellslinger with gloves you've covered in weakweed? That's cold.'

I took off the gloves and let my hands drift to the pouches at my side. 'You're going to reverse whatever it was you did to Seneira and the others, Dexan.'

'I'd love to, kid, but my clients wouldn't take kindly to that.'

'And who might they be?' Ferius asked.

Dexan shook his head. 'Sorry, can't tell you.'

'I think you can,' I said, pulling a pinch of powder in each hand, 'because otherwise you're going to feel just what Revian did before he exploded in a ball of flame.'

Dexan put up his hands. 'Okay, kid. You win.' Then a smile took over his face. 'Oh, wait, you don't.' He made a slight gesture with the first two fingers of each hand and spoke a three-syllable incantation I recognised as a more powerful form of the breath spell I use. The next thing I knew, Ferius, Reichis and I were all flying back through the air, slamming into the back wall of the building and falling to the ground.

'Don't feel bad, kid,' Dexan said. 'You put together a pretty good plan, all things considered. That weakweed you put on your knuckles before you punched me in the face was particularly inspired.' He reached up a hand and wiped his face. Not only did the greenish marks from the weakweed come off, so too did an almost clear waxy substance.

'You covered your face with mesdet paste to protect you from the weed . . . but how could you know th—'

He shrugged. 'Let's just say, I can be clever too.'

I got back to my feet and Reichis hopped up on my shoulder.

Suddenly he was sniffing at the air. 'Something's wrong here, Kellen. This skinbag's not alone.'

Dexan smiled. 'He can smell it, can't he? Clever little thing. Must come in handy when you get yourself in a jam. Of course, I have a friend of my own too.'

He touched the onyx bracelet at his wrist, and suddenly from the deep shadows at the other end of the room a creature with scaly hide and long, powerful jaws came shambling towards us. It took me a second to figure out what it was since I'd never seen one outside of pictures in books. Of course, in the books they never looked quite this big.

'Ah, heck,' Ferius said, getting to her feet and pulling out her deck of steel cards. 'This guy's got a crocodile?'

42

The Crocodile

Dexan took a step towards us. The crocodile, sensing violence was coming, snapped its teeth in anticipation. From his perch on my shoulder, Reichis snarled at the other animal, but it wasn't his usual eager, almost joyous challenge. This was higher-pitched, panicked. The squirrel cat was terrified.

'How did you know?' I asked, playing for time, glancing around the room, desperately searching for some distraction we could use to make our escape.

Dexan gave me one of his phoney smiles and shook his head sadly. 'Third rule of spellslinging, kid: never let love make you stupid.'

'You're lying,' I said, my fingers itching to grab at the powders at my sides. 'Seneira would never—'

'He's distracting you, kid,' Ferius warned. She had a half-dozen of her razor-sharp steel cards fanned out in her right hand. 'Stop playing his game.'

But I couldn't let it go. The thought that Seneira might have betrayed us, that she could be working with Dexan . . . *No, that's what he wants you to think.*

'That fake shadowblack,' I said then, working it out even as I talked. 'You can see what the victim sees, hear what they hear. That's why the attacks happen when they do: you're the one triggering them, so you can use the afflicted as spies.'

Dexan sighed. 'See, kid? This is *exactly* why you ought to be working with me. You're quick; you work things out. We'd make one hell of a team.'

Anger and outrage were rising up from my stomach, making me feel sick. 'You're the voice Seneira hears. You're the one saying all those horrible things to her.'

'Now, that's not entirely fair. I mean, sure, I had some fun for a while there – the girl's such a self-righteous little creature; how could I resist giving her a push now and then? But that was only at the beginning, before I gave control of her over to my clients. That's who's talking to her now, Kellen, and, believe me, you don't want to mess with them.'

'Who?' I demanded. 'Who are you working for?'

'Fourth rule, Kellen: never rat out the client.'

Without another word he touched the onyx bracelet on his wrist and whispered a two-syllable incantation. Suddenly the beast was racing towards us, jaws wide open. The sudden rise in Reichis's growl filled my right ear even as I pulled powder from my pouches and hurled it. '*Carath*,' I said as I formed the somatic shapes.

Fire exploded in front of me, so hot my own cheeks felt they might burn. Reichis screamed and leaped off me to the ground, suddenly rolling on the carpet to put out the flame that had caught part of his fur. Only then did I realise what had happened: my spell had failed. I stared down at the palm of my right hand, where an angry red patch of skin in a perfect circle was now throbbing.

'Sorry, kid,' Dexan said. 'Turns out that charm I stuck on you does more than just lead you to wherever I want you to go. It also keeps you from using magic unless I want you to.'

I leaped back, desperately avoiding the crocodile's snapping jaws as the animal lumbered towards me. Within seconds I was backed into a corner and I watched helplessly as the beast twisted its head and opened its mouth wide so that it could grab hold of my leg. A steel card flew through the air, partially embedding itself in the creature's scales just for an instant before falling to the floor. The crocodile turned, briefly distracted, only to come back at me.

'Die, you filthy reptile!' Reichis snarled, concern for me temporarily overpowering both his fear of the crocodile and his sense of self-preservation.

'Reichis, no!'

The squirrel cat landed on the animal's back and started raking at it with his claws, but to no avail. The beast's hide was too thick. The crocodile suddenly flipped over, rolling onto Reichis, who screamed in pain and surprise at finding himself on the floor, where he was most vulnerable. Another two cards struck the beast, but neither stuck. 'Ah, the hell with it,' I heard Ferius say.

Just as the crocodile was about to snap at Reichis, Ferius dropped her deck of steel cards and leaped onto the animal's back, covering it with her whole body, wrapping her arms and legs around its thickly armoured hide to keep the creature from being able to reach her with its jaws. The crocodile instinctively flipped over several times, trying to shake her off so it could attack her with its teeth. Ferius just kept hanging on, shouting, 'I. Hate. Wrastlin'. Crocodiles!'

I ran over and scooped up as many of the cards from the floor as I could, trying not to slice my own fingers open. I don't know how Ferius managed to hold them so easily without cutting herself, but it was a skill I hadn't mastered. 'Leave the croc to me,' she shouted, struggling to maintain her grip on the animal as Reichis hopped around, hackles high and hissing madly as he searched for a weak point to bite or scratch at. 'Get Dexan!'

I flung one of the cards at the spellslinger, though I doubted it would reach my target. Sure enough, he got a shield up. It wasn't particularly strong, and the card didn't so much bounce off as kind of hover before falling to the ground. 'Best you give up now, kid,' he said. 'Another minute or so and the Argosi and the squirrel cat are both going to be dead and it'll be your fault.'

I flung two more cards at him, and again they seemed to get stuck in the air for an instant, only to then tumble down. His shield was weak. If I could just distract him long enough, maybe it would fail. I reached into my pouches and tossed a pinch of each of the powders at him. The resulting explosion of flame burnt the tips of my fingers, but Dexan flinched, and for just a second I was sure his shield had come down. I heard Ferius grunting in pain, but I kept focused and hurled the next card, feeling a brief moment of victory as it embedded itself in Dexan's thigh. He screamed, but he wasn't the only one.

I glanced over to my right and saw Ferius on the floor, holding her arm which bled where the crocodile's teeth had bitten into her flesh, but the creature itself wasn't paying any attention to her, because right then it had its jaws around Reichis. The squirrel cat was screaming my name over and over.

'There now,' Dexan said, his voice strained as he plucked the card out of his thigh. 'Guess I had that coming.'

266

'Please,' I begged, my eyes glued to the crocodile's jaws that were holding Reichis helpless in their grip. Any more pressure and the squirrel cat would be crushed. I stared at the crocodile, wondering why it hadn't finished the job, and saw for the first time the swirling black inside its eyes. Whatever magic Dexan had been using on his victims, he was now using to control the crocodile. Reichis whimpered, and I saw him staring at me, eyes wide with terror, pleading with me to save him. 'Just let us go,' I begged Dexan.

'Let you go?' For the first time the glib self-assurance left Dexan's eyes, replaced by a burning outrage. 'I gave you the chance to be my partner, Kellen. My *partner!*'

He strode towards me, hands clenching as if he was going to choke me. Just before he got close, Ferius reached into her waistcoat and pulled out the eight-inch metal tube with the other three pieces inside, flicked it to its full extension, and struck Dexan on the shin.

'Damn it,' he bellowed.

Ferius brought her arm back for another swing, but Dexan's fingers twitched and the crocodile's teeth closed a fraction more. Reichis screamed again and I saw blood well in his fur. He went quiet, then passed out from pain or fear.

'Stop!' I dropped to my knees in front of Dexan. 'Please . . . Just tell me what I have to do.'

A version of Dexan's smile returned, though it was meaner than the one I was used to. 'Well, first of all . . .' He leaned down and his hand swung out and cracked Ferius across the jaw. On the floor as she was, there was no way to turn with the blow to dissipate its force. Her head snapped back and her eyes looked blurry, confused, but even I could tell she

267

was preparing a counter-attack. 'Try it,' Dexan warned, 'and the squirrel cat dies.'

Ferius's jaw clenched in anger, but then she nodded.

Dexan grinned at her. 'Now then, you asked what you had to do to save the animal?' He knelt down so he was face to face with Ferius. 'Well, it's easy. Just don't move.'

I didn't understand what he was getting at, but Ferius seemed to. She nodded again.

Dexan brought his fist back and punched her hard enough that his hand came back with blood on the knuckles. 'Whoa, now that hurts,' he said, then smiled as he punched her again. After the third time her eyes couldn't seem to focus on him. When he hit her the fourth time, her head shook like a drunk's and her mouth hung open.

'Stop!' I shouted.

'Almost there,' Dexan said, and swung at her again. This time when he hit her, she didn't move at all.

'You sick bastard!' I cried. 'Why are you doing this?'

He rose to his feet and came over to me, staring down at me like I was a child who'd disappointed him. 'I've told you before, Kellen: it's a tough world out there for people like us. You think *you've* had it bad? I've been on the run for ten years. Bounty hunters, hextrackers, war mages . . .' He sighed in mock disgust. 'You steal one too many sacred books and all of a sudden you're an outcast.'

'But . . . I thought you were hunted because you had the shadowblack like me.'

Dexan laughed, and raised a hand up to the scars around his eye. He pressed his thumb and forefinger into his cheek and pulled away what looked like scarred flesh. Underneath, his skin was smooth and unharmed. 'The scam works better if people think I cured myself first,' he explained.

'But if it was all just a way of making money, why did you kill Revian and Tyne? Why are you—'

'I got caught, all right!' Dexan shouted. He calmed himself before continuing. 'I got caught, Kellen. The people who were trying to find me, well, they got tired of me getting away and hired some real talent to come after me.' He shook his head again. 'They would've killed me right then and there, no trial or nothing. So I told them about my discovery, about the way I could make people think they had the shadowblack. Even bragged at the fun you could have using them to spy on their families to figure out just how much you could charge for the cure.'

A stupid move – even I knew that. For the first time, Dexan didn't strike me as a quick-witted rogue. Instead what I saw now was a con artist, not too bright but with a few cunning spells and a willingness to do anything to survive. 'You made a deal.'

'Don't give me that look, you ungrateful brat. I could've killed you and the Argosi *and* your pet the day I met you. I'm not a bad guy, but I need to get back into my clan, to be close to an oasis again to restore my connection to our people's magic. The mages who caught me said they could have my exile overturned. I'd be free to go home, to leave this hellhole of a territory.'

'So why are you still here? If you gave them the secret, can't they—'

'Doesn't work that way, kid. It took me a while to tune myself to the . . . well, I'd tell you but that would be breaking

269

rule number two.' He came closer and cocked his fist. 'Nothing personal, kid. Me, I think violence is barbaric, but my clients like to send a message.'

He only had to hit me once to keep me from getting up again.

43

The Worms

I awoke to find Ferius and myself both sitting on wooden chairs, our hands tied behind our backs. Her waistcoat and the belt holding my pouches were a few yards away on the floor. My fingers ached and I realised they were taped in a way that kept me from forming any somatic shapes. That was the one bright spot: Dexan hadn't figured out that I couldn't do any damage without my powders. Maybe if I could get loose I could bluff him somehow.

If I ever get out of here, I should really learn how to bluff.

On the table in front of us I saw several metal implements, but my eyes were mostly drawn to a particularly sharp knife.

'I tried to tell you, kid,' Dexan said, reaching up to a shelf and pulling down a blue glass box with lines of silver along its surface. 'Remember the first rule of being a spellslinger?'

Never mess with another spellslinger's business. 'Talk like a pompous ass?' I asked.

He chuckled. 'Clever. Brave too.' He turned to smile at me. 'Leastways you know how to give that impression, and that's almost as good as the real thing, right?'

I looked around the chamber, hoping to find something, anything, that could help us. Reichis was still unconscious, tracks of blood on his side and haunches from where the crocodile had got hold of him. The massive creature crawled around the back of the room like a sentry waiting for the next attack. I wanted to kill the animal for what it had done, but the swirling darkness in its eyes told me that it hadn't had any choice in the matter. It was a slave to Dexan's commands. One more reason why I had to find a way to end him.

'I'm curious,' he said, placing the box on the table. 'How did you figure out it wasn't the shadowblack?'

'Revian,' I replied. 'When I went back to look at his body after he died, the markings were gone. All that was left was a tiny pile of black ash next to his face. The shadowblack is part of the skin, so it shouldn't have come out like that.'

That seemed to impress him. 'See? Like I said: clever.' His hand came up, holding something about six inches long that gleamed. I flinched instinctively, expecting to see some kind of weapon. Instead, what he held was a small pair of silver tongs. 'You were right about the infection. It's not the shadowblack, but it's also not a curse. It's something far more . . . inventive.'

As I watched, he set the tongs down and carefully, almost as if he were following a ritual, opened up the blue glass box to show me the contents. At first I thought it was some kind of thick black oil, swirling from the box having been shaken, but then I began to make out individual strands, twisting, each separate from the others, dozens of them. 'They're a type of fluke; a flatworm, basically,' Dexan explained. 'Found a colony of them burrowing in a patch of volcanic glass a couple of miles north, near the mountains.' He pursed his lips in disgust. 'Vile things really. When I first saw them, a couple of years ago, I nearly blasted them out of existence.'

272

'Why didn't you?' I said, revulsion at the sight of the seething tangle of worms threatening to make me nauseous.

'I found a book some years back, an old Jan'Tep tome I got off a man who died not far from here. It mentioned a kind of charm that I'd never heard of before. I didn't think nothing of it at first, until I saw a picture of the creature needed for the ritual.' Dexan picked up the tongs and reached them inside the box to pull one of the writhing worms out. He dangled it in front of me. 'The book called them *obandiria neheris*, but I just call them obsidian worms. They sure are ugly, ain't they?' Suddenly he used the tongs to hold the worm down on the table and his other hand came up holding a knife. He cut the creature in half and a faint black mist filled the air between us. 'Try not to breathe it in if you can,' he warned. 'Makes you powerful sick for a few hours.'

'What . . . ? What was the point of that?'

'You ever cut worms in half as a kid?' he asked. 'Weird creatures. Some of them don't die – they actually just become *two* worms. My friend *obandiria neheris* here does one better. Both halves remain . . . well, connected somehow. Even across a hundred miles, they're still part of each other.' He lifted up the tongs, which still held one half of the worm. 'First step is to take this little guy and place him in onyx.' He held up a bracelet made of rough black beads, like the one he'd used to control the crocodile. 'Now watch this, Kellen. This is the first weird thing about them.' Very slowly, he touched the worm to the bracelet. As I watched in horrified fascination, it . . . slid . . . inside the stone, inch by inch until it was completely enveloped.

'How . . . ? How is that possible?' I asked.

Dexan shrugged. 'Who knows, kid? The underground metals in parts of this continent do weird things to some creatures.'

273

He nodded towards where Reichis lay on the floor. 'I mean, just look at your friend there. You reckon *that's* natural?'

'You gonna charge us for this little zoological demonstration?' Ferius asked groggily. Her eyes were blinking and I could tell she was fighting to clear her vision so we could find some means of escape.

'Hey, you're awake,' Dexan said. 'That's great.' He used the silver tongs to pick up the second half of the worm. 'Now, Kellen, you being a clever fellow, have you guessed what we do with this part?'

Ancestors, I thought, my eyes locked on the writhing, horrible thing dangling from the tongs. *Please, don't let him do this to me.* I'm pretty sure I screamed then.

Dexan started laughing. 'Come on, kid, don't be like that. What did I tell you was the first rule of being a spellslinger? Never, ever mess with another spellslinger's business. Besides, the way I hear it? Your father's got a good chance at becoming prince of your clan.' He turned to Ferius and started towards her, the worm still held in the teeth of the tongs. 'This Argosi pain in the ass, on the other hand, well, your kind don't have any friends at all now, do they, darlin'?'

Ferius's eyes went wide, but just as quickly she recovered and assumed her usual calm. 'You reckon that's the best way to play this?' she asked. 'Because I think you're missing out on an opportunity.'

I'd seen Ferius talk her way out of plenty of problems before, or, more often, talk her opponents into putting themselves in a position where she could overcome them. Dexan was having none of it. 'Don't you start that Argosi persuasion nonsense on me. You think I'm going to let you mesmerise me?' He reached out with his free hand and grabbed her jaw,

274

hard. 'You should know that I'm not a bad man really. I don't kill people unless I have no choice. I'm just a guy with a couple of spells and a few tricks up my sleeve, trying to survive as best I can.' With that he placed the worm on the skin just below her right eye.

Ferius tried to shake it away but Dexan was holding her jaw too firmly. At first nothing happened – the worm seemed to just slither around her eye socket. Then suddenly one end of it drove down through her skin, and Ferius Parfax screamed as if the obsidian creature was digging its way into her very soul.

She screamed for a long time.

I'm not sure how long it went on for. I was shouting at Dexan, begging him to stop, to pull the worm out. I threatened him too, though that didn't do any good either. I think he must have done something to knock me out, because when I woke up we were outside and our bonds had been removed. Ferius was stumbling around, unable to find her footing.

'It'll be like that for a few hours,' Dexan said, standing next to me. 'She'll seem drunk, and then the fever will set in. Don't bother trying to cool her down; it'll only make it worse. Best just to let nature take its course.'

'And then what?' I asked.

'Then she's mine.'

I turned and tried to hit him, but either he was too fast or I was too clumsy because I missed by a mile. He gave me a sharp slap across the face. 'Listen, kid, because this is how it's going to be from now on. You do *what* I tell you, you do it *when* I tell you and *how* I tell you. You want to know what happens if you don't?' Without waiting for an answer he lifted up his arm and stroked the new onyx bracelet. The

275

worm inside writhed as if it were swimming in the black stone. Ferius screamed again, turning to me, eyes blind even as I could see the creature that had embedded itself in her face began swirling beneath her skin.

'Stop!' I shouted, lunging for Dexan. He sidestepped and I tumbled face first to the ground.

After a few more seconds, his fingers drifted away from the bracelet and the screaming stopped. 'I can do this any time I want, Kellen, from anywhere. I can use silk magic to send dreams into her mind that will leave her so terrified it'll be as if someone had cut parts of her brain out. I can do other things too, awful things. Things I don't want to do unless you make me – unless you defy me.' He reached down and grabbed me by the collar before hauling me back to my feet. 'Or maybe, if you both behave for a year or two, I'll be a nice guy and use one of the rituals I've devised to destroy the worm and set her free.' He gave me a shake. 'Do we have an understanding now, Kellen of the House of Ke?'

Ferius would have taken advantage of the proximity to knock him down. She would have had something clever to say, some means of getting around this impossible situation. I just said, 'Yes. Yes, we do.'

'Good.' He held up a folded piece of paper and slid it into the front pocket of my shirt. 'Tell Beren this here's my client's final offer.'

Without another word he turned and walked away, showing me his back without the slightest fear that I might attack him because there *was* no reason to fear me.

Dexan had won.

He'd won it all.

WAY of STONE

The way of the Argosi is the way of stone.

Stone does not bend or sway, but rather stands resolute, preferring to shatter into a thousand thousand pieces rather than allow itself to be shaped by the will of another. Like stone, an Argosi stays firmly on their path. Though it may wind and twist in unusual ways, the path never allows itself to be moved. This is why an Argosi who knows the way forward never, ever backs down.

44

The Way of Cowards

I trudged down the road like a half-dead drunk, every step feeling like it might be my last even as I struggled to keep Ferius on her feet. She was heavier than she looked, or maybe I was just weaker than I thought.

'What's wrong with ya, kid?' she mumbled, her usual drawl now barely coherent. 'This ain't no dance I taught ya.'

I could feel the heat coming off her in waves, the fever burning her up, sweat soaking through her clothes. I had to stop to lean on every tree to catch my breath. Ancestors, but she looked so . . . wrong, somehow. Beneath her flushed skin I could see the black worm sliding and slithering around her right eye as one end burrowed its way deeper into her brain, taking hold there. Dexan told me that his 'clients' had given him a spell that could hide the markings, but he chose not to use it on Ferius. He *wanted* us to see it, wanted her to know it was there. Not content with infecting her, he'd made sure everyone would know what he'd done. Dexan had branded her.

The air was cold on my bare skin. I'd had to take off my shirt and turn it into a sling to carry Reichis. The poor little animal was still unconscious, lying in a heap inside the folds of my shirt, trickles of blood seeping from his wounds.

The sky in the distance was starting to change, the pure black becoming washed out by a trace of yellow-orange along the horizon. I was so tired it was all I could do not to just drop Ferius and Reichis and lie down on the ground next to them and hope something came along to put an end to us all. I'd failed them both, failed everybody, and the thought of carrying that with me was more than I could bear. I'm not sure what kept me stumbling down that long road towards Seneira's house, other than maybe the feeling that they had a right to know just how badly I'd screwed up, to spit in my face and send me packing.

Even before we got to her door, she came running out, her father beside her.

'Kellen!' she cried, and rushed over to help take Ferius's weight.

'Let's get you inside,' her father said, reaching an arm around my shoulders. That brief offering of support somehow made my legs go out from under me. He held me up, one hand catching the note that was falling from my shirt pocket. 'It's all right, son, I've got you,' he said, even though I could see the strain on his face from bearing my weight.

Seneira carefully picked up the improvised sling with Reichis in it. 'His breathing doesn't sound too bad. I'll see to him. I'll see to all of you.'

They were so concerned with looking after us that they didn't even ask what had happened, didn't ask whether we'd done what I promised or had just destroyed their family's hopes for survival.

I think that's what broke me.

*

Seneira and her father brought the three of us into a guest room and set Ferius down on the bed while they tended our wounds. They had to tie Ferius's hands to the bedposts because she kept trying to claw at her eye and Beren was worried she might blind herself.

'We've got to keep her from scratching at it,' he said, peering down at the black markings. 'The . . . worm you've told us about . . . seems to burrow deeper when she rubs her eye. I honestly fear the vile thing might kill her if she keeps at it.'

He left the room and returned a minute later with a small jar of clear liquid. 'It's a sedative from the hospital,' he said, pouring a spoonful into a large glass of water. 'It'll help her sleep.'

'Thank you,' I said. 'Thank you for everything.'

He brushed a hand against my cheeks, one after the other. It was an odd gesture, an almost absent-minded act of affection that Beren had probably done for Tyne a thousand times. Now his son was gone, and his own cheeks were red and wet from tears that would probably never stop coming.

I was searching for some words of comfort to offer him when he took his hand away and smiled wearily. 'You'll be all right,' he said, then went over to Reichis, whom Seneira had laid down next to Ferius on the bed, and petted him gently. 'He's a brave fellow, isn't he?'

The bravest you'll ever meet, I would have said if it wasn't for the fact that I didn't want to start crying again.

'Kellen?' Beren said, rising to stand once again.

I looked up. 'Yes, sir?'

He motioned for me to follow him. 'Maybe you and I should talk now.'

*

We sat around the small table in their kitchen. Beren offered me something to drink but I declined. He nodded as if that meant something to him.

'I found something in the pocket of your shirt,' he said, holding up a folded piece of paper. I'd forgotten Dexan putting it there. *Their final offer.*

'What does it say?'

'Nothing.'

I looked up at him. 'What do you mean?'

Beren's face took on more lines than I'd seen before. 'It was a message for me. They want the Academy to stay open, for me to keep my mouth shut and keep doing the work I've been doing.'

'But why would that matter to them? What do they gain?'

'I don't know, and at this point I don't care.' Beren crumpled up the paper and tossed it on the table. 'They also say you and your Argosi friend have to leave the territories right away.'

'I'm surprised they care one way or another what we do. It's not like I turned out to be a threat to them.'

Beren's gaze became hard, and for a moment crushing grief gave way to stern determination. 'Don't sulk, son. That's a boy's way. I need something more from you right now. For whatever reason, they want you gone.'

I nodded. I guess we'd come to the point at last. 'You're right. I'll leave tonight as soon as I can transport Ferius. Is it . . . Is it all right if I say goodbye to Seneira?'

He shook his head. 'No, Kellen, I don't think so.'

I suppose I should have seen that coming. But then he surprised me. 'You have to take Seneira with you.'

'With us? Why?'

284

'Because I'm not going to keep the Academy open, Kellen. I've already begun preparations to shut it down. The students will start leaving as soon as I can arrange for their safe passage back to their home countries. A few of the masters might choose to stay, and, well, that's up to them. But those kids are going home before this Dexan and his employers can hurt any more of them.'

'But they'll—'

Beren cut me off. 'I will deal with the consequences when the time comes. But my daughter . . . she needs some kind of chance at life. Even if she can get far enough away from here that our enemies can't get to her through that thing in her eye . . . well, wherever she goes, folks will think she has the shadowblack. Then she'll need to run, to hide, to find some new place.'

Run, hide, find somewhere else to do both all over again. The way he talked it was clear to me he had no idea what that was going to be like for Seneira. Then he reached over and took my hand. 'You can help her do that . . . No,' he corrected himself, 'the two of you will help each other. She cares about you, Kellen. One day she might even fall in love with you.'

'She doesn't—'

'I know I'm asking a lot of you, son, asking you to set a course for your life without even a day to think about it, but, well, asking is just what I'm doing.' He tried to hold himself together, but I could see his lower jaw start to tremble, and his next words came out as a whisper. 'They took my son, Kellen, don't let them have my daughter.'

It felt odd . . . wrong . . . to have this powerful and important man talk to me as if he were a beggar pleading for a few coins. Worse, I didn't think what he proposed was even possible. 'Seneira's not going to leave you, sir. Not from what I've seen.'

He sniffed, then gave a soft chuckle. 'She's a wilful soul, that's for sure.' The bitter scrap of laughter faded as quickly as it had began. 'I've already talked to her, Kellen. Go see her. She's expecting you.'

I found Seneira in her room, a small travelling case open on her bed. She was examining a rough-spun shirt before placing it inside. 'Is this too much?' she asked. Her voice was flat, neither angry nor sad nor any other emotion I could discern, as if she'd lost the capacity to feel anything any more.

'Too much what?'

She pointed to the case. 'I've seen people travel with a lot more, but I know it'll be different for us.'

'Seneira . . . your father needs to make a deal with Dexan, with his clients, find some arrangement that—'

'He won't beg, not if it means putting those other kids at risk. My father's going to do what he thinks is right, what will keep people safe.' She closed the lid on the travelling case. 'You and I have to do the same.'

'I don't understand.'

She turned to face me, determination set in her jaw. 'You said it yourself: Dexan is just a lackey working for someone else. And I don't think they would risk killing my father even if he *does* close the Academy, not when they can look for some other way to use him. My father is smart, and strong; he built the greatest centre of learning in a town everyone else had long forgotten, in a country no one cared about.' Something changed in her expression. 'But he won't have a chance with me here. Not when someone could use me the way they used poor

286

Revian . . . the way they used Tyne. That's why I need to go, get away from this place, go so far their spells won't reach me.'

I found myself just staring at her, suddenly missing the bravery and belligerence I'd got used to seeing in her eyes, the cleverness that always seemed to appear in the smallest twitch of her lips, the compassion with which she treated everyone around her. But for all those absences, it was the paleness of her skin that drew my gaze. She'd never had to spend long days under the hot sun. Her fingers were smooth from a life of study, not labour. Seneira was like me in a way – the me from months ago who hadn't yet lost everything and learned to live with almost nothing.

'It's not what you might think,' I said. 'The life of an exile, of an outlaw, it's not glamorous or exotic – it's awful. Most days it's dull and tiring, except when you're running, terrified that this time you're going to end up dead. People don't like wanderers and drifters – not even here in the borderlands – and from what I've heard from Ferius, it's even worse in other places. It's not a life anyone would want, Seneira. You spent . . . what? A few days, and with Rosie watching your back? Imagine day after day, year after year of it.'

She listened patiently to my litany of complaints about the horrors of the road, then said, 'I'm sure that's all true, Kellen, but you know what I think?'

'What?'

She took my hands in hers, and then, as if she were fighting desperately to swim up from the bottom of a deep, dark lake, she kissed me for a long time. 'I think no life can be so bad so long as you have someone to share it with.'

287

45

The Hootch

It didn't take long for Seneira to finish packing. There's only so much you can carry when you're travelling the long roads. We could've left that very hour if it weren't that Ferius was still in the throes of the obsidian worm fever.

'Hey, Kellen,' she said, eyes half-opening as I walked into her room. 'Come to rescue me?' She pulled at her bonds. 'Mind taking these off so's I can get a drink? I'm powerful thirsty.'

'They were just to keep you from hurting yourself.'

'Silly kid, why would I want to hurt myself when I've already got so many other folks tryin' to do it for me? Now take these restraints off.'

'You should sleep awhile first. Let yourself—'

'Let myself what, kid? Get used to this crawler under the skin of my right eye?' Again she pulled at her restraints. 'Take them off, Kellen. I ain't gonna scratch out my own eye. I need it for something first.'

Not feeling as if I could refuse her, I did as she asked. When I was done, she sat up groggily. 'All right, now where are those boots of mine?'

'Ferius, I need to talk to you. I need to tell you the plan.'

She smiled in a way I found kind of patronising. 'The plan? Sure, kid, tell me all about your plan.'

I did, explaining what Beren was intending and what the rest of us would do that night.

'Sounds sensible,' she said. 'Good thinking. Excellent plan. Now, how about those boots, kid?'

Something struck me about her tone. 'Ferius, you're coming with us. You, me, Seneira and Reichis are leaving tonight, before—'

'No, Kellen, that's *your* plan, not mine. You and the girl –' she looked down at Reichis, still curled up asleep on the bed – 'and the squirrel cat if he wants, you all get out of here fast as you can. Me? My dance card's got a fella's name on it that I mean to scratch off once and for all.'

'Are you crazy? Dexan will kill you!' I strode over to a chest of drawers and pulled a small mirror from its stand to hold it in front of her. 'You see that thing around your eye? He can use it to hurt you. If those bracelets he uses have any kind of blood sympathy or iron attraction spells charmed into them, then he'll know when you're nearby. You won't get within fifty feet of him before he ends you.'

She made a show of looking in the mirror and fixing her hair. 'Reckon that might be so. Probably worth laying some money on it if you can find someone dumb enough to take the bet.'

She wasn't listening. Ferius was falling back into that stupid habit of pretending everything was some big joke and that she'd just swagger on up to Dexan and trick him into giving up. 'Come with us,' I pleaded. 'The four of us can survive if we just –'

She rose up from the bed, visibly unsteady but not letting me support her. 'Kid, I've been trying to teach you for months what it means to be an Argosi. It ain't some set of tricks or skills, it's not even a philosophy. It's a path, Kellen. That's what makes a person an Argosi: finding your path and never straying from it.' She slipped her black leather waistcoat back on and took out her metal flask. 'And *my* path runs right through that son of a bitch.'

'Don't do this,' I begged, practically starting to cry. Yeah, I guess I was laying it on a bit thick, but, well, I needed to put on a good show.

She tilted her head as she looked at me, then reached out a hand and ruffled my hair. 'You're a funny kid sometimes, you know that?' She unscrewed the cap of her flask and took a long drink. 'All right, best you and the girl set off now, Kellen. I've got some serious dancin' to do.'

'Will you two shut up?' Reichis groaned. 'I'm trying to die here.'

'He okay?' Ferius asked.

I nodded. 'Seneira took care of his wounds. She said they were too shallow to do much damage.'

'Good, that's good.' She took another swig from the flask before sealing it up and putting it back in her waistcoat.

'Nothing will stop you from going after him, will it?'

She smiled. 'Not a thing, kid. Not one, and if you respect me at all, you'll understand that . . .' She looked confused, then sat heavily back down on the bed. 'Whoa . . . who set this room to spinning?'

'Must be the fever,' I said.

Ferius glanced over at the night table, and the small vial of sedative that was two teaspoons short of what it should have been. 'Damn, Kellen . . . you drugged my hootch?'

I nodded.

'That's . . . That's just . . .' She fell back and I caught her in

290

time to turn her around so her head was on the pillow. Her eyes were already fluttering closed as she muttered, 'You're the worst apprentice I ever had.'

Reichis got up and shook himself off, then started inspecting his wounds. 'So what now? We toss the Argosi in the back of a wagon and run for it?'

I wanted to. More than anything in the world right now the thought of getting away from this place, of starting a life with Seneira, pulled at me like iron magic. But what kind of man would I be, what kind of life could I give Seneira, if I let my friends down? 'No more running,' I said. 'Ferius is right: an Argosi never backs down.'

'Neither do squirrel cats, but I thought –'

I pointed to the black marks around her eye. 'It's a safe bet that if Ferius goes anywhere near Dexan, he'll know she's coming, through his connection to the worm. He'll kill her before she can so much as toss a card at him.'

Reichis stared up at me, then shook himself again and his fur went from grey with silver stripes to black with traces of red. 'So you and me are gonna . . . ?'

I nodded. 'Yeah. You and me, partner.'

He looked as if he was trying to decide whether to come with me or just leave me there and go find a business partner who *didn't* get himself into life-or-death situations every five minutes. I wouldn't have blamed him; none of this was his fault. After a minute of watching him I couldn't stand it any longer. The thought of doing this without him was threatening to make me lose my nerve. 'Well?' I finally asked. 'What's it going to be?'

He got up on his hind legs and stared down at the cuts on his side, then up at me. 'I am seriously going to kill that damned crocodile this time.'

291

46

Whisper Magic

Reichis and I made our way back to the edge of town and returned to the lush swampy forest that should never have been able to thrive in such a dry climate. I'd got so used to the wide open desert of the Seven Sands that the way the foliage grew so thick, with everything closing in around me, felt eerily threatening.

'So, you've come back to talk at my spirits, eh, spellslinger?'

I glanced around, trying without success to see where the voice had come from. 'I need your help, Mamma Whispers. I need your magic.'

She walked out from behind a tree, a young girl – a child – who had no business looking so at ease in this strange, forbidding place. She gave a shake of her head, almost toppling her ragged top hat. 'I told you, spellslinger, Mamma Whispers doesn't have no magic. She just whispers to the spirits, and sometimes they listen.'

Reichis chittered on my shoulder. 'Somebody needs to tell "Mamma Whispers" that she talks like an old lady.'

She tilted her head and then laughed. 'Well, maybe some-body ought to tell the squirrel cat that *he* talks like a gap-toothed frontier bandit.'

'You can hear what he says?' I'd never encountered anyone other than the Dowager Magus who understood his growls and chitters.

'I told you, boy, I don't got no magic. The spirits, though, they tell me things.'

I went to her and knelt down, taking one of her small hands in mine. I had no idea if this was going to ingratiate me to her or get me killed, but I felt like a gesture of some sort was necessary. 'The man who's behind the shadowblack plague, I have to stop him, but he's hidden somewhere and I can't find him. Could your spirits help me track him?'

She took her hand away. 'Spirits don't belong to nobody but themselves. You want their help, you gotta learn to ask real nice.'

'Can you show me?'

'Well now, I don't know.' Suddenly she twirled around and her voice rose to a loud bellow. 'Any spirits here want to talk to this spellslinger? He ain't a bad one, I think, just stupid sometimes.'

Not the most hearty endorsement of my virtues.

'Well?' she shouted again. 'I asked if any spirits want to take pity on this boy. Maybe show him a better path through this nasty world?'

'Could we—'

She cut me off with a wave of her hand and a dirty look, so I shut my mouth. With her arms outstretched like the arrow on a weather vane, she kept spinning around, alternately whistling and whispering into the night air. 'Ah, ah, ah,' she said at last, bobbing her head. 'I hear one now. Yes, yes. A strong spirit. Bold. A touch foolish though –' she opened her eyes and glanced at me – 'but maybe that's to be expected.'

293

'Uh . . . thanks?'

She came closer. 'Now we gotta teach you how to talk to them, yeah? Have to show you how to whisper, whisper, whisper to them.' She grabbed my forearm and looked down at one of the bands there. 'You work some breath magic, spellslinger?'

'I do, a little.'

'That's good. That's real good. This here spirit, she's a sasutzei: a wind spirit. They like the breath magic best – better than the other nasty kinds you Jan'Tep mess with.' She looked up at me and her eyes narrowed. 'But you gotta learn to make the whispers just right, you understand? What we do, it ain't just words. Anyone can make words. We make whispers – totally different thing. You think you can do that?'

How was I supposed to answer a question I could barely understand? I had a sense that my answer mattered, to her and to this sasutzei spirit. 'My friend is hurt,' I said. 'Other people are hurt too. I think . . . I think there's something very bad happening out there and I need to know what it is so I can put a stop to it.'

Mamma Whispers shrugged. 'So what's that mean to me?'

'It means I'll do anything it takes to help my friend, so stop wasting my time and teach me the damned spell.'

Her eyes went wide for a moment, then the young girl who called herself Mamma Whispers leaned her head back and laughed up at the heavens. 'Ah, the spirits gonna like you, spellslinger. I think you gonna whisper real good.'

For all her backwoods mysticism, Mamma Whispers was right about one thing: whisper magic was nothing like the Jan'Tep incantations I knew. The spell – if you could call it that – wasn't made up of words or syllables, but almost impossibly

294

subtle movements of breath, through the mouth, passing by the lips, sometimes whistling through the front teeth.

'You're doing it wrong,' she said.

'How? I'm trying to do it exactly like you showed me.'

She shook her head impatiently. 'That's the fool's way. Stop trying to be like everybody else. Let the whisper come from your belly, from your need, from your promise to do what you say you'll do.' She wagged a finger at me. 'The spirits don't like liars, so stop trying to lie to them by pretending to be me.'

Okay, that made sense.

No, of course it didn't.

'Just tell her,' Mamma Whispers said, her voice gentler now. 'Tell the sasutzei what you want. *That's* the spell.'

'I need to know where the obsidian worms are,' I said to the night air around us. 'I need to see where they come from.'

She slapped my arm surprisingly hard. 'Not with words, with whispers.'

'But you said—'

'*I said, you said* . . . Stop *saying*! The spirits, they don't like loud things. That's why they come out here where it's quiet, where no people are. They don't need you talking at them, just *whisper!*'

If it had been as simple as just *whispering* the words, that would have been easy. But it wasn't, as I discovered when she smacked me again. 'That's just talking quiet.'

Finally I tried something else. I tried to just *think* of my need – not as words in my head or even pictures, but as the need itself, the simple desire, to understand the obsidian worms, to be able to see them. As I did this, I found my breathing changed, and I let myself whisper *without* making the words, letting my need speak for itself.

'Ah,' Mamma Whispers said, 'that's good. That's real good, spellslinger.'

Reichis growled. 'Something's happening. What's going on?'

'You be quiet now, mister squirrel cat. The spirits got no troubles with you.'

'I don't feel any different,' I said, but all of a sudden my right eye – the one *without* the shadowblack – started to itch. At first it was nothing; like a light breeze blowing on it, but then the sensation increased in intensity until it felt like someone was melting ice on the surface of my eyeball. 'What's happening to me?'

'You asked to *see*, and now the sasutzei is trying to show you.'

I blinked furiously, trying to get rid of the sensation, but then suddenly the pain went away and I saw the grey-green of the trees and grasses again, only . . . I saw something else too: a thin black strand, like a spider's web, glimmering in the air before me. It travelled from far to the east of us, from somewhere in town, all the way through the air to the west until it faded into the distance. 'What am I seeing?' I asked.

'You wanted to follow the black worms, so the sasutzei, she's showin' you the thread that connects each half together.'

'So I can . . . I can trace it, follow it to find where it leads?'

'Maybe,' Mamma Whispers replied, 'but maybe you need to stop looking so close.'

'What do you mean?'

'Look around you, spellslinger. Look all around.'

I did, and then I realised that there wasn't just one black thread. There were dozens, everywhere, passing through us, above us . . . 'How could Dexan have implanted so many worms into his victims? There would be a massive panic!'

A dark look passed across Mamma Whispers's young face. 'They're too clever, the ones behind these dirty tricks.' She tapped me on the temple. 'They let you see one or two of the victims to make you and the Argosi believe you know what's goin' on, but they use nasty magic to hide the other infected so you never see how far their evil work has already spread.'

So this wasn't just about blackmail schemes or even revenge. Whatever was going on, Dexan's clients had something much bigger planned. 'I have to go,' I said. 'I have to follow these threads to find the man responsible.'

'Go on then,' she said. 'You carry a spirit now.' Mamma Whispers chuckled as she tapped first my left cheekbone then my right. 'Now you got the shadowblack in one eye and the sasutzei in the other!'

Reichis sniffed at my face. I pushed his snout away. 'How long will the . . . sasutzei stay with me?' I asked, not sure how comfortable I was having some strange spirit take up residence in my eye. I had enough trouble with disturbing visions already.

'Oh, she stick with you as long as you keep her interest, boy. Whisper to her once in a while, and maybe she show you what others don't see. Just be careful you don't ask for the wrong things, spellslinger. The sasutzei, she gets powerful angry sometimes.'

Great, because all I'd needed to make my life complete was to have an angry spirit inside my eyeball.

'Go on,' she said, pushing me away with her small hands. 'Go on to your noisy world with your noisy troubles. Go be a hero.' She glanced around as if searching for something. 'Or maybe a dead man. I don't know which.'

297

47

The Threads

'What are we doing here?' Reichis asked as we stood outside the tall central tower of the Academy.

It had taken me several hours to follow the threads out of the deep forest into town and finally back to this place. Most of the time I couldn't see the threads at all, but then if I stopped and whispered my need, the sasutzei spirit in my right eye would give me another brief glimpse of them. I counted more than a dozen of the black gossamer filaments leading here.

'What could Dexan's clients possibly want with the Academy?' I asked aloud.

Reichis clambered up my leg, then leaped up to perch on my shoulder. 'Maybe they want to shut it down. Though why not just kill Beren instead of wasting time infecting a bunch of dumb kids?'

'The people who come to study here aren't dumb,' I said somewhat defensively as I thought back to Cressia, Lindy, Toller and the others. 'They're smart and ambitious. They come from some of the . . .'

Reichis poked at my cheek with his paw. 'What? What is it?'

I'd been about to say that the students here came from the best families from across the continent, but that wasn't precisely true; what their families had in common was that they were all rich and influential. Daroman courtiers, Berabesq clerics, Gitabrian merchants . . . 'Ancestors . . . I had it backwards: the Academy isn't where the threads lead, it's where they *begin*.'

'What's *that* supposed to mean?' Reichis asked.

A bell chimed and sound erupted from inside the massive tower. Soon hundreds of students would come rushing out, off to wherever it was students went after class hours. Some of them would have the obsidian worms buried inside their eyes and not even know it, attributing their symptoms to a passing fever, unaware of what now lived inside them.

Poor Beren. He'd built this place to be a beacon of hope and peace – a place where children from all over the continent would come not just to study their chosen subjects but to learn about the Seven Sands and its people, to find common ground with them and maybe one day support their bid for sovereignty when they returned to their own countries. But whoever Dexan was working for meant for the students to take something else home with them. 'Tyne kept saying that whenever he had an attack someone was listening to him, but I think what he really meant was that they were listening *through* him.'

'So Dexan could use the worms to spy on the families of the victims even in their own homes?' Reichis let out a whistling sound through his teeth. 'You could do a lot with all that information.'

I nodded. 'It gets worse. Remember how they used Revian as an anchor? They cast those ember spells through him, even though that entire house was protected with copper and silver wards.'

'So the kids whose worms are hidden by Dexan's spell . . . when they go back to their own countries . . .'

'They'll become spies on their own people. Maybe even assassins.'

Reichis gave a low growl. 'So what do we do?'

'The bracelet – the one Dexan made when he put the worm inside Ferius – he must have others, one for each victim. If we can find his real hideout, we can get the bracelets and destroy them so that he can't use the worms any more.'

'Okay,' Reichis said. 'But he's been smart enough to keep his lair hidden from us so far.'

I let my need rise up inside me again, and whispered to the sasutzei spirit in my right eye, pleading with her for guidance. This is what my life had come to: I was now begging my own eyeballs for help, and even *that* didn't feel strange. The strands from the obsidian worms appeared before me again, but I could see many of them glistening brighter, all leading in same direction. 'I think I can track him now.'

'Great, so then we just need to somehow get past a crocodile to beat a guy who just kicked our asses so badly that the only reason we aren't dead is because he didn't care enough to kill us.'

I shook my head. 'Last time I did it wrong. I tried to beat him at magic, but he's too strong for me.'

'So then what?'

I grinned down at the squirrel cat. 'How do you feel about a little burglary job?'

*

We followed the glistening black threads that the sasutzei revealed to us to a set of caves hidden in the hills outside of town. It made sense, now that I was there: those caves were probably where he'd found the onyx he needed for the bracelets. They probably also had a lot of iron deposits, which would make it hard for hextrackers to find him here. Then again, since they already had, it no longer mattered how well hidden he was.

Reichis and I crept up the path and then all around the caves that led into Dexan's home until we were sure we'd accounted for all the possible entrances and exits.

'Ready, partner?' I asked as we prepared to go in.

He hopped up on my shoulder. 'You know, Kellen, I'm pretty sure you're about to get us killed in a bid to save Ferius and a bunch of strangers even though the odds are terrible.'

'Yeah? So what?'

I felt something odd and furry against my cheek. Reichis – *Reichis* – was nuzzling me. 'So I'm starting to think that maybe you're all right, kid.'

48

The Heist

'Almost there ...' Reichis said, carefully rotating the lock's small wheels.

'You said that already. Six times.'

He glanced over at me from where he stood on his hind legs so he could reach the lock that held the back entrance to Dexan's lair. 'You *really* want to do this again?'

'Sorry,' I said.

Reichis resumed his work. I'd laid a circle of copper wire on the ground around us to counteract any warning charms that might have been inscribed onto the lock. I figured as long as we kept it in the circle, the spell shouldn't be able to reach Dexan.

Eventually Reichis got the lock open, and we left it within the wire.

With the door open, I was about to go in when I felt Reichis tug on my trouser leg. 'What?' I asked.

He pointed with one paw near the floor just inside the entrance. At first I couldn't see anything, but when I knelt down to squirrel-cat height I could just barely make out the thin wire running from one side of the doorway to the other. 'Tripwire,' Reichis explained, and hopped over it into the dark

302

space beyond. After a few seconds he called out, 'Hey, Kellen, you should see this. Kind of a clever trap. There are actually six different wires running across the floor, and if you trigger any one of them, a small lever turns a pulley connected to a large—'

'Can you disable it?'

A pause. 'Well, sure, but don't you want to hear how it works? I mean, it's pretty cool the way the blade will just take your head off and all.'

'Maybe next time,' I said.

'Your loss.'

A few minutes later I heard a crashing sound that nearly gave me a heart attack. 'Reichis?'

'What?' he asked, poking his head out the door.

'What was that?'

'A big mother of an eight-foot-long steel blade crashing to the floor. What did you think it was?'

I followed him inside, fumbling around until I found a glow-glass ball suspended near one of the walls. I set my will on it, and after a second or two managed to get a somewhat pathetic but still helpful amount of light.

'Nice place,' Reichis said.

He wasn't kidding. What should have been a dank cave turned out to be an extremely large and elegant open room with polished marble floors and walls reminiscent of a Jan'Tep sanctum. Large display cases stood in various spots around the space, filled with books and charms and any number of interesting artefacts. A door in one wall led to a bathroom. Reichis, of course, was immediately entranced by the tub. 'Will you *look* at this thing? It's huge.' He started fiddling with a tap on one side. 'Running water too.' He hopped back off the edge of the bath and followed the copper pipe to a small wood stove. 'Hey, fire this up for me, would you, Kellen?'

'Are you serious? We're on a heist here, Reichis, and you want to take a bath?'

The squirrel cat started sniffing around the room. 'Not unless I can find some butter biscuits, I don't.'

'Come on,' I said. 'Let's find the onyx bracelets he uses to control the worms. After that I promise I'll buy you all the butter biscuits you can eat.'

'Deal,' Reichis said, then added more quietly, 'sucker.'

As we began searching the vast room with all its curios and furnishings, I became confounded by the fact that Dexan – someone I would have expected to be constantly on the move – had created something so . . . permanent for himself.

'Any luck?' I asked Reichis.

He glanced back at me from where he was hanging off the top of one of the glass cases. 'There's kind of a lot of ground to cover here, Kellen. What about asking that thing in your eye?'

I shook my head. I'd tried several times since we got here but the sasutzei wasn't responding. Maybe some of Dexan's own wards interfered with it somehow. I rubbed at my right eye and felt nothing there. I'd probably asked it for help so many times on the way here that the spirit had got bored and abandoned me entirely.

'What about one of those Jan'Tep magical whammy things?' Reichis asked.

I almost laughed. 'When have you ever seen me successfully cast a seeking spell?'

Reichis went back to rifling through the shelves and grumbled, 'I can dream, can't I?'

We kept searching for an hour, making rather a mess of Dexan's palatial home, when all of a sudden the glow-glass ball I was carrying to illuminate the room flickered out.

'Hey, a little light here?' Reichis said.

Unfortunately I couldn't make the glow-glass ignite again. Worse, I was pretty sure I knew why. I looked down at the red mark on my palm and felt the sting of Dexan using it to block my magic.

'I told you the charm would go away by itself in a couple of days,' Dexan himself said, stepping into the room. 'If you'd just waited until then, you might have had a chance.'

I started to reach for powder from the pouches at my belt, but stopped myself when the burning in my palm increased.

'Oh, you're not going to start with that again, are you?' Dexan asked. He sighed theatrically. 'You know, it's hard to believe, but even after all the nonsense you've put me through, I still can't quite get myself to hate you, Kellen.'

'That's nice,' Reichis chittered, climbing up another of the cases to gain the height he'd need to glide down and attack. 'Tell him the feeling ain't mutual.'

'Unfortunately,' Dexan went on, 'I really can't allow you to keep breaking the first rule though.'

I reached into my pockets and took out some of Ferius's steel playing cards. At least *those* Dexan couldn't interfere with.

'Should've become my apprentice when you had the chance, Kellen,' Dexan said. He made a simple somatic shape with his right hand, and this time I could see the slight shimmer of the onyx bracelet around his wrist. The sounds of thick claws at the end of four short legs clacked against the marble floor, along with the rustling of a heavy tail being dragged behind.

'Great,' Reichis said. 'He brought the damned crocodile.'

305

49

The Fight

'You know what your problem is, kid?' Dexan said as he approached, his massive crocodile lumbering close behind.

'Bad timing?'

He shook his head. 'Self-deception.'

'How do you figure?'

His hand formed the somatic shape for the lightning needles I'd seen him use on Revian's house mage. I had no idea what it felt like to be hit by those and no desire to find out. He could sense my discomfort. 'You keep fooling yourself into believing you can be someone other than a spellslinger, Kellen, but that's who you are. It's what we both are! Exiles. Outcasts. We've got our little scraps of magic and our wits and that's it. When you forget that – when you let yourself believe you can join the Argosi or fall in love with some rich girl and move in with her and her papa – you lose the one advantage you have.'

'Which is?'

'Knowing how the world really works.'

He took another step closer, his hand still holding the somatic shape even as the onyx bracelet on his wrist shimmered again. The crocodile opened its mouth and let out a hissing sound that made my guts go cold.

Reichis and I had spent most of the climb into the hills discussing how we might deal with the beast. Two possibilities had presented themselves, neither of which were particularly promising. In the end it was Reichis who'd made the decision between the two.

I backed away. Quickly. 'You're wrong, Dexan. I might be an outcast like you, but that's not all I have to be.'

He shook his head in disgust. 'Look at you! Seconds from meeting your own death and yet you're still refusing to face the fact that this – right here –' he spread his arms to gesture at the surroundings – 'this is the best somebody like you or me can hope for. A little money, a nice place, maybe some comfort, at least until our own people hunt us down and take it away from us.'

'That's a pretty lonely existence,' I said, retreating.

'That's the life of a spellslinger, Kellen. People either want to kill us or use us as tools. That girl you like? Even if you *could* cure her, all that would do is make her leave you behind. Why would someone like that want to be with an outlaw spellslinger cursed with the shadowblack? And that woman? Ferius? She's an *Argosi*, Kellen. They're loners, every one of them. Sure, she'll let you follow her around for a while, but then that "path" of hers? Well, it'll take her to places you don't want to go, and when it does, she'll walk right out of your life and you'll never see her again.' He gave a chuckle. 'Damn, kid, you don't even have a proper familiar. Just a squirrel cat who probably steals everything he can get his paws on.'

'Got that right,' Reichis chittered.

Suddenly something small and shiny hurtled through the air towards Dexan, letting out a high-pitched chime as it struck his forehead. It was the bell from the charm we'd tried to buy.

The distraction was just enough for me to get one steel card thrown. I'd aimed for Dexan's neck, which was a bad idea since it wasn't a big target. Still, the card sliced his cheek and I got a loud yell for my troubles. Then he set the crocodile on me.

As the creature advanced, I scrambled backwards, readying myself for what Reichis had dubbed 'the bloody-tongue manoeuvre'. Just as the crocodile opened its jaws, I flung one of Ferius's steel cards into its mouth. The first one missed, clacking against the brute's teeth only to fall to the floor, but I fired off a second one and that one went right inside. Instinctively, the creature bit down, and gave a roar as the sharp steel edges bit into the soft flesh of its mouth.

Dexan was only momentarily distracted, his fingers went back into the somatic shape of the lightning-needles spell. He opened his mouth to utter the incantation, and I knew I was a few syllables away from a rather unpleasant end.

Reichis leaped down from his perch on the glass case, limbs spread wide so that the furry membranes of his glider wings blocked Dexan's view. The squirrel cat wrapped his paws and feet around Dexan's face, clawing into him to hang on.

The crocodile was snapping its jaws open and closed, trying to dislodge the card. I didn't have long before the creature would give up on that endeavour and turn his attention to me, but in the meantime I raced past it and made a running leap for Dexan. 'Reichis, now!' I shouted.

The squirrel cat sprang away just as I tackled Dexan to the floor. It felt almost satisfying to be on the attack for once, instead of just being the guy who gets beaten up all the time. But Dexan was a foot taller than me and a good fifty pounds heavier. Within seconds he'd managed to throw me off, and I landed hard against one of the display cases, sending it toppling to the floor, the glass doors shattering into thousands of pieces.

'You stupid little ingrate!' he spat, getting to his feet. 'You think just because I'm a spellslinger I don't know how to fight?'

I scrambled to my feet. 'Oh, I'm sure you know how to wrastle,' I said, 'but me, I'm more of a dancer these days.' I held out my hand and showed him what I'd taken from him.

Dexan glanced at his wrist and saw the onyx bracelet he used to control the crocodile was gone. He made a grab for me, but I ducked low and came up on the other side of him, tossing the bracelet to Reichis, who leaped up and caught it in his teeth. The crocodile, mad with confusion and rage, now freed from Dexan's control, came after all of us.

'Are you sure about this, Reichis?' I asked again, preparing to throw another card at the creature's mouth. I doubted it would fall for that twice.

'He's mine!' Reichis growled, leaping onto the crocodile's head and grabbing onto the ridges with his claws.

Squirrel cats really don't like losing a fight, and Reichis is especially prone to acts of revenge. As the crocodile began to flip over to shake off his unwanted guest, Reichis leaped off. The crocodile tried to snap its teeth at him, and in that instant Reichis threw the bracelet into the beast's mouth.

The crunch of the bracelet shattering inside the massively

powerful jaws was followed by the creature suddenly halting its frantic movements. The black swirling inside its eyes stopped and the beast stared at us, gaze clear for the first time. I wasn't sure what to expect then, whether it would die or perhaps still be just as wild. What Reichis had theorised, and I'd hoped, was that the beast, once free of the magic controlling it, would turn its attention to the man who'd made it suffer for so long.

For once we got lucky.

The crocodile started scrambling along the marble floor towards Dexan, who ran backwards while frantically grabbing for something inside his pocket. Suddenly he pulled out what looked like a small glass figurine which he crushed in his hand, grimacing from the pain of the glass cutting into his palm. The crocodile collapsed on the floor. Blood began to drip out of its eyes and mouth.

'That's the difference between you and me, Kellen,' Dexan said, wiping the tiny slivers of glass from his hand. 'We're both spellslingers, we're both wily, but I've been at this a lot longer than you. Did you think I wouldn't have prepared something just in case I lost control of the beast?' He raised both his hands and thin tendrils of blue lightning slithered around his fingers.

'There's something else that makes us different, Dexan: I have . . .'

I didn't get to finish my sentence because at that moment Dexan dropped like a stone, unconscious. Behind him, Ferius, with Seneira at her side, stood over him and slowly closed her extendable metal rod. 'Oh, I'm sorry, kid,' she said. 'Were you going to say something?'

'Yeah.' I knelt to let Reichis clamber up my arm to my

shoulder then walked over to Ferius and Seneira. 'I was going to say that the difference between me and Dexan is that I have friends.'

Ferius gave me that smirk of hers. 'Friends, eh? So why did you take off without us like that?'

'Because you'd never have let me do this my way.'

'Damn straight, because I'd have known you'd end up in a position like this.'

I nodded. 'Just like I knew you'd come find me.'

50

Ending the Worms

It didn't take us long to find some copper binding wire to use on Dexan. I made sure to wind it around his fingers just as he'd previously done to me, so that there was no way for him to form any somatic shapes.

'You'll never find those bracelets, kid, not if you search this place for a hundred years. So you'd better start treating me nice or negotiations could take a long, long time.'

His smug self-confidence made me want to hit him very badly, but though I tried to whisper to the spirit that now lived in my right eye, the sasutzei remained silent. 'What will it take?' I asked Dexan.

'Wait,' Reichis said, and clambered up to my shoulder. 'Let me try something.'

'What?'

'Just listen and do exactly what I tell you.'

He explained his plan, and though I didn't understand how it was going to help us, I had no better ideas so I followed his instructions. I knelt down, grabbed Dexan by the collar and gave him my best version of a smirk. 'You're a sucker, you know that, Dexan? Did you really think we'd risk our lives coming here if we didn't already know *exactly* where you'd hidden the bracelets? We took them before you got here. Frankly I'm surprised you hid something so valuable in such an obvious place.'

His eyes showed a glimmer of concern, but then he just laughed. 'Hate to tell you, kid, but you're terrible at bluffing.'

'He's right,' Reichis chittered. 'You are pretty bad at it.' He leaped off my shoulder and ran along one of the carpets up to the back wall. 'On the other hand, that moron's poker face is just as lousy as yours.'

'What's going on?' Seneira asked.

'Squirrel-cat magic,' Reichis said, and had me translate the rest while he scampered up a set of shelves and began probing with his claws along the rough-hewn stone wall behind them.

'When I told Dexan we already knew where he'd hidden the bracelets, his eyes went to their hiding place.'

'I was watching him and I didn't see his eyes move at all,' she said.

Neither had I, other than the briefest flicker, but apparently Reichis was better at this sort of thing than we were. 'Over here,' he said excitedly. Ferius carried on tying Dexan up while Seneira and I joined Reichis at the back wall. There, up in the left-hand corner, was an outcropping of stone no different than any other part of the wall so far as I could see, but when I placed my hand there, the rock was as soft as silk cloth. The covering gave way, allowing me to reach past it and take hold of a wooden box about the size of an old book. As I removed my hand, the cloth went back into place, seamlessly becoming part of the wall again. Inside the box were at least two dozen onyx bracelets, each with its own slithering form inside: the other halves of the obsidian worms magically bound to those inserted around the eyes of Dexan's

313

targets. Every bracelet had the victim's name inscribed along one edge.

I started rummaging through them, and before long I found the one with Ferius's name. 'Here,' I said, handing the bracelet to her as Seneira took the box from me and began searching for her own.

Usually Ferius is hard to read. She wears a look of cool self-satisfaction on her face whether she's angry, happy, sad or scared. But it was rage I saw there now – rage like I'd never seen on anyone before. That's when I finally understood the most important thing there is to know about Ferius Parfax: there is nothing in this world or the next that matters to her more than being free. *That* is the path of the wild daisy.

Wordlessly she took the bracelet and threw it to the floor. With the heel of her boot she smashed it, grinding it into fragments even as she screamed from the pain. I could see the worm beneath the skin around her eye squirming, shuddering, shattering into thousands of tiny black particles, like grains of sand. Finally Ferius stopped, and what was left of the worm came oozing out of her eye like blood from a wound. She wiped at it furiously, determined to remove every last trace. When she was done, her gaze turned to Dexan. I think, despite her Argosi vows, she might have murdered him right then were it not for Seneira's sudden cry.

'I can't find it! I can't . . . Where is mine?'

She was still rifling through the box, desperately trying to find the bracelet with her name on it.

'Sorry, little girl,' Dexan said. He almost sounded sincere. 'They sent for it three days ago – a falcon, if you can believe it. My instructions were to tie the bracelet around its leg, and as soon as I did, it flew off back to its master.'

314

'Why? Why me?'

'They like you, girl. Big powerful diplomat's daughter, one day a diplomat yourself. They picked you and a few others to be . . . special cases. Reckon you're going to be real useful to them.'

She looked at me, terrified, desperate for someone to tell her we could fix this. I went back to where Dexan sat on the floor. 'There has to be another way. You said it before, you were practically bragging that you had rituals to destroy the worms. "Rituals" plural, not just one.'

'Guess you must've misheard me, kid. Without the bracelet, there's nothing you can do.'

Nothing *you* can do? Why say it that way? Why not 'nothing *I* can do'?

Reichis came over, sniffing at Dexan. 'He's lying.' Another sniff, then a growl. 'He's holding something back.'

I didn't know how he could tell, but since it was the only hope we had, I knelt down to face Dexan again. 'The squirrel cat thinks you're holding out on us.'

'Well, guess you shouldn't rely on a dumb animal to think for you.'

Reichis snarled and puffed himself up. 'Give me five minutes alone with him, Kellen.'

I gave Dexan the most menacing look I could muster, which probably wasn't much. 'Maybe you're right. Maybe all Reichis is picking up is the stink that sticks to a man who'd turn people's children into spies and slaves.' I got back up to my feet. 'So I apologise in advance if it turns out he was wrong.' I looked down at Reichis, who was already grinning that terrifying feral grin of his. 'You're always talking about eating eyeballs. Here's your chance.'

The squirrel cat crept up to Dexan as if he were a mouse about to be pounced on, then starting crawling up his leg, growling all the while. The spellslinger tried to shake him off, but the squirrel cat dug his claws in and kept going. Ferius locked eyes with me. The shock from before had worn off now and I could see she was telling me she wouldn't allow us to torture Dexan. Fortunately, even without clawing out someone's eyes, Reichis can put on quite a show when he puts his mind to it. He'd barely licked the guy's eyelids before Dexan started screaming for mercy, 'All right, all right! I'll tell you! Just get him off me!'

'Best give him a chance to speak, Reichis.'

The squirrel cat looked up at me. 'He doesn't need both eyeballs to tell us how it's done, does he?'

Dexan was babbling now. 'There is something, another way to get rid of the worm, but it's dangerous. And I want a deal first.'

'What kind of deal?' Ferius asked.

'You let me go. You let me leave here and you let me take three of my bracelets as insurance. It's a tough world out there and I might need a favour from someone powerful one day.'

Ferius put a boot against his chest. 'Boy, you ain't gonna set your will on another child ever again. You cure the girl, and we'll let you go on with your miserable life for so long as the earth can tolerate your footsteps upon it. That's the best offer you're gonna get.'

The first hint of a sneer started to find its way to Dexan's face, but then he saw the way Ferius was looking at him. There's this thing she can do – I don't know what it is because it isn't magic and it sure isn't normal – but I've yet to see

316

anybody who could match that stare. 'Fine,' he said, and looked up at me. 'Just keep the crazy woman and that damned squirrel cat away from me.' His eyes went to Seneira. 'It's gonna hurt.'

'I don't care,' she said, almost shaking with anger and fear. 'I just want this thing out of me.'

'You know how Jan'Tep counter-banding works?' Dexan asked me.

The question took me by surprise. Just the thought of what my parents had done to me still made me sick to my stomach. I nodded.

'Well, it's kind of like that. It's tricky work and needs a breath spell to channel the flow of the inks to keep the patient from dying along the way.' He nodded at his bonds. 'So you'd better get these off me before my hands start to cramp up.'

I'd been about to start untying the knots when Seneira said, 'No.' We all turned to look at her. 'You say it takes spells? Then I want Kellen to do it.' She reached out and touched the tattooed band around my forearm. 'You can do breath magic, right?'

It was the only magic I *could* do, but this was different. 'Seneira, I've never done the procedure he's talking about. Working with banding inks is dangerous. I could end up blinding you, or worse!'

'I don't care. I won't have that man lay hands on me, not if there's any other choice in the world.' She took my hand in hers. 'Please, Kellen. I trust you not to hurt me.'

Great. Now if only I trusted myself.

51

The Procedure

Seneira and I sat facing each other in the wreckage of Dexan's lair. I'd set up a small table between us with the necessary instruments. Two sets of metallic inks bubbled and boiled in tiny glass containers over twin braziers, the flames flickering red and blue. 'Are you ready?' I asked.

She nodded. 'I'm ready.' Seneira was doing a good job of keeping the quavering out of her voice, but the fear was plain as day in her eyes. This was going to hurt, and she knew it.

I'd made Dexan go over every step of the process three times, making sure he didn't change any details in each recounting. Ferius kept an eye on him while Reichis, who had wrapped himself around Dexan's neck, chittered a near-constant stream of threats into his ear. Despite having no idea what he was saying, Ferius pretended to relay every word. Most of her guesses were pretty close to what the squirrel cat was saying. I guess he really is predictable sometimes.

I dipped the first needle into the container of liquefied copper. Dexan hadn't lied when he'd said the procedure was similar to the counter-banding my parents had done to me, which made my hands alternately want to clench in anger

318

or shake with trepidation. The critical part was the breath spell I'd use to channel the inks as they entered the skin around her eye. Once the needle pierced flesh, I'd have to guide the molten metal into the worm, killing it without burning Seneira's flesh . . . or blinding her for life. But it was this, or forever be under the control of whoever had been behind this whole ugly business.

As I raised the first needle up to her eye, Seneira leaned back out of reach. 'Wait . . . Kellen, stop.'

I thought she was panicking, now unsure if she could go through with the procedure, but it was something else entirely. 'Kellen, I can feel them . . . the mages who have the other part of the worm. They're trying to talk through me.'

'Hold them off,' I said. 'It won't be long, I promise.'

'No. I'm going to let them do it. Maybe something they say will help us figure out who they are.'

I'd seen what it looked like when they insinuated themselves inside her mind before. The sickening pain on her face had been almost too much to endure. 'They're not going to reveal themselves, Seneira. This is just some—'

She shook her head. 'I don't care. Maybe you're right and we won't learn anything, but I want to do it anyway.'

'Why?'

Seneira reached out and took my hand, making me set the needle back down on the tray. 'Because I want you to deliver a message to them from me.'

'Hello, Kellen.' The voice was Seneira's, but the diction, the way her mouth moved, belonged to someone or something else entirely.

I said nothing in reply, staring at her face, watching every

319

twitch of the lips, every slight raise of the eyebrow or subtle smirk rising from one corner of her mouth.

'Come now,' she said. 'Don't play the silent, petulant child. You must have many questions.'

'I don't.'

'Really? I very much doubt that.'

I laughed, partly to disguise my own discomfort at watching Seneira being used in this way. 'I already know you won't tell me who you are and I already know what you've come to say.'

Seneira's eyes narrowed to slits. 'Tell us.'

'You want to make me an offer.' I nodded back to where Dexan was tied up. 'Like the one you made him.'

A smile crept onto Seneira's face. 'Oh, better than that. True, we would have permitted Dexan to enter one of the oases, to renew his connection to the raw source of Jan'Tep magic, but for you we would give so much more.'

'A pardon,' I said, having fully expected this. 'The end of the bounty on my head.'

'A chance to grow up without fear of being hunted, to return to your home. Freedom, instead of captivity. Comfort, instead of fear.' Seneira leaned forward just a bit. 'Life, instead of death.'

I considered the words that had been spoken, every one, until finally I said, 'Thank you.'

The head tilted, 'Ah, but not so quick. First there is what you must do for us. You will cease your interference in our affairs. You will leave this place without revealing what that little swamp witch's spirit spell has shown you about who we have taken under our control and you will kill the spellslinger Dexan so that he cannot reveal what he knows.'

That last part was tempting, but . . . 'I don't think so.'

Anger flashed on her features. 'Do not attempt to negotiate with us, child. You have—'

'No, you don't understand. I wasn't thanking you for the offer before, I was thanking you for the clue you gave me about your identity.'

'Oh?'

I nodded. 'I already knew that only mages of the highest order could work the spells needed for what you've done here, and only someone of tremendous influence could have corralled so many bounty hunters to help you track down Dexan. Only lords magi have that kind of power and authority. But then you gave me the thing I was missing: you said I could *return to my home*.'

'You disbelieve us?'

'On the contrary, it makes perfect sense. The thing is, no Jan'Tep clan could ever make that offer on behalf of another clan, which also explains why your accent is so close to my own.' I leaned forward and stared into Seneira's face, but into the gaze of our enemies. 'You're lords magi of my own clan.'

Even before I received a response, I imagined their faces. Ra'meth, if he was still alive, Te'oreth, An'atria, Ven'asp. I hoped Osia'phest wasn't involved. I'd always liked the old man. I picked up the small shallow case containing the remaining onyx bracelets. Then I picked up a small hammer I'd found among Dexan's things and smashed the bracelets into pieces.

Seneira's jaw stiffened and her eyes widened in rage. Her hands started to reach out for my neck, but she was still in there, her will too strong to allow them. 'We will kill the girl in front of you,' the voice said, its timbre changing, deepening, the words echoing inside the chamber. 'We will send ember magic through her to kill you and those with you.'

A glow began to emerge from her eye, red and fiery with traces of an icy blue as though lightning were building up inside a ball of flame. I feared we'd pushed our enemies too far, but then the magic died down, and Seneira, sweat dripping from her brow, said, 'I. Think. Not.'

She was incredible, resisting their control with only her raw will, denying them access to her as an anchor for their spells. I knew she couldn't do it forever though, so I relayed her message. 'Stay out of the Seven Sands, My Lords Magi. It can be a far more dangerous place than you might expect.'

The glow disappeared entirely, and for a moment I thought they'd gone, but then the voice said, 'There is a special hell for those who betray their own people, Kellen of the House of Ke. You dishonour all those who have loved you.'

I considered that last threat, something about it bothering me – like words I couldn't make out on a page or an itch I couldn't scratch. 'I've never wanted to hurt my people,' I said, then looked into the swirling black within Seneira's eyes that somehow carried all the way across the endless miles back to my enemy's own. 'But I'm going to find out who you are one day and kill you all the same.'

Seneira's mouth opened to speak, but then her fists clenched. 'No, I think that's all we want to hear from you.' She blinked her eyes then looked at me. They were green again, and filled with tears. 'Do it now, Kellen, burn this atrocity out of me.'

I dipped the needle back into the molten copper, and for the next hour I did what had to be done; the deed was

322

difficult and dangerous, and listening to her screams as the worm twitched and seethed beneath her skin was almost more than I could bear as I struggled to perform the spell, but I didn't waver, not once. Her courage kept my hand steady and my mind focused.

When it was done, the tiny black ashes of what remained of the worm slid down the tracks of her tears. She wiped it all away with the sleeve of her shirt. For a while she was silent, then finally she said, 'Thank you, Kellen.'

I should have felt relief that she was safe, and gratitude because things could have gone so very badly. Instead a fury seethed inside me. My people – my own people – had done this, were doing it still to the others whose bracelets they possessed. All to bring a new form of the shadowblack – the darkest legacy of my people – into the lives of innocents. The black markings around my own eye began to smoulder with a heat that was soon matched inside my chest. My left eye kept blinking uncontrollably, and each time it did, I saw a vision – of fire, of destruction. Murder and mayhem with me at its head, destroying my enemies. Burning them alive. Killing. Killing. Killing.

'It's all right,' Seneira said, her voice closer than I'd expected. I was on my feet and she was next to me, her head on my shoulder, holding on to me as if a wind were about to blow me away. 'It's all right.'

As gently as I could I separated myself from her, the darkness still burning behind my left eye. 'You shouldn't be near me right now.'

She seemed unfazed. 'Why is that?'

'Because I have the shadowblack. The real shadowblack, not the thing they put inside you. There's . . . There's some-

323

thing terrible inside me that's just waiting to come out, and I don't know how long I'll be able to hold it back. I'm not who you think I am.'

Seneira reached a hand to my face. I flinched, but she carried on until her finger was tracing the winding black lines around my eye. 'Maybe you're not who *you* think you are either, Kellen.' She took her hand away. 'There's one thing I know about you for sure though.'

'What's that?'

She kissed me on the cheek. 'You're a far better person than you think you are.'

I didn't know what to say to that. I never do.

Seneira hugged me once more, then said, 'Come on. My father will have realised we're gone and he'll be worried.'

'I can't go,' I said, exhaustion starting to set in as it always did after one of my episodes. 'I have to keep searching in case Dexan has any more onyx bracelets hidden around here.'

'Okay,' she said, 'but you'll come back to my house straight afterwards. Don't deny my father the chance to thank you.'

Not knowing what else to do, I nodded.

Ferius, Reichis and I spent the next few hours searching Dexan's things, much to his dismay. Ferius found a journal Dexan had kept, listing the names and family details of his victims, along with a notation on a half-dozen of them that we figured out meant the bracelets were now in the possession of Dexan's clients.

'They'll get to you, you know,' he said to me as we were preparing to leave. 'You don't know what it's like out there, Kellen.'

'Now weren't you goin' on braggin' about what a successful spellslinger you were?' Ferius asked with a chuckle.

Dexan spat. 'It's not any kind of life. It's running from town to town, hoping some bounty hunter doesn't kill you in your sleep. It's scratching the dirt looking for anything – anything at all – to give you an edge the next time you have to fight. People don't trust you, and you can't trust them.' He looked up at me. 'Believe me, kid, you're going to regret not taking the deal they offered. Those mages, whoever they are? They're going to kill you.' He pulled at his restraints. 'That's if I don't get to you first.'

I walked past him and reached down to pick up his black frontier hat with its copper and silver glyphs set in the band circling its circumference. 'What are you doing with that?' he demanded.

I set it on my head and felt it slide down just a little low on my brow. It was too big for me and probably looked ridiculous, but I didn't care. 'It's called the Way of Water, Dexan. You tried to kill me, so I get to keep your hat.'

52

The Offer

That evening we did indeed return to Seneira's home, and after a lot of explaining and a supper that ended in Reichis burping various compliments at me that he expected be promptly delivered to the chef, the house settled into a weary silence. Seneira and her father seemed determined to put on a brave front for Ferius and me, but you could see the sorrow of Tyne's absence in every glance they shared.

'Well,' Ferius said, catching my eye, 'it's gettin' late and the kid here needs his beauty sleep somethin' awful so I reckon we'd best—'

'Actually,' Beren interrupted, setting his hands down on the table, 'I was hoping to exchange a word or two with Kellen in my study.'

I couldn't think of a reason to refuse. Seneira had said *nobody* ever went into her father's study, so I guess this private chat was meant to be something of an honour. Or maybe a consolation prize.

'Some nice stuff in here,' Reichis chittered quietly, as his eyes went to the assortment of sculptures and artefacts adorning the dark oak shelves. 'Some *very* nice stuff.'

I'd told him to stay outside but, well, he doesn't take orders very well. 'Stop drooling,' I said, giving him a gentle kick in the butt.

Beren took a seat in one of the room's thickly padded chairs and motioned for me to do the same. 'You're a remarkable young man, Kellen of the Jan'Tep.'

'Kellen Argos,' I corrected, though that didn't sound right either any more, but I didn't want anyone ever mistaking me for one of the mages whose cruel machinations had very nearly brought ruin to the Seven Sands.

Beren nodded. 'Of course, of course.' He reached over to a small table for a crystal glass bottle and poured its dark amber contents into two glasses before handing one of them to me. 'Pazione,' he said, as if the word should inspire awe in me.

I took a sip. Now bear in mind that my experience of alcohol consisted of having got drunk once in my life, right before facing the lords magi of my clan to await their judgment, but this was maybe the most remarkable thing I'd ever tasted. The flavour was a mix of peach and some kind of spice that seemed to burn then cool then burn again on the tongue before finally settling into a deep warmth that soothed my throat going down.

Reichis, peering down over my shoulder from his perch on the back of the chair, sniffed at the glass, then said, 'Gimme.'

The thought of letting a squirrel cat drink from my glass felt uncivilised – not to mention unhygienic – but hells, the little bugger had almost been eaten by a crocodile a few hours ago. Reluctantly I held up the glass to him. He dipped a paw in and licked it. 'Oh, that's good,' he said, and his fur shivered briefly before settling into a brownish-amber colour almost

327

identical to that of the contents of my glass. He dipped his paw into the pazione three more times before I pulled it away from him. Reichis drunk is never a good idea in polite company.

Despite how disgusting it is to drink after a squirrel cat's been at it, I took a second sip. It was even better than the first.

Beren must have caught my expression of wonder. 'My own private supply,' he said, then took a long drink himself before setting the glass down on the arm of his chair. 'I'm pretty sure it's the most expensive thing I ever bought, after the Academy of course.'

'What will happen to the Academy?' I asked.

He sighed wearily. 'I'm not sure, Kellen. You can't imagine how much wealth it takes to keep it running. The money required to persuade the best teachers and masters to come live in the borderlands, the envoys we have to send to try to convince influential families from Darome, Berabesq, Gitabria, even a few Jan'Tep now and then . . . It's a lot to deal with.' He slumped back in his chair looking suddenly exhausted. 'More than that, it's the time and work of keeping it vibrant, and convincing my own people that it's not a threat to their way of life. Trying to keep everyone safe.' He caught my gaze. 'You could help with that, you know.'

'Me?'

'Don't act so surprised. You're clever and resourceful. You're a lot tougher than you look, or than you seem to think you are. I'd feel a lot better reopening the Academy if I knew you were going to be part of it, Kellen.'

I'm not sure why, but I couldn't seem to make sense of his words. I wasn't drunk and I was pretty certain the pazione wasn't poisoned, but the idea of what he was offering was too much for me to hold in my head. 'You'd be a student,' he explained, no doubt noticing whatever confused expression had settled onto my face. He held up a hand. 'Tuition free. Everything paid for. You could become a military strategist or a designer of contraptions or, heck, a philosopher if that's what you want. I'd be grateful for your help.'

Visions of myself striding along the Academy's marble halls ignited within me. I pictured myself rushing into those gilded classrooms, quietly taking a seat among brilliant students my age who'd come from all over the continent. Respected scholars would stand before us, sharing their wisdom and remarkable knowledge, then stepping back, amused, as we, the leaders of tomorrow, debated and argued over deep philosophical questions. I felt as if contraptions and devices would be a subject I could be good at, but philosophy was the discipline that fascinated me most. Among my people, foreign philosophers are respected even if they don't have magic. Spellcraft used to be called natural philosophy, in fact.

But one thing you learn quickly in the borderlands: nothing comes for free. 'You mentioned something about keeping people safe. Does that mean you'd want me to be some kind of guard?'

'Nothing so formal. By my way of thinking, just having you there will make things safer.' He gave Reichis a rueful smile. 'You and that remarkable squirrel cat of yours, assuming you can keep him sober.'

I turned my head and only then noticed that Reichis had been surreptitiously dipping his paw back into my glass. 'Well, it's not like you were drinking it,' he mumbled, staring back at me glassy-eyed.

Beren gave a polite cough to get my attention. 'What I'm

asking, Kellen, is that I be able to come to you, from time to time, if I think something unnatural is going on at the Academy – something that quick mind of yours might be more suited to investigating than my own.'

'What about Ferius?' I asked.

Beren's face took on an oddly compassionate expression. 'The Argosi are wanderers, Kellen; they never stay in one place for long. I think you know that, and I also think you may be coming to realise that there's more to life than following whatever road happens to appear before you.'

I took another sip of the amber-coloured pazione. Once again the remarkable cascade of sensations came over me, ending in that calm, warm feeling that was the exact opposite of sleeping on cold, hard ground wondering when you'll next be attacked by bounty hunters.

Beren's offer was more tempting than even he could know. To be safe, to have a place to live, to not always fear what's around the next corner. The truth was, I was terrible at being an outlaw; I liked comfort and security, and studying things that made sense.

'There's something I'd need from you,' Beren said, sensing I was leaning towards accepting his offer.

'What's that?'

'Seneira.'

That took me aback. 'I don't understand.'

'I think you do, Kellen.' He stood up straighter in his chair and looked as though he was bracing himself for a fight.

'She's . . . Seneira's loyal to a fault. Once she sets her heart on something . . .' He kept pausing, which was odd, because I was sure he'd planned this entire conversation out before-hand. 'She loved Revian, you know, loved him something

330

fierce ever since they were kids. Our families had arranged for them to be married next year, and even when it turned out he . . . well, he loved her back, but I don't think it was ever going to be in the way . . .'

'He's trying to say the kid liked other boys,' Reichis said, scooping up another pawful of pazione from my glass.

'Yeah, I figured.'

Beren must have thought I was responding to him. 'Revian was an exceptional young man. I'd have been proud to have him as a son, less so a son-in-law; it would have been half a marriage. Seneira's mother and I, before she passed on . . . When you've had a great love, the kind that changes your whole life? Well, you can't imagine your children having anything less.'

I wasn't sure what to say to that, but Beren went on. 'My daughter, though, her word is stronger than any steel I've ever found. She'd have gone through with it anyway.' His eyes caught mine. 'Just like she'd stick with you, even though she doesn't have the shadowblack and you do, and even though that means you'd be cutting off the future that's awaiting her.' He leaned forward in his chair and stared me straight in the eye. 'You'd be safe here though, Kellen, at the Academy. We'd protect you just like you'd help protect us. It's a good life I'm offering you, son. But you have to let Seneira find the destiny that's right for her.'

Reichis let out a growl. For a brief instant I wondered why, but then realised he was picking up on my emotions. I felt like throwing the glass into Beren's face, shouting at him and telling him what he could do with his offer. I might have too, except that there wasn't a trace of meanness in his eyes, not an ounce of judgement against me or anything about me.

331

He rose from his chair. I did the same. 'Just think on it tonight. The local puffery are determined to throw a big parade for you in the morning, to show their gratitude for all you've done for us.' He shook hands with me. 'Whatever you decide, Kellen, it's been one of the great honours of my life to meet you.'

I did something stupid then, something so embarrassing I can only figure it must have come from some deep desperation I wasn't even aware was bubbling up inside me: I hugged him.

Without even missing a beat, Beren hugged me back as if it were completely normal, as if we'd known each other our whole lives. That made me feel even worse somehow. Beren wasn't some controlling patriarch. He was just a parent, a father who had lost his own son just days ago, not trying to lock up his daughter but just wanting to make sure she was free to find a path to her own happiness.

I would have liked to have had a father like that.

53

The Path

I'd planned to leave any decisions about my life and the Academy for the morning after whatever party or parade the local notables insisted on throwing for us. The Jan'Tep don't have parades, but Ferius said those kinds of grand gestures make people feel good about themselves. Reichis figured it would be a good opportunity to pick a few rich people's pockets. Me? I just wanted to enjoy a long luxurious sleep in a proper bed – with silk sheets and actual pillows.

Comfort. It's not for everybody, but I sure don't mind it.

I'd just settled into a nice warm daze when I felt a hand on my arm. For just a brief second I thought it might be Seneira, but before I could even decide how I felt about that, I heard that annoying frontier drawl half whispering, 'Rise and shine, kid. Time for me to vamosey on out of here. The road's calling.'

'"Vamosey" isn't a word, Ferius,' I grumbled, shrugging off her hand and turning to nestle deeper into my pillow. 'Nobody "shines" in the middle of the night, and the road isn't calling. It's asleep, like everybody else.'

Even as I tried to force myself to drift into unconsciousness, I waited for whatever clever reply she had in store for me.

When none came, I sat up in the bed and rubbed at my eyes. When I opened them again, she was gone.

'Wha's up . . .' Reichis muttered, stretched out alongside me in the bed, front paws reaching out as if he'd been dreaming of chasing falcons in the air.

I didn't answer, because it suddenly occurred to me that during the past few weeks I'd said a lot of rotten things to Ferius; I'd given her any number of reasons to part company with me. Now that we'd dealt with the shadowblack plague, maybe she was ready to be free of me and this had been her way of saying goodbye. She hadn't said it was time for *us* to vamosey – whatever '*vamosey*' was supposed to mean. She'd said *her*.

I jumped out of bed, dislodging Reichis and earning me a loud hiss followed by him suddenly jumping into attack position, front claws out and sleepy eyes opened wide. 'Who's out there? Who'd dare interrupt the sacred dream sleep of a squirrel cat? Show yourself, dead meat!'

'Relax,' I said, hurrying to slip a shirt over my head and putting on my trousers. 'And get your stuff.' Reichis's 'stuff' consisted of his bag of stolen shiny objects, which I noticed was considerably more swollen than it had been when we'd first arrived.

'We leavin'?' he asked, looking mournfully back at the bed. Then he looked up at me and I could see in his eyes that he understood. 'Or just saying goodbye to Ferius?'

'I . . .' I stuffed my own few belongings back into my pack and slung it over my shoulder before putting my boots on and sticking Dexan's hat on my head. 'I don't know, but come on.'

He snatched up his little velvet bag in his teeth and leaped onto my shoulder.

I raced through the hallway and headed for the stairs as quietly as I could, trying my best not to wake anyone. As I passed by Seneira's room, I paused for just a second, wondering if I should sneak inside and gently wake her to say something.

'Creepy,' Reichis warned in my ear.

I guess he had a point.

Down the stairs and out the back door, I found Ferius leaning against her horse, arms folded across her chest and a trail of smoke drifting up towards the starry sky from the red dot of her smoking reed. 'Were you really going to leave without me?' I asked.

She didn't reply, but nodded towards the barn, where a second horse was saddled and ready to go.

Reichis sauntered over and leaped up onto the horse's back, sorting himself out to lie on his preferred spot just ahead of the saddle and muttering a warning to the poor animal that he better make it a smooth ride.

I hesitated, looking back at Seneira's big white house and the promise of good food and effusive praise that the morning would bring. More importantly, her father's offer of a life at the Academy pulled at me. A place to live, a chance to study and a purpose that would let me see myself as something passably noble: Kellen, defender of the Academy. Okay, I'd work on the name some other time.

And what did Ferius have to offer? Long winding roads and convoluted frontier mysticism; hard living and a future that had no clear direction; no promises of who I'd be or what I would become. The choice should have been easy, and yet . . . it wasn't. Maybe it was because Ferius had saved my life so many times, or because some of those ridiculous lessons of hers in dance and music and swagger were finally sinking in. Mostly, though, I didn't want to say goodbye, because, crazy as she was, Ferius Parfax was the strangest and most daring person I'd ever known, and if I stayed behind, I was more sure than I've ever been about anything in my whole life that I'd never meet anyone like her again.

As if she could sense my indecision, Ferius dropped her reed to the ground and stamped it out with the heel of her boot before mounting up on her own horse. I walked over and stared at mine. 'Well?' I asked Reichis. 'You reckon we should follow her into even more mayhem?'

'Don't give a shit,' he mumbled, nestling his head in the folds of the thin, furry gliding flaps that ran between his front and back legs. 'Sleeping.'

Ferius was already on the move, so I put a foot in the stirrup and hauled myself up to the saddle.

Once I caught up with her on the road heading out of town, I asked, 'Why did we have to leave in the middle of the night? Those people were going to throw us a parade or something.'

She kept her eyes ahead of her. 'Yeah? What would that have been like?'

'I don't know,' I grumbled. 'Nobody's ever thrown a parade for me before. I guess it'd be a lot of people cheering for us and telling us how great we are. Seneira's father said they had some kind of ceremonial plaque or sculpture they give to those who've done great deeds for the Academy.'

A sliver of a smirk settled itself on her lips. 'Well, when you put it that way . . . it sounds even more boring than I thought.'

'What about Seneira? We never said goodbye!'

It seemed like a pretty good counter-argument. I mean,

why would you leave before even settling things with someone you cared about? But Ferius just asked, 'What were the last words she said to you?'

I thought about that for a second. 'I think she said, "You're a better person than you think you are."'

'Yeah. Kid, those sound like pretty good parting words to me.'

The simple truth of that settled on me like a cold, lonely night. Seneira had her own life to live now; a future full of fine and important people, of diplomatic missions and vital trade agreements. Someone would come into her life who *wasn't* an itinerant Jan'Tep outcast with a bounty on his head and a curse around his left eye. Someone who could share a proper life with her. Someone who wasn't me.

Seneira *had* said goodbye.

'Besides,' Ferius went on, 'you really want to carry some big-ass plaque in your saddlebags from here to Gitabria?'

'Gitabria?' Just the word on my tongue felt uncomfortable. And dangerous. 'That's where we're going?'

'That's where *I'm* going, kid. Dexan's journal showed most of the Academy students who've gone home with those darned worms in their eyes come from there. Those kids need seeing to before whoever's got the other half uses them for whatever magical shenanigans they got planned. Best put a stop to that nonsense before it gets troublesome.' She finally turned to look at me. 'Fancy raisin' some hell with me?'

Shenanigans. Nonsense. Troublesome. She made it sound like nothing more than children being quarrelsome instead of what it really was: a consortium of deadly Jan'Tep mages, with a plot that could stretch across the continent and the means to destroy anyone who got in their way.

337

Ferius kept staring at me, even as our horses settled into a gentle walk along the sandy road, waiting for a reply. 'Well, kid? You decided what you want to be when you grow up?'

Behind the glib words was the question that had been eating me up inside ever since I'd fled the Jan'Tep lands. All I'd aspired to was to get away from the people who wanted me dead, to find somewhere safe or some path I could follow that would ensure I didn't have to be afraid any more. More than anything, I'd wanted someone to tell me who I was, and what I was going to be. I looked down and was surprised to find Reichis, eyes open, watching me, waiting.

'My whole life I'd planned on being a Jan'Tep mage like my mother and father,' I said. 'To spend my days learning and crafting new spells with my people, maybe even to become a lord magus one day. That life is gone forever, isn't it?'

'Reckon it is,' Ferius said.

'And I probably won't become a proper Argosi like you, will I?'

'That's up to you . . .' She held back for a moment, then said, 'But I'm guessing not.'

'And Dexan was the only other spellslinger I've met, and he turned out to be a liar and a thief.'

'Hey!' Reichis growled. 'Don't go insulting liars and thieves.'

My horse shook its head, nearly dislodging Reichis, who proceeded to chitter a number of rather nasty threats in its ear. Our mount promptly reared just enough that I had to hang on to the saddle and Reichis went tumbling to the ground, before the horse stopped and waited politely for the squirrel cat to hop back up. Apparently certain rules were being established.

I found my gaze drawn to the sand, the quartz so pure it

reflected the night sky above us like a giant map of the stars; an infinite number of lights, each one a guide to a different destination, not one of them demanding I follow it to the exclusion of all others.

'Guess I'm always going to be part Jan'Tep,' I said finally, 'even if they never want to be part of me.' I felt something in my chest that had been tight for a long time finally start to ease. 'Reckon I'll be part Argosi too. How else am I going to keep up with my dancing lessons?'

Ferius grinned and brought her horse closer to mine. 'Gonna make a passable musician out of you too.' She unslung the little guitar from her back and handed it to me. 'Go on, kid, play us something grand.'

I stared at the thing. 'How? You haven't taught me how to play.'

'That's cos I'm hopin' you'll figure it out on your own.'

I let go of the reins and strummed a couple of opening chords I'd seen Ferius play in the past. The resulting noise was pretty awful, but I kept on trying anyway. 'I figure I'll need to be part spellslinger, since some folks keep insisting on trying to kill me.'

She nodded. 'That's fair.'

I was about to try a tune on the guitar when I felt a tap my knee, and I looked down at Reichis, whose expression was making it clear I was in a great deal of personal danger. 'Yeah,' I finished up, 'I'll probably have to learn to be part squirrel cat too.'

'Damned straight,' he said, curling himself back up to go to sleep. 'If I leave things to you two morons, we'll just keep risking our lives and end up with nothing to show for it.'

'What'd he say?' Ferius asked. When I translated, she

said, 'Well, not nothing. Kellen got himself a nice new hat.'

Reichis opened one feral eye and looked up at me, then closed it again. 'Guess it *is* a pretty cool hat.'

We rode slowly but steadily all through that night, the stars above us and the glistening sand below. I would bungle various chords on the guitar while we took turns singing – even Reichis. We made up preposterous songs about our adventures, sometimes cheering each other on, sometimes, like when Ferius sang a soft, whispering lament for Revian – a young man I had hardly known but whose death was burned into my soul – I even cried, almost as if I was a decent human being. Mostly, though, we laughed at our own exploits, because when you thought about it, the three of us had to be pretty much the craziest bunch of lunatics the Seven Sands had ever seen. Somewhere in that long night of song, of laughter, of tears, I somehow found myself.

My name is Kellen Argos. I am the Path of Endless Stars.

Acknowledgements

The writing of the second book in a series can be a dangerous road for any author, full of pitfalls and hidden traps. Fortunately for me, a number of kindly Argosi wanderers helped keep me on the right path.

The Way of Thunder

Writers are perpetually asked where they get their ideas, to which most of us reply with some variation of: 'Umm . . . everywhere . . . kinda . . . I mean, I sort of just . . . Next question, please!' Even more important than coming up with an idea, however, is giving it the right shape. I do that by talking those ideas through with the following experts:

- my darling and endlessly insightful wife, Christina de Castell
- my occasional writing partner and constant narrative sage, Eric Torin
- my friend and fellow traveller on the long roads of novel writing, Kim Tough.

The Way of Water

Right, so now I've got the ideas down, I've written a draft, but where to go next? How can I subtly (or not so subtly) change the flow of the story to make it better? They don't make a compass for writers, so you have to ask for guidance along the way. I'm grateful to the following perceptive people for their wisdom and advice:

- my editor, Felicity Johnson, who never tells me what to do and yet somehow I'm pretty sure I end up doing just what she thinks I should . . .
- my publisher, Jane Harris, who, in addition to providing the title for the third book, persuaded me to allow just a little romance into poor Kellen's life
- the chronically astute Dramatica expert Jim Hull of narrativefirst.com
- the perpetually enthusiastic (and occasionally murderous) human embodiment of the squirrel cat, Nazia Khatun
- the shrewd and sensible Simone Hay. I promise to put more fights in the next book!

The Way of Stone

There's a strange magic to the way all the loose ends of a manuscript suddenly become something real – something permanent – when the right people get their hands on it. My gratitude to:

- Talya Baker, for helping shape my messy prose into coherent sentences
- Melissa Hyde, who spotted not only typos but also plot holes
- Sam Hadley, for his outstanding illustration (and for showing me what Seneira really looks like!)
- Nick Stearn, who not only makes the covers beautiful but makes the process tremendously fun

- Jamie Taylor, for putting it all together into the book you now hold in your hands.

The Way of Wind

One of the saddest truths of the publishing world is that many books never get read simply because readers don't get to hear about them. Luckily for me, some very fine champions gave their all to bring *Spellslinger* to the attention of the world:

- my wonderful agent, Heather Adams (and her almost-as-wonderful husband, Mike Bryan)
- Mark Smith, who is bold, fearless, and still owes me a private jet
- Annabel Robinson, Sophie Goodfellow and the rest of the FMcM team who put actual fire into the launch of *Spellslinger*
- the excellent sales team at Bonnier Zaffre, who are no doubt tired of saying, 'Well, it's kind of like a western only there's magic and no cowboys... but there's a talking squirrel cat. What's a squirrel cat, you ask? Well ...'
- if you're reading this in something other than English, then know that a brilliant translator was forced to make my rambling prose sound elegant in your language
- of course it never would have gotten to them were it not for Ruth Logan and Ilaria Tarasconi, who convinced publishers in many countries to become spellslingers themselves
- the many, many kind reviewers, bloggers, and booksellers who went the extra mile to read the book, rush to meet print and web deadlines and introduce readers to Kellen, Ferius and Reichis. May you all get your own squirrel cats one day!

344

The Path of Endless Stars
The real magic of a book, of course, only happens when readers take the time to read it, bring their own sense of wonder to the story and then cast their spells on friends and family, inspiring them to read it as well. It's through that act of sharing one's excitement and enthusiasm that the book really comes to life, and to all of you who take the time to do so, you have my eternal gratitude.

If you'd like to write to me, you can reach me at www.decastell.com or follow me on Twitter @decastell

HOT KEY BOOKS

Thank you for choosing a Hot Key book.

If you want to know more about our authors and what we publish, you can find us online.

You can start at our website

www.hotkeybooks.com

And you can also find us on:

We hope to see you soon!